Whacked

Whacked

JULES ASNER

WEINSTEIN
BOOKS

ISBN: 978-1-60286-017-9

First Edition
10 9 8 7 6 5 4 3 2 1

For my sister, Denise

Whacked

ONE

On the day she died, the body of Marilyn Monroe went missing for ten hours.

Usually the speculation around the circumstances of her death focuses on whether she accidentally overdosed, committed suicide, or was murdered. And if she was murdered, who would have wanted the thirty-six-year-old sex symbol dead? Was there a Kennedy conspiracy? Marilyn had been romantically linked to both President Kennedy and his brother Robert. And why was Kennedy cousin Peter Lawford one of the first to be called to the scene?

Eunice Murray, Marilyn's housekeeper, found her a little after 1 AM on August 5, 1962, dead of an apparent overdose of barbiturates, which included pentobarbital (sleeping pills) and chloral hydrate. The police weren't called to the scene for over four hours. Murray told the authorities she had to wait to get the okay from the Twentieth Century Fox Publicity Department and that it took a "bit of time."

Officers knew as they drove up the private driveway to the bougainvillea-covered home that Marilyn lay inside, dead. Murray greeted police at the door with two of Marilyn's physicians, Ralph

Greenson and Hyman Engelberg. They escorted detectives back to Marilyn's bedroom. The housekeeper seemed calm; she was even doing laundry, which was kind of weird considering it was five in the morning.

From the bedroom doorway, officers could see Marilyn's nude body lying facedown in what investigators call the "soldier's position." Her arms were by her side, her legs stretched out, and her face was burrowed in her pillow. This arrangement was odd for someone who had overdosed, because ODs almost always have convulsions and vomit before they die, and their body is left usually on their back, their limbs twisted. OD'ing on pills ain't pretty, but if you want to off yourself, it's less messy than blowing your brains out.

Most female suicides don't shoot themselves in the head.

Investigators found no glass by Marilyn's bedside for her to have used when she swallowed all the pills, and many of the police files and interviews conducted after her death have disappeared.

But I'm *most* fascinated by the hours that Marilyn's body seems to have disappeared—starting when the corpse left her house off Sunset Boulevard in Beverly Hills to the time it was checked into the LA County Morgue—over six hours later. Normally the drive would take half an hour, maybe forty-five minutes—but six hours?

I'd been told by someone who should really know that the transportation of her body was intercepted by members of a secret society of necrophiliacs. My person-in-the-know said that a lot of money changed hands so that several members of this society could have sex with her dead body.

Once Marilyn's body arrived at the morgue, there were more tales of postmortem sex. Every nurse, coroner's assistant, and janitor in Los Angeles claimed to have known someone who had some. There was even a song by that guy Tom whatever-his-name-is. So that was proof it was true.

"Totally true," I said to myself as I hit "save" on my laptop.

I pushed back from my desk and reached my hands toward the ceiling, trying to stretch out the knot in my back that came whenever I hunched over the computer writing. I wondered if I should try that new cupping technique I saw in *Us Weekly*. Cupping isn't really new—it's been around for centuries—but ever since Gwyneth showed up at a movie premiere with her back looking like a Nebraska field scored with crop circles, cupping had been the new old thing that people on both coasts were rushing to try to ease their joint ailments.

My thoughts of Marilyn and Gwyneth were interrupted by a sharp knock on the door. I straightened up, smoothed my hair, and yelled, "Come in," hoping it wasn't anyone with a question. Today was my first day back in the office after being gone all week and I was playing catch up and feeling even more overwhelmed than usual. Plus, my boyfriend, Dave, had some sort of surprise planned for tonight and had persuaded me to kick out of work early, so I was trying to get things here a little under control before trying to sneak away.

Tommy from wardrobe poked his head from around the door. "Hey, Dani, you got a sec? I want to show you some options real quick."

"Sure," I replied, relieved it was just a question about wardrobe and not my boss, Steve Jacobs, wondering why my revised pages for the show weren't finished.

"Do you think this is too much? For when we catch the guy at the end of Act Two?"

Tommy held up a T-shirt that read, "Crack open a cold one." I stared at it in disbelief.

"It's a real shirt they sell," Tommy said. "I got it off a necrophilia Web site."

"Crack open a cold one?" I repeated. "Jesus, and I thought *I* was sick. They actually have shirts?"

"Yep."

I didn't want to think about how Tommy knew where to find the shirt on such short notice. All of a sudden the premise for my "Marilyn" episode made me feel very tired.

"I don't know," I told Tommy. "We're kind of pushing it with the whole story line anyway, and we might push the network censors over the edge with the . . . shirt. I really don't want to do anything to make them start looking at this episode any closer."

Tommy tried not to look hurt. "So, too much?"

"Way too much. Just put the guy in something normal from the Gap or Aberzombie."

Tommy shrugged and turned to leave, my pun totally going over his head. I had a feeling the shirt would find a home in Tommy's closet.

"Jesus Christ," I murmured to myself when the door was closed. Being a writer on a show was tough, but making a judgment call like that was easy.

Glancing at the clock, I hunched back over my laptop, back to Marilyn, whose unaccounted-for hours I was transforming into an episode of the show I wrote for, *Flesh and Bone*. I knew the Marilyn story inside out, because when I first moved to Los Angeles and got a job out of college, I was a second assistant to a major recording star who was obsessed with her. Being the second assistant didn't mean I got to travel with the star on private jets or shield her from the crazy fans who would sleep on the pavement outside her hotel when she was touring. Instead, I did things like buy her tampons, pick up the mess when her dog had an "accident," and make sure her soy milk was sugar-free. She was convinced sugar would zap her energy levels. I always got her the soy milk with sugar and just told her it was sugar-free.

Every morning I'd fetch her latte before rushing up to her glass mansion at the end of one of the bird streets above Turner's Liquors on Sunset. She did Bikram Yoga every morning for ninety minutes and I had to be there when she was finished. The routine was always the same. Walking into her private yoga room, I was always knocked flat by the 110-degree heat. Then I was enveloped in the overwhelming smell of sweat. I tried not to think of it as BO or I'd gag, but it was pretty pungent. She would walk toward me with one hand outstretched, the other wiping down her soaking wet body with a 500 thread count towel.

Weighing the Starbucks Venti cup in her hand, she'd gauge through the recycled cardboard cup if the temperature was just right. If it was too hot, she'd make me hold the lid until it cooled off and then hand it back to her so it could seal in the perfect temperature. If the latte had gone cold, I'd have to rush down the hill for a fresh cup.

When I placed the order at Starbucks, they'd ask me my name, and my employer always told me to say "Norma Jean." I could have said my name, but she didn't want to see "Dani" scrawled in crayon on the side of her latte. "Norma Jean," my recording star, didn't want me to use her real name, because she thought the barista might know it was for her and spit in the cup when no one was looking.

Sure, when I got *her* herpes medication refilled at the pharmacy I had to use my name, but for the coffee I had to let her be "Norma Jean." I was twenty-five and making a thousand bucks a week and didn't want to point out she was bonkers.

"Norma Jean" was completely obsessed with Marilyn. In her living room, high above the overstuffed red velvet couch, was a giant framed sepia print of herself in profile, frozen with her eyes closed and head thrown back, her homage to Marilyn. "Norma Jean" was obsessed with the story of Marilyn and the necrophiliacs. "Dani, you just don't know what it's like to have people want a piece of you, any piece of you," she'd tell me.

"I can't imagine. It's one more awful thing about being so famous," I'd reply gravely.

"The thing is no one ever *tells* you what will happen when you're famous. There's no class you can take or school that will prepare you—it just happens and then your life gets so crazy that you can't help but think this wasn't what you signed up for."

"I know you must feel like you're being hunted sometimes."

"You have no idea. Do you know if those paparazzi didn't have cameras around their necks I could have them arrested for stalking, but because they're *press*"—she sneered the word—"they can do what they want, because it's a God-damn-fucking-freedom-of-the-press-constitutional-thing!"

"They're vultures," I replied.

"And let me tell you, they're going to hunt me until I'm dead—they're going to chase me like they did Diana, and they won't be happy until they get photos of me lying on the pavement after a car accident, and then they're going to follow me to the hospital to have sex with my helpless dead body."

She was starting to get a little manic; she always did when she mixed Diana and Marilyn in the same rant. I tried to calm her down. "That's why it's so good you have The Plan."

She nodded vigorously. "The Plan is my only hope for being able to rest in peace. No one is going to violate my body when I'm dead!"

To make sure The Plan would work, we'd have drills, the way they do in New York in case there's another terrorist attack. "Norma Jean's" dead body was never to be left alone; her sister or brother would be the first to be called, and they would handle all details of contacting authorities and overseeing transportation. We were ready for the day when "Norma Jean" kicked it, so that her impeccably maintained body wouldn't be defiled. The Plan made her sleep well at night. Sometimes I'd put an Ambien in her Yogi Tea before bed so she really slept well.

"Norma Jean" hadn't had to use The Plan yet. She was still out there among the living, although I'd bet there wasn't much of a heart beating behind her left foam-covered saline breast implant.

I had no guilty feelings about turning her personal drama into an episode of the show; I'd decided it was karma paying me back for all of the clean urine samples I personally provided for "Norma Jean's" court ordered maintenance tests. I turned to my computer screen:

NORMA JEAN
You don't have any idea what it's like to be famous.
They're going to hunt me down just like they did
Diana.

ASST. #2
I know, it's terrible. It's like you're a caged animal.

NORMA JEAN
That's why we have The Plan. The Plan will give
me the dignity in death that I deserve.
No one is going to defile me!

I scrolled ahead to when Norma was nice and dead, and the show's detective was on the scene.

Interior of a holding cell. Day. A uniformed policeman enters, accompanied by MAGGIE BLACK. They pull out two chairs and seat themselves next to the interrogating officer, then focus on Asst. #2.

MAGGIE BLACK
So was she afraid for her life? Did Norma Jean have
reason to believe that someone was trying to kill her?

ASST. #2
She did have enemies . . . I mean, you don't get to
be that successful without . . . trampling on some

people with your stilettos. But it didn't seem like
anyone would want to KILL her.

MAGGIE BLACK
But she talked about her own death frequently.
Would you say she had a fixation about death?

ASST. #2
Yes, she did seem fixated on death. She was terrified
at the thought of what they did to Marilyn—after she
died. She was very concerned about someone trying
to do anything to her body after she passed on.

One of the first rules of police work and case investigation that I'd
learned by shadowing the real investigators was that random acts of
violence were actually pretty rare. If someone got murdered, the murderer was likely someone the victim knew. So the investigators would
concentrate on the immediate family of a victim, then move on to the
boyfriend or coworkers. They think of it as a circle and work their way
outward.

For this episode, the cops would put pressure on Assistant Number Two and she would eventually crack, spilling out her hatred for
Norma Jean and admitting she murdered her.

Assistant Number Two wouldn't have sex with the dead Norma
Jean—*that* would be over the line. We'd just throw in Norma Jean's
obsession with necrophilia and that she needed The Plan.

The necrophilia thing would just be played up big because it was,
well, sweeps. Sweeps are the all-important ratings periods that oc-
cur four times a year and measure shows' viewership. These numbers
then dictate what the network can charge advertisers for commer-
cials during the show. We always planned on doing our biggest and
most exciting shows during these sweep weeks. Not only was it

sweeps, but this was the first time I'd ever written a show all by myself, and I was feeling edgy about it.

Our production schedule could be brutal, and sometimes we shot different episodes simultaneously, which could sometimes be hard on the actors, who would get confused over what dead body they were supposed to be squinting at on the metal autopsy gurney.

The turnaround time for a one-hour episode was usually fourteen days. The director and crew would prep the episode for three days, then shoot for a week straight. The rest of our time would be gobbled up in editing and all of the postproduction work required to make a show perfect. The Marilyn show was being rushed through shooting and postproduction because the network was so excited about the story line. I'd missed most of the shooting because of my trip, but there were still a couple of last-minute scenes that were being rewritten and shot, with the show set to air in only eight days.

The network executives had even come through with the extra money for us to cast Jennifer Love Hewitt as Assistant Number Two. Love, as she liked to be called, was the star of her own hit show on CBS, *The Ghost Whisperer*, but they had wrapped shooting for the season. In a recent interview featured in *InTouch Weekly*, Love had proclaimed herself *Flesh and Bone*'s "number one fan." Steve Jacobs made a few calls and rushed her over a copy of the shooting script. Love *loved* that the role played against her nice girl image, and committed to playing Assistant Number Two right away. The suits at the network loved the idea of featuring one of its biggest stars on a highly promoted sweeps episode. Everybody won.

The remnants of my lunch, a turkey sandwich (hold the mayo) from Quiznos, lay next to my computer. This reminded me to enter my points online. Quickly saving out of the show script, I navigated over to the Weight Watchers' Web site. Because I was a member, it dumped me right into the calorie manager page. I selected the date and the day's blank menu page filled the screen. Dragging the cursor over to the breakfast category, I entered in what I'd eaten that day. Half a scone from Starbucks and a latte—that right there was ten points. Those scones were a killer—even when you just ate half they were still as big as a football. The Quiznos sandwich had been a smarter choice for lunch and clocked in at seven points. I frowned at the screen; I was left with only three points for the rest of the day. Sighing, I saved my food intake points and gathered the carcass in the sandwich wrapper, tossing it in the trash bin under my desk. I'm sure whatever surprise Dave had planned for me later was going to involve eating something. So I was probably going to have to dip into my Flex Points for the week to get through the day.

It was almost 2 PM. I sent a longing gaze at my office phone; I'd already left two messages for Dave, hoping to nail down more exact plans about what we were doing later, but he'd never called back. Calling a third time just seemed desperate and sad.

I pulled out my makeup bag and squinted critically at my reflection. The circles under my eyes weren't going anywhere, and I was definitely showing a little fraying around the edges. I worked long hours, and couldn't keep up with all the maintenance LA required. I might have to start seriously thinking about the whole injection thing. Thank God I had my mother's full lips, the one thing I was thankful to have inherited from her. No collagen needed there. They say you should really think about starting all of the fillers young. Some actresses were starting to go for Botox in their early twenties.

"Damn those little bitches," I said to my reflection. I pulled my face back a few inches from my mirror, a much more flattering distance. Those twenty-year-old waifs were ruining it for all of us who weighed over ninety-five pounds. Somehow the new ideal in beauty had become fried fake hair and bad skin, atop a skeletal frame with plastic boobs. I guess the airbrushing helped those girls look somewhat human on their magazine covers. But airbrushing couldn't help any of them with the chronic halitosis from all the bingeing and purging. I'd heard about that dentist in New York who specialized in making new teeth for those bulimic girls who'd had a river of stomach acid eat away their tooth enamel. He had a secret door so his patients could slip in unseen, and he kept a reflexologist on staff to rub his patients' feet while they were being worked on. Fifty grand for a set of perfect new chompers that would rarely eat solid food.

The phone rang. "It's Dani," I said, briskly picking up, hoping it was Dave finally calling me back.

"Hey . . ." It was my friend Lauren. "Why the busy voice?" she asked.

"I've just got a shitload of stuff to do after being gone all week."

"Anything new with the guy?"

"When you say 'the guy' do you mean Dave?"

"Yes, I mean Dave, unless you've found a better guy yet," she replied dryly.

Lauren didn't like Dave. She always called him a "total dick," after something he had said to her at a barbecue at our mutual friend Ina's. Lauren had never fessed up about what he'd said, so I gave up trying to get them to like each other—I just tried to keep them seated far apart whenever we went out together.

"The two of us have both been so busy with work. There's hardly been time to hang out. He said he's got something special planned for us later; a surprise."

"If he really wanted to do something nice for you, he would dig deep and finally come up with an engagement ring," Lauren snarked.

"C'mon, get off the ring stuff. That will come. I'm not in any rush."

"Yeah, right."

"What's with the attitude, girl? Are you having your period?"

"No, but it's been practically two years now that you've been together. I just think he should get off his ass and marry you like a decent guy. He's never going to meet anyone better than you."

"True, true," I admitted. "But right now, since I'm not even sure if I'm going to see him tonight, I don't want to set myself up for a big letdown. I can't start counting on a diamond ring for lunch, ya know?"

"Okay, but if he does step up to the plate, call and let me know."

"I sure will. Now you go back to being on the rag."

"I know I'm being bitchy. Sorry. I have to go interview someone stupid now."

"So that's why you're in such a nasty mood. Are you going to interview a Housewife who's Desperate?" Lauren was a television reporter for *MoreTV*, a twenty-four-hour cable channel devoted to all things celeb. She'd had the dream gig, flying off to glamorous places like the Cannes Film Festival or interviewing James Bond on the set of his latest film. Recently though, *MoreTV* had shifted its focus from being the "CNN of entertainment news" to chasing celebutards, following around rejects from *American Idol,* and debating which stars from *Desperate Housewives* were feuding. This had not pleased Lauren.

"Yes, I *am* off to see a Housewife—we're going to the Dog Park up on Laurel Canyon so she can share one of her passions with me," Lauren replied.

"I bet she'll tell you her dog is her child. Do you want to bet me?"

"That is a bet I won't take," Lauren said. "Call me if you get engaged."

Lauren hung up and I turned back to the mess of my desk.

"Hey, Dani, your mom's on the phone," my assistant Azita called out to me from her desk outside my door. "Do you want her?"

I didn't need my mom's toxic juice spraying all over me on a catch-up day like today. Thank God I'd been on the phone with Lauren and not picked up the second line when it was blinking. "Can you tell her I'm in a meeting, an *emergency* meeting that I'm needed in?" I yelled back.

"Sure, no problem."

The last time I'd made the mistake of picking up my mom's call at work, she'd broadsided me with the latest news about my dad. "Well, you're going to find out sooner or later, so I guess I should let you know that your father is dating a Russian," she'd told me.

"Really? I'd asked. "Is this someone he met from one of his magazines?"

"No, I think they met online. She's one of those women they call a 'Natasha.'"

"Her name is Natasha? Like Boris and Natasha?" I'd asked.

"No, she's like a hooker, I think, but she needs an American man for her green card."

"So Dad's getting married to give this 'Natasha' a green card?"

"I don't know if your father is getting *married* again, but they are very serious," she'd added gravely. "I hear she has a daughter who's around ten or twelve that your father adores."

"Oh my," I'd replied.

"You know, that's around the age you were when we divorced, so I think he has a lot of guilt associated with those feelings of abandoning a girl close to your age."

"Yeah, that's great to hear, Mom." I had stood up from my chair and gazed longingly at the open doorway of my office. "I'm ten minutes late for a meeting, so I've got to run."

"You have to go?" she'd wailed. "But I had some questions about the show that was on last Sunday!"

"Oh, they're waving me in now, Mom, I'll call you over the weekend or something."

"Okay, I love you, Dani."

"Me too," I'd answered, hanging up quickly. Bringing up my dad was a dirty trick. I don't think either of us knew exactly why we weren't speaking—we just stopped, and his hundred-dollar birthday checks had stopped a long time ago.

• • •

Thinking of my parents spurred me into the office kitchen in search of some comfort food. I scoped out the fridge to see if there was anything worth eating. Thinking of my Weight Watchers points, I glumly swiped a yogurt someone had left unguarded. Turning to leave, I saw Evil Janet staring at me stonily from the doorway to the kitchen. I called her Evil Janet because she *was* evil, eternally dressed in black, skulking around the office and always eating some sort of mystery food out of yellowed Tupperware containers. Evil Janet was another writer on the show, but she was treated like some sort of visiting dignitary because she used to write on *CSI*—and not on one of the crappy spin-off *CSI* shows—but the good one that takes place in Vegas.

Evil Janet had already had two shows on this season with sole writing credit and I'd silently relished it when Steve told her that the episode she'd been working on featuring a child kidnapping was pushed down a week in the schedule to make room for my Marilyn show. I guess necrophilia trumped child abduction. Hee, hee, hee.

"This is my yogurt," I said, my eyes daring her to wrestle the Yoplait container from my grasp. My heart started racing; I was jacked up on enough caffeine that I could totally fight her. Shooting me a dour look, she turned in the doorway and left. I shivered. A few months ago, Azita had told me she'd seen Evil Janet shaking a coffee can in the office kitchen. She then put the coffee can in the back of the freezer and left. Curious, Azita waited until she was gone and then opened up the freezer. Inside the coffee can were some twigs and herbs and three names written on small scraps of paper: my name, Steve Jacobs's, and George W. Bush's. Azita got scared and threw the can away, but she was convinced that Janet was trying to place some sort of spell on us. This totally scared the shit out of me and I tried to give Evil Janet a wide berth when we crossed paths in the halls. I always wondered how I ended up on a short list with George W.

I meandered back to my office, carefully trying to avoid my boss. Spying Azita, I mouthed the words to her, "Where's Steve?"

She smiled and mouthed back, "Gone home early for the Jewish holiday."

"Cool." I smiled back.

"Very cool." She parroted.

Knowing I wouldn't have to go all ninja to get out of the office early undetected was a huge relief.

Steve Jacobs could be an exacting boss, but he was also a very nice guy. I'd first met him when he taught a television-writing course at the UCLA Extension, and he gave me my first break four years ago on his bikini jiggle fest *High Tide*. Cheesy, but incredibly successful, it was the top-rated syndicated show in sixty-nine countries, and it made Steve a very rich man. I started by photocopying scripts and quickly worked my way into the writers' room to become a writer's assistant. Being a writer's assistant entailed filling the latte orders, but I also had a chance to learn something. Every day I would take notes of all the script changes and make sure the scripts got out on time to the crew and actors. When I got home (late) I would stay up working on my own scripts, with *Court TV* playing in the background, until I passed out.

Flesh and Bone was my first "official" gig as a staff writer. I was kind of a late bloomer; most of the writers on staff were in their twenties, not "just turned thirty" as I liked to think of myself.

My boyfriend, Dave, was always telling me Steve was being so nice to me and giving me a break to write on the new show because he wanted to get into my pants. Dave was a self-declared expert about this kind of stuff, because as a successful director, he knew "how things worked in this town."

But whatever Steve's motives, I knew I had to make this gig work. I'd been out of town all week until yesterday, visiting with some new FBI show advisers. With so many forensic shows on the air, having these kinds of technical experts in the credits really helped our credibility with viewers. So in the middle of all the craziness of getting the Marilyn show ready, I had to drop everything and go to Quantico to meet with their team of forensic specialists. Around the office, I acted slightly exasperated about the last-minute assignment, but for someone like me who was a little sick in the head when it came to a fascination with crime scenes, the trip was awesome. It was my very own forensic porn.

Being away from Dave had been hard. I was a little addicted to talking to Dave several times a day. Every time I heard the familiar ding of my Crackberry from the bottom of my purse telling me that I had a message waiting, I'd scramble through everything to get it, hoping it was Dave. Last night, I had been so eager to see him when I landed that I thought of driving straight over to his house, but decided I could use the detour home to defunk. It was a good thing I did, because when I got home I found Dave sitting on my couch with a bucket of KFC.

"Hey, baby," he said, smiling. "I missed you so much, and thought you could use a little KFC and some kisses to welcome you home."

"That's sooo sweet of you!" I didn't really like KFC (ten thousand Weight Watchers points) but still, it *was* sweet of him.

But last night our romp in the bedroom began with a soft beginning for him and a softer ending. That was a first. Nothing makes a girl feel worse than not being able to get a guy off. I mean, c'mon, I'm naked and under you, or in this instance on top of you, and you totally lose your boner?

Dave stared up at the ceiling. "I'm sorry, baby, I've just had a lot on my mind with work and everything. . . ."

"It's okay." I tried to brush it off. "I guess we just need to practice more. I won't go out of town so much." I was a little flushed and trying to catch my breath; I'd been working hard to make it happen.

Had I gotten too fat on the trip? I hadn't been able to work out and there'd been plenty of pizzas ordered in for lunch at Quantico. Maybe Dave was disgusted with my being a little extra lumpy. Stretched out next to Dave, I pulled the sheet to cover up a bit. I didn't want him to think there was a beached whale lying next to him in bed.

When I reached down to try and arouse him again, he grabbed hold of my hands. "Don't do that!"

His sharp tone took me aback. He held my hands together halfway down his torso. "Just don't."

"Okay, I mean, sorry, I understand you have a lot on your mind."

He rolled onto his side, facing away from me. I felt so hurt and shut out that I just stared at his bare back. I didn't want to cry. I hated crying in front of a guy. I took in deep breaths, in through the nose, out through the mouth, just like in yoga. I wanted to talk more, but after flying all day I was beat. Dave's back to me was his signal that there would be no more conversation about what just happened.

Dave rolled back toward me and pulled me to him. "Don't worry, it's only temporary." He brightened. "Hey, do you think you could kick out of work early tomorrow?"

"Mmm, I've been out all week, and there's so much going on with the Marilyn episode." I traced my finger on his doughy tummy. No six-pack here, but that would be kind of gross. I didn't have a six-pack, so why should I expect someone I was dating to be able to bounce a quarter off his?

Dave grabbed my wandering finger again, holding my wrist still. "Make it work." His hazel eyes were sparkling now. "I have a surprise for you. Something special I've planned for a while."

"Can you give me a hint?"

"Just dress comfortably. I'll pick you up at work. You'll love it, I promise."

He was so adorable that I almost forgot about Mr. Softy. "Okay,

I'll make it work. . . ." I said. Then he pulled me toward him for a salty kiss.

Heading back to my office after my yogurt break, I passed a framed cover of *TV Guide* from earlier in the month. "Maggie Black" was the cover story. Haley Caldwell, the actress who played Maggie on *Flesh and Bone*, was posed as provocatively as possible for a TV coroner who was dressed in something she would wear to perform an autopsy. She stared out at me, and with her dark hair and blue eyes, even I had to admit there was a bit of a resemblance between us. I'd already taken a lot of shit when the article came out, because *TV Guide* had taken some behind-the-scenes photos for the story and run a shot of me working with the other writers with the caption "Maggie Black's alter ego?" That probably earned me a couple of extra twigs in Evil Janet's coffee can.

Haley did look great on the cover. The network was always trying to get us to sex her up. We'd get notes like, "Can't she dress a little fleshier?" But there were only so many scenes you could write about finding dead bodies on the beach that would necessitate "Maggie" wearing a tank top on the job.

Haley was a typical actress success story; she had toiled away for years on daytime television, which led to a role as "the best friend" on a hit sitcom. She thought she would forever be designated the best friend, the Rhoda. But then she had a brow lift, full body lipo, a chemical peel, and hair extensions (the best extensions, the kind made from the hair of virgins in India). Haley was her very own episode of *Extreme Makeover*. Her publicist attributed her metamorphosis to her macrobiotic diet and her newfound devotion to Ashtanga Yoga.

Haley was cool, although she had her diva moments; after all, she was a star and this show made millions for the network. We just had to be careful with close-ups right after her regular Botox, collagen, and Restylane injections. The bruises would read on camera for an entire week.

Back at my desk, I started trying to make the normal chaos of my work space not so embarrassing. I thought about calling Dave to see where he was, but restrained myself, because a third call was just plain desperate.

I tried to focus at the computer screen, feeling tired and overwhelmed.

"Hi, princess." Azita poked her head in the doorway. "Did you see that sick T-shirt of Tommy's?"

I rolled my eyes. "I know. Sick."

"Well, besides that . . . Look who I found!" she trumpeted, pulling Dave by the hand into my office.

"Hey, baby. You ready?"

Dave grinned at me from the doorway. Just seeing him there blew me full with pride. I still got that gooey feeling looking at his mop of unruly hair and hazel eyes. His smile lit up his whole face, and I grinned at him like a high school girl meeting up with her football hero crush.

Dave was definitely more established in TV than I was. He had worked as a director on probably a dozen different shows. He also talked about his *work* more than I did at home, which was fine. Someone once told me that all directors had a God complex, so I just kind of let him run at the mouth when he described the complexities of shooting the barrel of a .357 Magnum gun in close-up. I liked it when he came by the office. I had an actual office on a show, which is rare, and I didn't mind showing it off to him. It was nice for him to see that I was also on my way to being successful.

"So should I leave you two lovebirds alone?" Azita asked.

I loved Azita. You could describe her sense of style as "jailbait." I'd never seen her in anything but a cheerleader-short miniskirt paired with T-shirts formfitting enough to let you know that under that sheer cotton were real twenty-five-year-old breasts.

"And before I forget, I also have the McGuire research and photos for you," she said, sashaying in front of Dave to put the file on my desk. I didn't mind her teasing manner—that was Azita. I did mind how Dave glanced down her backside, focused on her pert ass, and lingered there.

Azita could be trouble, but she'd never make a move on, or allow a move from, my man. She was the all-around office superstar—but the sad thing was that she really wanted to be an actress. I knew that next week she was testing to be a series regular on *The Young and the Restless*. Secretly I was hoping she wouldn't get the gig. I didn't want to lose her here, and besides my selfish motivations, I wanted more for her than just a photo op in *Us Weekly* of her shopping at Kitson.

"Later, boss lady. Bye, Dave." She turned and left and Dave turned with her, his eyes still on her ass. Guys have no clue how obvious they are.

Soon enough, Dave settled his attention back on me. "Hey, baby . . . your surprise awaits." He came around the desk to finally kiss me hello. I knew he was trying to cover his ogling, and closed my eyes for his kiss.

"Yes, I'm ready, but are you sure you don't want to invite Azita?" I couldn't help being a little sarcastic.

"Don't go being like that on such a special day." Dave's hands roamed down my back and grabbed onto the back pockets of my new jeans. "Remember, I have a surprise for you." He kissed me again.

Now I felt bad. "I know. Maybe I just don't think my ass was ever as tight as hers . . ."

"Your ass is tight. Here, let me feel it," Dave said, using both hands to give me a hard squeeze.

"Don't!" I yelped. His squeeze was so sharp it bordered on being a double-handed pinch. I tried to wiggle away.

"Um, excuse me, Dani?" Hearing the voice from the doorway, Dave and I sprang apart like a couple of kids caught playing doctor.

"Oh . . . Hey, Rich," I stammered out.

Rich Pisani's huge frame filled the doorway. Rich was one of the technical advisers on *Flesh and Bone*. A retired LAPD cop, he was retained by the show for whenever we had a question about real police procedure. Rich mostly kept to himself, and the rumor was that he'd resigned from the force after taking a bullet for someone. Being a consultant was a good gig for him, but I knew he also did security for celebrities, as well as some private-eye work on the side.

"What's up?" I asked.

Dave, unfazed, turned his attention to the bookcases, choosing to ignore Rich.

Rich hesitated in the doorway, eyeing us warily. "You left me a message that you had some questions for me, about something you're working on."

"Oh, shit." I had totally forgotten that Rich and I had made a plan to meet. I did have a couple of things I wanted to go over with him, but it was for a show several weeks away, and it wasn't Marilyn-related, so it could wait.

"I'm sorry to blow you off like this, Rich, but I was just headed out," I said, shooting a glance at Dave, who, after removing his hands from my ass was now shaking a snow globe I had on my desk, captivated by the falling flakes. "Um . . . Rich, this is my boyfriend, Dave."

"Nice to meet you, Dave," Rich offered.

"Back at you, man," Dave answered, barely glancing at Rich.

Embarrassed by Dave's semi-rudeness, I moved behind my desk and began powering down my laptop. "Rich, are you cool if we do this next week?"

He shrugged. "Sure, if that works for you. I just thought there was some urgency because you were working on deadline."

"I was . . . I mean, I *am* on a deadline, but I just can't today . . . okay?"

I don't know why I felt so awkward. The girls in the office all swooned over Rich. They even had a nickname for him: "Detective McDreamy." Whatever—I didn't see it.

"We can reschedule for next week, Dani. It's no problem." Rich gave Dave that universal nod that all guys exchange. "Nice meeting you, Dave."

"Yeah, bye, man." Dave answered.

Rich smiled at me. "Have a good weekend, Dani. We'll talk next week."

"Thanks, Rich." I turned back to Dave, still absorbed in the snow globe. "Baby, I'm almost ready to go. Let me just collect my things." I started packing more files and my usual junk into my bag.

"So where's the famous Steve Jacobs?" Dave prodded, picking up a crystal skull that was a leftover gag gift from some office party.

"It's quiet this week for the Jewish holidays. I think Steve left early because it's Passover."

"Really?" Dave half laughed. "I didn't know Steve was a Super Jew."

"I don't know if he's a Super Jew either, but come on, it's Hollywood and it's the Jewish holidays. Half the town didn't even come into work this week."

"He's such a dick," he muttered, this time not to me but to the crystal skull.

"No, he's not a dick. He's great. You just don't like him." We'd had this conversation before.

"He's just been great to you because he wants to fuck you."

I stepped around the desk, took the skull out of his hands, and placed it back on the desk. "Could you please cool it with that stuff? Anyone could hear you."

"Well, they would just agree with me that it's true."

"So I'm a lousy writer who's got a gig only because the boss is just biding his time waiting until I'm free, and then he's going to pounce. That's Steve's plan, you think?"

"No, he's just keeping you around because you've got a great ass." Dave smiled, looking very pleased with himself. He'd somehow managed to check out my assistant's ass, kind of insult me, and then definitely insult my boss, and now he was back in good with me with the "great ass" comment.

"You are impossible. Let's get going. I can't wait for my surprise."

TWO

Exiting the lot, we headed over Barham back toward LA, with the warm San Fernando air blowing through the open windows. We dropped my car off at my place just off Highland. As I climbed in next to him, Dave smiled at me, looking immensely satisfied, sitting low in his vintage 1964 VW Bug. He hadn't said a word since we started driving.

"You're not going to give me any clues?" I was fishing for any kind of clue—after all, this was what I did for a living.

Dave just smiled.

I grinned back and tried to relax and enjoy whatever was to come. I deserved something special after the trauma of last night in bed. So here we were, racing through Hollywood to who knows where. Dave leaned back and smirked at me. He was going to give me nothing.

"You didn't buckle up. I want my baby to be safe," he said. I was always bad about buckling up. I dug into the leather seat to find the buckle, reaching the two sides to click together, but not quite making it. In one week I couldn't have gotten *that* fat.

"Either I've gained weight, or someone very skinny was in the passenger seat recently."

"What are you talking about?" He frowned, looking at the two parts of the seat belt not quite meeting across my jeans.

"A passenger recently pulled this seat belt very tight." I waved the two stubby ends of the belt. "What gives? Who's the skinny hottie you've been driving around town while I've been away on business?"

"Yeah, right," he sneered. "I just had the car detailed this week— you know how they move things around." Dave reached across the bench seat and gave my knee a squeeze. "You're the only baby I drive around. You know that."

The car did smell of Armor All and glistened from a recent wax. Funny.

We had a good story. I'd been waiting at the bar at LAX for a weekend flight home to Arizona. My original flight had been canceled and I had time to kill until the next one. Dave was sitting two seats away from me having a beer, awaiting his flight. I'd noticed him right away because he was hot. Not in a metrosexual way, or the way my girlfriends all thought of as hot. His hair was dark and slightly overgrown, with long bangs that I watched him push off his face.

I judged him to be around thirty-two or thirty-three. He wasn't that well put together: sneakers, jeans, and baggy leather coat. But that was cool. I never liked a guy to spend more time getting ready than I did.

Looking at him, I was glad that I'd put on my good-butt jeans before heading to the airport. Halfway through my Amstel Light, I kept my eyes straight ahead and waited to see if he would make his move. I didn't have to wait long. I could feel the movement of air next to my barstool; someone was inching in. I glanced to my left and saw Cute Guy placing his computer bag on the bar and signaling to the bartender for another beer. The bartender called back to him, "We'll make it a large for a dollar more."

Cute Guy answered, "Sure."

Not bad. It was only 5 PM and he was on the large beer—my kind of guy. A few minutes went by as I tried to appear engrossed in my Jackie Collins novel. He silently sipped his beer next to me.

"Excuse me."

I turned to face Cute Guy. Looking directly at him, I felt a bit like I'd been punched in the stomach.

"Hi."

"Hi," I said cautiously.

I immediately started fantasizing about what our children would look like, but I also reminded myself to be careful. I had no idea if he was a crazy.

"Look, I know you don't know me and I can't think of a single line, but I just wanted to talk to you, so hi." He extended his hand. "I'm Dave Gallagher."

Dave's hand was still outstretched waiting for mine, so I offered up my hand and he gave it a solid squeeze.

"I'm Dani Hale."

He was pretty cute. Really cute. Living in LA, I'd learned that the cheeseballs who hung out in bars always came up with some lame line they'd stolen from that month's issue of *Maxim*. The last time I had been subject to a pickup line while waiting at a bar alone, a guy had come up to me and blurted out, "Hey, little lady! You know, if you were a booger, I'd pick you." For me, pickup lines had always fallen into the "eww" category. I'd smiled to myself at Dave's simple hello and handshake.

Dave and I traded details. He was a TV director. I told him I was a writer for TV shows too, inflating my résumé only slightly; I was still working my way up the ranks in the writers' room at *High Tide*.

"Are you from the East Coast?" I asked. "I think I'm hearing a bit of an accent."

"Yeah, South Boston," he answered, tipping his beer back for another sip. That's when I noticed the freckles splayed across the hand gripping his beer. Salmon and beige flecks that reminded me of spots on a puppy's tummy.

"I hear the south side of Boston can be tough."

"For some," he answered. "Where'd you hear that?"

I smiled. "I've just read a lot of interviews with Mark Wahlberg." This made him laugh and we both kept smiling. The long wait for my flight that I'd been dreading evaporated, and I was surprised when I heard the muffled announcement that my flight was boarding.

We exchanged numbers. He gave me his home number and asked for my e-mail, saying he wanted to forward me a link he thought I'd like. He solemnly shook my hand good-bye and, when he slightly pressed his thumb into the palm of my hand, I got instantly wet. I smiled all the way to the gate.

That was almost two years ago. Friends thought we were some sort of fairy-tale couple that would eventually marry, buy a house in the hills, and spawn. "Think how fate brought you into each other's lives," my friend Ina would say. "It was destiny for your flight to be canceled. You guys were meant to be together."

I'd let most of them think we were Hollywood's version of Camelot. The truth was that this past year had been bumpy. We'd definitely had our hills and our valleys. Dave was moody, which I tried to shrug off as his hotheaded Irish way. He was also very critical of whatever project I was working on and the way the higher-ups treated me. Dave said he had to be honest with me about all this stuff "because I love you so much," and it upset him when people at the office treated me so "shitty." He liked giving me advice about work. Early on, he'd disappeared on me for a couple of weeks with no phone calls or e-mails. I thought he'd gone back to an ex-girlfriend or decided he wasn't into being in a relationship. When he reappeared he told me he "just had to get my head together" and that he *was* ready to be in something this "big."

We made a left on Sunset and headed east. We roared through Little Armenia, past the huge Scientology Center, before grinding to a stop in bumper-to-bumper traffic when we reached Silver Lake. At a dead stop, I had an idea where we were headed.

"Are we going to a Dodger game?"

"Yes," Dave said. He exhaled, a tiny bit deflated. "But I'm not ruining the surprise. We would have been there in ten minutes anyway."

Okay, a Dodger game, I told myself. I guess that's a surprise. And maybe Lauren was right—maybe something surprising would happen *at* the Dodger game.

Growing up in Boston, Dave lived and breathed the Red Sox. Dave's loving baseball meant *I* loved baseball. So kicking out of work early on a Friday to go to a Dodger game was great.

We parked in the farthest part of the event parking lot, in a deserted stretch of empty spaces. "Are we in a different zip code from the stadium?" I asked.

"I just don't want any drunk people nicking my car," Dave muttered. "I'm still pissed about the dent in the back." Some "maniac," as Dave called him, had bumped his car when he ran into Kinko's to send a FedEx, and I'd been hearing him talking for weeks about "getting in a part" to help fix the side back panel.

Dodger tailgaters had been in position for hours, grilling hot dogs and all sorts of eats in their parking spaces. Fathers were playing catch with sons. Women like me, girlfriends tottering in high heels, were hiking with their dates up to Dodger Stadium. Halfway up the path, Dave stopped me. I held my breath.

"I want to take your picture—the light is so great right now."

He carefully positioned me, took a step back, then moved me to the left a little. He had always taken lots of pictures. He was always telling me to smile, or freeze, or wave. I just chalked it up as a "director thing."

"Okay, now, smile!"

I tilted my head to the left and smiled huge.

"Beautiful!" he said, stowing the camera in the pocket of his jeans and leaning in to kiss me quickly. Dave grabbed my hand and pulled me behind him the rest of the way to the turnstiles. The tickets had been courtesy of his lawyer, and the seats were great, ten rows back on the third base line. This was a big game; the Dodgers were playing the Giants. There were almost as many San Francisco fans in the stadium as there were locals.

We settled into our seats and ordered our first round of beer from the vendor guy. I grinned at Dave as I bit into my Dodger Dog. I purposely let a little mustard smear on my cheek so he could smudge it off with his finger.

As the national anthem sounded through the tinny loudspeakers, Dave's hand rested on my knee and he gave me a little squeeze. The night was beautiful, and I was glad we had arrived early. I hated getting to a game too late to hear the national anthem. It was like running late for a movie and missing the previews; you felt like you were missing a big part of the show. I sipped my beer and watched Nomar Garciaparra step into the on-deck circle and begin going through his notorious routine to warm up. He swung the bat, tightened his gloves, touched each shoulder, and tightened his gloves again. I was sure sport shrinks across the country must have analyzed the slugger's routine, trying to label it obsessive-compulsive or strictly superstition. Nomar stepped out of the box, walked it off a few steps, and then stepped back to begin the routine all over again.

"That guy's crazy," Dave commented into my ear.

Dave loved Nomar when he played in Boston, but after he left the team and they went on to win the World Series the following month, he always blamed Nomar for being the curse that plagued the Red Sox (although he played there for only nine seasons, and the "curse of the Bambino" had hung over the team since 1918).

"Nomar wears number five, and I read somewhere that all of his rituals are in groups of five," I told Dave. "He taps his sneakers five times, he'll tug the gloves five times, and he even signs autographs in groups of five. If he signs for six people, he'll keep going until he reaches ten signatures."

Dave was unimpressed. "I've never read that, and I'm the one who grew up in Boston and has watched this guy play for years," he said, his eyes on the field.

"Yes, I know . . ." I answered patiently. I didn't want to get into a "thing" about it. Dave could be the "keeper of all knowledge" when it came to sports stuff; I'd just sit here and be the girl. "Anyway, Nomar is number five, and Joe DiMaggio wore the number five for his entire career," I went on. "Did you know that after Marilyn's death, Joe claimed her remains as her next of kin, even though they'd been divorced for eight years? Her mother was alive but institutionalized, and he stepped forward to claim her body and make the funeral arrangements." As I talked about Marilyn's funeral I felt myself becoming more animated.

Dave just stared at me. "I can't believe you're talking about dead Marilyn on a gorgeous day like this. I planned today to get your head out of the Marilyn Morgue."

Now I felt bad. "I'm sorry, baby. I can't help thinking about the Marilyn stuff because of the show. You know it's a big deal for me to get the Marilyn show on air."

Dave scowled. "Dani, I just want to have a nice day; I wanted to do something nice for you . . ."

"And you did. This is great." I leaned in for another warm kiss. "Let's not fight—let's just watch the game and eat, okay?"

"Okay." Crisis avoided. He took some of my curly fries and turned his attention back to the action on the diamond. I munched on my hot dog and decided to forget about Weight Watchers points until tomorrow, when I could start starving. The thing I loved most about going to a sporting event was the food. It was a regular chow-a-palooza with beer, hot dogs, Cracker Jacks, and more beer. Late in the game, with the Dodgers leading by two runs, Dave left to get one last bag of peanuts. He was gone for a while. Maybe he was off making arrangements to have the cameraman film us kissing to show on the Jumbotron. Swiveling in my seat, I looked around for him. My heart started to beat faster, thinking of what Lauren had said on the phone. Could he actually be planning the dreaded scoreboard proposal? As itchy as my finger was for his ring, I wasn't sure if I could face Lauren with that kind of proposal story.

I decided not to worry. Choosing to relax and feeling just a little buzzed, I took in the lush field and stadium. It really was beautiful here, and I told myself I was happy. I felt a tap on my shoulder and turned to see Dave holding a pink Dodgers hat.

"Everyone should have a Dodgers hat!" he said. He adjusted the back of the cap and handed it to me. "Turn it over," he urged.

I turned the cap upside down and read aloud what he'd written in large black Sharpie inside the brim. "For Baby—Baseball! I love you, XO D."

"Thank you, baby!" I exclaimed.

It would squash my hair, and wasn't a diamond ring, but that was okay; it was really sweet. Dave took his seat and I noticed that in the row behind us four women in their mid-forties were sitting together. They were obviously related. Sisters, I bet.

"That was so sweet!" one of them gushed, touching my shoulder. "I wish I could get my husband to do something like that for me."

I smiled, embarrassed. I didn't want to rub in anyone's face how nice it felt to have someone to do such thoughtful things for you.

I chomped happily on my Cracker Jack and sipped my third beer. Nomar hit another homer over the right field wall, bringing in two more runs. The Dodgers were now ahead by four. Smelling a victory, thousands streamed toward the exits. We had no intention of leaving so soon.

Now that the seats were emptying out, I saw a couple seated a few rows in front of us. They were both decked out from head to toe in Dodgers regalia: hats, jackets, banners, everything. I watched Grandma Dodger take a foil-wrapped sandwich out of her bag and give half to Grandpa Dodger. It was obvious this was their routine. You knew their story just by taking them in for a few seconds. They were season-ticket holders and had been coming to games together for years and years. First they brought their kids, then their grandkids. But on days like today, being here was their tradition, their treat for each other.

"Do you think that'll be us one day?" I boldly asked Dave, pointing to the elderly couple.

"What do you mean—old and crazy and going to baseball games?" Dave asked. "Definitely!" He came in close and kissed me. "Here's to old and crazy!"

I smiled, lingering in the kiss. When Dave pulled back slightly I kept my eyes closed. "Kiss me again," I said, and he did.

After the game, Dave drove me to my place, where I picked up my car and followed him back to his house. We passed out on top of the covers in bed with bellyaches like a couple of kids. I slept with a smile, thinking of our being "old and crazy."

It was a great night. I was sure we'd have sex in the morning.

THREE

Dave nudged me gently. "Hey, beautiful. I have to go to practice."

Saturday mornings were Dave's "guy time," playing basketball with his buddies. I smiled sleepily. "Okay, I'll see you later."

He trailed his fingers through my hair and kissed me one last time on the neck before grabbing his keys and heading to his car. The gate leading to the sidewalk banged closed behind him and then I heard the distinctive metal-on-metal slam of his car door and the engine revving up.

I smiled again to myself, thinking how great he was. The Dodger game was fun. It was thoughtful and special. I rolled over and pulled the sheets up to my neck. I could still feel the warmth next to me where he'd been a few minutes earlier. There'd been no AM sex; he'd been in a hurry to leave. I counted on my fingers how many days had gone by since we last did it. The softy incident two nights ago didn't count. With no action since I'd been back from Quantico, we last did it the night before I left. That was eight days ago. That was a long time. I knew we'd never gone a week without doing it. Don't guys count the days? Don't guys always want sex? It just seemed weird that he was fine not waking up a few minutes early to give me a good shag before he left. Dave owed me after the Mr. Softy incident; the baseball game didn't make up for that disappointment.

My eyes drifted around the room at his stacks of comic books, framed movie posters on the walls, and the clothes on the floor that he'd worn last night. Even though work had been going great for Dave, he'd lived in this small bungalow for three years, a miniature log cabin with a small bedroom and attached office. It was one of those great finds you had to hear about from a friend; you'd never read an ad for a place like this on craigslist. The pizza man always had a tough time delivering because the house was off a small street up Beachwood Canyon, partially hidden by a giant oak tree. Dave's house was cozy in the winter, when we'd light a fire and snuggle in to watch a good movie. Dave always said that when he moved again, it would be into the house that he would live in for the rest of his life. His place was an okay bachelor pad, but it was definitely an interim living arrangement. On the far wall he'd put an old wooden table he used as a desk, where he kept the whole setup he called his "command center": computer, fax, printer, plus a million different chargers for his cell phones and various other junk.

As sleepy as I'd been kissing Dave good-bye, suddenly I felt very awake. I blinked and stared at his computer. Dave had left his PowerBook out.

Big mistake.

The screen was up, but it was dark. The computer was sleeping, the way I should be sleeping. I felt the blood pounding through my veins. I pushed back the covers and swung my legs out of bed. As I walked toward the computer, I could feel its force field drawing me in. I sat down and pressed the power button and heard the familiar Mac start-up sound.

My first stop was to scan through his recent documents. Nothing new there, just some script changes for his upcoming show and a few saved e-mails from his brother back in Boston. There really wasn't anything interesting, and it felt like a bust. I couldn't believe I'd pulled my naked self out of bed, just to sit here with shivering nippies at ten in the morning. Not wanting to feel like a total failure, I double-clicked on his address book.

"You have 857 contacts," it told me. The page was open to the letter R and the most recently pulled-up name was Amy Robbins.

This stopped me. I started searching my memory. Amy? Amy Robbins? Who was Amy Robbins, and where the fuck was the 404 area code? I grabbed the cordless phone on the desk and dialed Information. The line rang once before the operator picked up.

"Excuse me, but can you tell me where the 404 area code is?" I asked.

"Sure, just a moment. . . . The 404 area code is in Georgia. Would you like me to connect you to Information there?"

"No!" I snapped and, thanking her, slammed the phone down.

Dave had never mentioned an Amy. He never mentioned anything about Georgia. I started circling the ideas through my head. I knew there was something, a glimmer I could almost remember. Then it hit me. When Dave and I met for the first time at the airport, he'd been on his way to Georgia.

Staring past the computer screen, I let my own thoughts spin. Maybe when we met he'd been going to Georgia to see this Amy, a girlfriend he was serious enough with to commute across the country to see. Maybe he'd continued their relationship after we started dating. I thought of how Dave had disappeared for those couple of weeks in the beginning. Maybe he wasn't sure if he wanted to be with me at the start. Maybe he had both things going at the same time. He could have taken me out for dinner, and then gone home and had hot phone sex with Amy.

I tried to calm myself with some deep-breathing techniques I'd seen on *Oprah*.

Maybe when Dave and I met that first time at the airport he'd been going to Georgia to tell Amy it was over—that after all they had meant to each other, it just couldn't work long-distance anymore. Maybe he had CDs to give back to her. He could have mailed them, but he'd really wanted to see her in person for the breakup.

Well, whatever it had been, I was going to take care of this *now*. Turning back to Dave's laptop, I opened up Amy's address card and changed the last two digits in her 404 phone number. Then I saved the card so the entry would update into the memory.

After changing her number, I scanned through the rest of Dave's contacts. For any woman listed that I didn't know, I changed one digit in her number.

This all made me feel great. Now I was sure that there wouldn't be any more calls to "old friends" that could possibly rekindle some smoldering feelings.

Content that I'd done well with the address book, I started thinking about cupcakes from Sprinkles in Beverly Hills. Oprah also talked about this kind of urge—the stress of thinking about Dave with this Amy chick was a "trigger."

Oprah talked a lot about recognizing our triggers, and how if we could recognize our triggers we could help control our choices. I knew it was too early for Sprinkles to be open, so I diverted my attention from sugar to my other addiction: real estate. Dave and I had talked about moving in together, but we really wanted to wait until we could buy a house together and make it a "big" move. Maybe if I could find the perfect place I'd be able to nudge him toward all the "big" stuff.

I grabbed one of Dave's flannel shirts from his drawer and slid it over my head. The faded plaid barely covered my ass. Opening the front door, I peeked my head out, scoping out the scene to see if anyone would see my slightly bare butt as I rushed out to grab the newspaper from the front step. The coast was clear and I darted out and then rushed quickly back inside the house with my prize.

Because it was Saturday, I knew the week's big real estate section would be in today's paper. A few open houses would clear my head of this Amy business.

I didn't knit or take any cooking classes, so driving around and looking at open houses on weekends was the closest thing I had to a hobby. Real estate agents had a name for people like me, "lookiloos": people who toured houses but never made an offer. I would drive around the hills of Hollywood and flats of Hancock Park, checking out houses and imagining the next chapter of my life with Dave. I'd do the combined-income math for the two of us in my head.

I'd recently cleaned out my savings and bought a new shiny BMW, and one of the best things about having the new car was being able to park directly in front of an open house. When I'd driven my Honda, I soon figured out that the Realtors knew there was no way I would be able to afford a two-million-dollar home. Realtors were as tough as interrogating cops when it came to sizing up potential buyers. They'd covertly spy through wooden shutters as the scruffy couples streamed up the sidewalk early with their Starbucks cups, and I felt like a pathetic single version of those losers. Open houses were a lot like Noah's Ark—everyone was paired off two by two. The BMW (even though it was an entry-level model) gave me enough cachet to walk in with my head held high. Gone were the days when snotty Realtors would pull the color Xerox copies out of my hand and say, "I really need to save these for the *serious* buyers."

I had my whole shtick down. Checking out real estate was a lot like going on a blind date. You needed to have pat answers that portrayed you in the best possible light and got you through to the next level. Ms. Realtor would ask, "Is this for yourself?"

"No, it's for me and my fiancé," I'd reply with a little laugh—like, how could I be looking for a place to live in alone? Obviously, someone like me was attached. I didn't feel bad about the fibs, because I knew the ring from Dave would come someday.

Ms. Realtor's eyes would drift down to assess the size of the stone on my finger. I could attribute my ringless finger to my being in my weekend-casual look, fresh from a hike, no jewelry necessary. "Are you working with a Realtor?" she'd ask.

"I am working with someone, but she's out of town, which is why I'm on my own today," I always answered.

If she was really dubious, Ms. Realtor would keep pressing me. "Really? Who? What office?"

I'd give the name of someone I had met at a cocktail party through friends, and the next day Ms. Realtor would call me to verify that we were working together. Whatever.

Now, flipping through the Open House section, I skipped past the houses I'd already toured. None of them were perfect for Dave and me, and besides it was a seller's market now, not really a great time to buy. I was hungry to find the "just on the market" place that no one had toured yet.

One advertised house on Chiselhurst in Los Feliz had just been redone for three million; I'd toured the house a few weeks before and it still reeked of kimchi from the previous owners. When I wrinkled my nose and asked the Realtor about it, she acted blasé. "Just get some candles," was her advice.

I continued my listing-scan and came across an interesting new house for sale up on Outpost. I knew that street well—tons of celebrities lived "in Outpost" as people called it: Will Ferrell, Matthew Perry. Celebrities were good for your resale value. One of the writers from the show, Jimmy, got up early to hike the steep street every morning, risking the busy cars whizzing past him during morning rush hour, so he could ogle Charlize Theron. I guess she read the paper on her porch naked, and even with her property surrounded with heavy foliage, he had a spot he used to peek through. Somehow I had a feeling he may have ripped out a few handfuls of leaves to aid his spying. Guys are pathetic.

Jumping in the shower, I let the water pound my face and I swore to myself that I wouldn't think about Amy Robbins. I did a quick cleanse, mostly washing off the Dodger game from the night before. I didn't have to wash off any sex; it *had* been eight days. I saw that I'd started gnawing my fingernails this morning. My fingertips were sore and red.

The open house on Outpost was close to Dave's log cabin bungalow, and I had time to grab a coffee and doughnut on the way. I balanced the cup between my thighs and convinced myself that eating a doughnut in the car somehow took away some of the Weight Watchers points. My fingers sticky on the steering wheel, I carefully wound my way up Outpost. I didn't have to check the address in the paper; the Porsches and Mercedeses were double-parked in front of the neighboring driveways. This was a hot house.

For me, walking into a house was always an emotional experience. My fascination with lookilooing went back to lonely car rides at night with my mom. "Do you want to drive around the nice neighborhoods?" she'd ask. This was a special thing for us, a treat. We'd slip into the car and head south up Baseline Road to the luxury community called The Lakes. It was the most exclusive neighborhood in Tempe, bordering a man-made lake. Most of the homes had their own docks, although there were little more than wooden rowboats moored to them. Up and down the culs-de-sac we would cruise. We always had to take U-turns slowly because our '77 Chevy had a shitty turning radius. Also, the muffler was a little loud, and occasionally drapes would move aside as the owners checked to see who was idling in front of their house at 11 PM.

"Imagine how nice your life would be if you lived here," my mom would say. "They must be pretty happy—these homes cost a hundred thousand dollars."

This was while my parents were still together. The drive home would be time for her monologue, which always started with, "If only your father made better money. . . ."

Even more than my mother, I was very specific about my dream home, and this Outpost listing had huge curb appeal. My dream home would be classic California Spanish and built in the '20s or '30s (the best decades for Spanish), with hardwood floors and two fireplaces, a media room, and renovated bathrooms and kitchen. I would need four bedrooms: one master suite for me, one for an office, one for a guest room (for whom, I had no idea), and one for the baby (who would one day come). I wanted the house's character to be intact, but with all the modern amenities of a home built in this millennium, complete with Viking range and Sub-Zero.

I didn't make eye contact with the Realtor. I wanted to convey that I had every reason to be here and that her pesky questions were just getting in the way of my browsing. Figuring my usual combined-income math in my head, I calculated that we could *just* make the payments on this place if we were buying it together.

My first stop was the master bedroom. I headed straight for the closet, always a dead giveaway about the occupant. I checked out the wall of shoes first. Prada, Gucci, Jimmy Choo. No one paid retail for all those shoes; they alone told me that the owner of this house was some sort of TV star, probably on a hit sitcom. This woman could have given Imelda a run for her money. Boxes and boxes of matching plastic containers. Each box had a taped Polaroid of the pair of shoes inside. Very organized, although I knew the owner of the house hadn't gotten all this together on her own. Maybe she had a second assistant take care of the shoes? Probably not, I told myself—TV stars usually have only one assistant.

The bedroom was serviceable, with a high, sloping ceiling and a plasma screen attached to the wall. A lit fireplace off to the side crackled invitingly, and a couple of potted ficus softened up the rough edges.

The bathroom needed a lot of work—it was cramped—although

the listing in the paper had boasted of "original tiles." Scoping out the bathroom of a stranger is one of the best voyeurism rushes you can get. I closed the door behind me for privacy, acting like I was trying to take in the full size of the room. I quickly opened up the medicine cabinet, and sure enough, Miss Nice Shoes had a bit of an anxiety problem, judging by the half empty bottle of Xanax with the patient name scratched off the label. I saw the tube of Valtrex and realized the herpes medicine was probably the reason for a lot of the anxiety. I was always shocked that people would leave their prescription medications in the cabinet. Xanax was a hot commodity and thirty of those shouldn't be hanging around for just anyone to snag.

I opened the bottle and counted out eight into my hand and stuffed them into my jeans pocket. Now eight bad things could happen to me and I would be okay. The pills would also come in handy if Amy Robbins suddenly descended on Los Angeles from Atlanta.

I closed the cabinet and then stopped short.

"Oh my God," I whispered to myself. To the left of the sink taps I spied the holy grail of skin products, a giant tub of Crème de la Mer, the one that cost over a thousand bucks. I picked it up gravely and carefully, as if I were handling a Fabergé egg. Feeling the weight of the jar in my hands, my heart hammering in my chest, I carefully unscrewed the top. I'd never been able to afford Crème de la Mer. I dipped my fingers lightly into the cream and warmed the dollop between my hands, the way I had read about in *Vogue*. I patted my face with the cream and stared hard at my reflection in the mirror. I guess I was expecting immediate results, but I saw nothing except a shiny face.

My fingers were greasy and the big tub slipped in my hand as I carefully glided it back to its home on the sink. It would be bad to drop it on the floor of the bathroom. From the weight of the jar I knew the crash would be huge, and I would look very guilty—not with egg but Crème de la Mer all over my face.

This place wasn't right for Dave and me; it was set too close to the street and I wouldn't have wanted to deal with the work on the bathroom. Suddenly I couldn't get out of there soon enough.

Starting my car, I worried that maybe they had security cameras and had seen me using the face cream. Maybe the actress who lived there would scan through the footage later and recognize me. Maybe she worked on the same lot where we shot *Flesh and Bone*. I had visions of a wanted poster of me distributed to real estate offices across Beverly Hills. Maybe I should lie low and give the open house thing a rest for a while.

FOUR

I didn't go back to Dave's after my open house adventure. I went home. Being in my own space was a relief. Lucy was waiting at the front door for me and had no problem letting me know how mad she was; I could hear her plaintive meow as I fumbled with the keys. I'd been at work all day yesterday and had made a pit stop after the baseball game only to pick up my car; I'd poured her a double bowl of kibble so she wouldn't starve, but she knew she'd been neglected somewhat for twenty-four hours.

Guiltily I headed straight for the kitchen and picked up her bowl. The sound of her kibble hitting the bottom of the dish made her happy. She purred and bonked her head against my calves as I set the bowl down for her. All was forgiven. I watched her dig in. She was so happy, and food did the trick—she didn't have to count Weight Watchers points, or count the days since she last got laid. She didn't worry about women named Amy in Georgia.

Heading to my bedroom, I dragged the laundry hamper out of the closet and started sorting through my dirty clothes, making neat piles of the whites and the darks. My stuff from the trip was still in my suitcase, so I emptied that too. Working the long hours on the show made me slack off when it came to taking care of my usual stuff.

I was shuffling down the hallway toward the washing machine when the phone rang. I knew it was Dave and I let everything tumble to the floor so I could make a clear shot at grabbing the phone off its base.

"Hi," I answered breathlessly.

"Dani, is that you? You don't sound like yourself."

I could practically hear my heart drop as quick and heavy as a bowling ball on my foot.

"Hi . . . Mom." *Shit*, I thought, *why didn't I check the caller ID?* My mother's calls to the office were easy to cut short; I just used the "running late for a meeting" excuse. But Mom calling at home on the weekend was death. "Sorry, Mom, I was running from outside." Already I was in the hole and apologizing.

"Why would you be running? You hate exercise."

"It's a long story," I replied.

"Well, anyway, I just want you to know that I really loved the show last week."

"Oh, really?" This was surprising. "Well, thanks so much, I'm glad."

"Honestly, Dani, I don't know where you come up with these things. You've always had such an imagination." She always talked about my imagination—it didn't seem like a compliment. She pressed on. "Joe, who I take computer classes with down at the center, was asking me why you never have your name up there on the screen alone. Why do you always write shows with someone else? Can't you write a show on your own?"

I closed my eyes and tried to silence my heavy exhale so she wouldn't hear it through the phone. *Patience*, I told myself, *patience and love.* "Mom, there's a staff of writers. Usually it's a group effort, and screen credit gets figured out accordingly."

"When did you have your name on the screen by yourself? I've never seen that."

I had just answered her question; she obviously thought I couldn't work alone, so it was not as though I would be able to change her mind.

"Actually, Mom, we're going to air a show next week that will have my name alone in the credits. It's kind of about Marilyn Monroe's death and it's a big sweeps show for us—so the computer guy doesn't need to worry about me, okay?"

"Really?" She sounded doubtful.

"Yes, really."

"So, if you wrote it on your own, does that mean you get paid more money?"

This made me smile; now I had her attention.

"Yes, it is more money when I write a show on my own." I was treading carefully; if she had any idea how much more I was making for the Marilyn show, she'd definitely be hitting me up for another loan. "Jennifer Love Hewitt is going to play the lead guest star role. It's going to be awesome!"

"Why would Jennifer Love Hewitt want to do *your* show when that show she's on is so good? You know she can talk to dead people?"

"I know she can talk to dead people. I know she's 'The Ghost Whisperer,' but she loves *Flesh and Bone* and is doing the show that I wrote all on my own."

"Well, I guess we'll have to be sure to watch the show then."

I decided to let it all pass. I asked her how she was, knowing she was never that great.

"I was really expecting my commission check from work to be bigger this month."

Mom worked at Crate and Barrel and lived and died by her commission. She was always thinking it would be more, and she always ended up short at the end of the month. Mom was part of C&B's team of "Design Specialists" and often made house calls to some of her bigger clients. Now she moved on to regale me with stories of her clients in Scottsdale, where she had gone on vacation this month, and how they had a safe in the house for the wife's jewelry.

Mom didn't ask any more questions about me. I was in robot mode with my prompts, and she just kind of talked *at* me, which was fine, because when she grilled me it could be *really* draining. "I know how you just get caught up with Dave and forget things," she said, "so I wanted to remind you that I'm going to be in LA in a couple of weeks, and . . ."

I *had* forgotten, thanks to my trip, the Marilyn show, and all the obsessing over Dave's Mr. Softy. Damn her.

"Well," she went on, "you told me you'd put it in your calendar before, but I know you forget, so be sure to make that lunch reservation."

I never forgot anything; I was sure it was in my calendar and that I would have noticed the notation and freaked out the day before. Maybe it was best not to think about seeing Mom until it was right upon me—that way, I wouldn't have to stress myself out dreading the get-together.

Clicking open my iCal, I saw it was in there. I wrote myself a yellow Post-it note to call for a ressie.

"Got it covered, Mom. . . . Can't wait to see you. Bye."

"Oh, wait, I wanted to tell you that I've found the perfect new haircut for you."

"I like my hair, Mom."

"Have you seen Misty Decker's hairdo? She does the weather here on Channel Three?"

"We don't get Channel Three here in LA. That's your channel in Phoenix. We have different channels here."

"Well, it would really look fantastic if you would just give it a shot.

You know how dry and coarse your hair looks all the time. This would really help you. That Misty is just so cute."

"Okay, Mom, thanks."

"All right then, love you, proud of you."

"Thanks, Mom, me too."

After putting the laundry in the washer, I ignored the pile of research materials on my desk. Focusing on the fridge, I start cleaning out the moldy veggies. I didn't know why I bothered buying the healthy stuff. Dave called while I was dumping the chunky soy milk.

"Hey, baby," I answered. "How was the game?"

"We sucked ass, but it's cool. I got in a great workout."

"So what's going on for later?" I asked, thinking about the eight days.

"Yeah, that's why I wanted to call right when I got home. You know, I've got so much to do with the show this week—I really need to stay in and do my homework for the shoot on Monday."

"Really?" I was stunned. It was Saturday. It seemed like having the afternoon today and all tomorrow before going to work on Monday would have been enough time for Dave to prep. But I didn't want to seem needy. "I wanted to hang out," I said. "You know I've been missing you so much what with my being away all last week. Are you sure you can't get together?" I tried to have my voice radiate a sexual invite.

"Yeah . . . I just can't. You know what it's like when it's busy at work," Dave said.

"Sure, no problem. I actually might have plans with some friends." I put that out there to see how it would hang in the air. I didn't say who my plans were with.

"Where are you going?" Now he seemed a bit more alert.

"Mmm. I think I'm just going to meet up with a bunch of people near the beach in Santa Monica, maybe get drinks at Shutters, and then walk across the street to the Ivy."

"Okay, so you're going to be at the beach—cool." He seemed relieved. "You know, you're the best, Dani. I'll come by in the morning and we'll go to Viktor's for breakfast, cool?"

"So you're not going to church?" I asked.

Dave was Catholic and his spirituality was very important to him. When we first started dating he asked me if I had a problem with him being so religious, and of course I told him I didn't. He tried to go to church most Sundays, and I respected his commitment to his heritage and faith, but secretly I couldn't stand it when going to church interfered with our Sunday brunch plans.

"No, not tomorrow."

"Cool. I love you," I tried to say brightly, and clicked off.

I wondered if Dave might actually have been worried about my going out on my own on a Saturday night. Well, let him worry—it just proved that after almost two years, the relationship was still fresh, which was a good thing. I had no plans, but I didn't want him to know that I couldn't call anyone to get together because it was Saturday night and everyone was already booked up with their boyfriends. A guy doesn't cancel on his girl on a Saturday. Bachelor parties are the rare exception.

I wondered again if he was going to call Amy, or try to—maybe she was visiting from Atlanta—and wondered if Dave would get it on with her, with no Mr. Softy in sight. But thinking this way was as murderous as eating a whole bowl of trans fats, so I told myself to put my paranoia out of my mind. I decided to follow Dave's example and work that night. I had TiVo'd some specials on cable about forensic police work and an autopsy show on HBO. It was fascinating to see how the cops nabbed the bad guys. Never doubt the importance of one hair or a vaginal swab containing seminal fluid—any physical evidence can lead to catching the perpetrator.

So at 8 PM, I grabbed a beer and air-popped some popcorn and soaked it heavily with Molly McButter before settling in for a cozy night. Considering that Dave had bailed on me, this was the best I could do. I stared at the television as viscera and mayhem flickered past me. Cool.

I woke up with a start. The TV was really loud. I didn't know how long I'd been asleep, but judging by the small pool of drool that had trickled down my arm and settled into the sofa cushion, I'd been out a while. Checking the clock, I saw it was past two, and realized I had slept through my plan to call Dave and let him know that I had come home from my beach adventures and hadn't gotten into any trouble. We'd talk in the morning. Leaving the couch, I used my night vision to navigate down the hall to my bedroom. Lucy was waiting, an inky stain of fur against my duvet. At least I wasn't getting into bed alone.

I dreamt about losing my new laptop. I lost everything: the script I had been working on, all my addresses, my date book, and my huge iTunes library. What a nightmare.

The next morning Dave and I went down the hill to get breakfast at Viktor's Coffee Shop. Dave always said you really know you're "a half of a two" when you have someone to get brunch with on a Sunday. I went to church with him plenty of times. Trying to be a trouper, I'd even bought two conservative dresses and a pair of sensible shoes suitable for wearing next to him in the pew. I'd always resented the shoes; they reminded me of something the mother of the bride would wear. So I'd sit next to Dave and stand on cue with my feet sweating in my closed-toe shoes, longing for a waffle and latte.

Judging from Dave's just-rolled-out-of-bed shirt and jeans, I could tell he had indeed skipped services today.

"So, how was your night?" he asked as he carefully cut the egg yolks away from the egg whites and moved them to the side of the plate. Dave always ate his eggs that way. Then he would dip his toast into the yolks and mop everything into his mouth.

"It was good. We had a good time. Even though I live in Los Angeles, I sometimes forget there's an ocean here. You know how I never go west of the 405," I replied.

"So who was there?"

Fuck Julia Roberts—I could have won an Oscar for this performance. "Oh, just the girls. Lauren, Ina, and Rachel who works with me on the show."

"No guys?"

"No, no guys," I assured him. "Why do you ask?"

"Well, it's just kinda out of character for you to go out like that. All night I imagined you driving down Ocean Avenue in your new fancy car, with your sunroof open, having a great time."

"Are you mad that I went out? You're the one who wanted to stay home and work on a Saturday night—and what's your beef with my BMW?"

"No; no beef," he said, holding up his palms to ward me off. "I just figured you might be out hooking up with some guy or something."

"Baby, what are you talking about? You're crazy!" I reached across the table and took his hand. "You know you're my whole world." I squeezed his hand for emphasis.

"So you weren't out messing around on me last night?"

I really couldn't believe this. He was so adorable. If only he'd known what I'd really done last night. Dave was beautiful in the mornings, with his unshaven stubbly face and hair still damp from the shower. "No, I was not messing around on you last night."

I'd mimicked his words back to him. This made him smile.

"Okay, so this means we can go back to your place and have afternoon sex?" he asked brightly.

He was so great. I had no idea he would be that insecure. Now I was smiling as big as he was.

"Let's go."

Only we didn't go to my place; we went to his. We had after-noon-daylight sex, which had always seemed a bit naughty. I stared up at the ceiling while I let him do the work; he should, after all the trauma I'd been through, worrying about Mr. Softy. He was al-most finishing, and I wasn't even close. I thought that Amy would have to be a blond; who'd ever heard of a brunette named Amy? I thought of Marilyn sashaying through *Gentlemen Prefer Blondes*. Maybe gentlemen do. Dave finished. I didn't, but it was okay—I'd been close. Nine days, thank God.

I was catching my breath, still tangled in the sheets. Dave dismounted after a few minutes to grab a drink of water in the kitchen.

"Shit!" I heard him yell, followed by the banging of drawers, open-ing and closing of cabinets.

"What's wrong?" I called out.

"I just wanted to make you dinner tonight. I was thinking of mak-ing a kind of baked ziti thing to have while we watched *The Sopra-nos* later."

"You mean you're making me Fuckin'-Baked-Ziti?" I teased.

"Yep, that's what the real Sopranos eat."

Talking about Fuckin'-Baked-Ziti made me smile; it was part of our boyfriend/girlfriend lexicon.

"I went to the Mayfair yesterday to buy the food, and I thought I had a couple of bottles of red wine here, but there's nothing," he called out to me.

"It's no big deal. I can run out and get some. The show isn't on for hours." I started to sit up.

"No, no, no." He came back in the bedroom, crossed over to me, and pulled the sheets back up. "You're going to relax. This is for you. Take it easy for once—you've been working so hard."

Dave tucked the duvet around my chin. "You deserve this—

you're my baby. I'll go to the store. I'll be there and back in twenty minutes." He leaned down and kissed me. "You can time me."

"Okay." I smiled back mushily. I'd just gotten laid and I'd almost had an orgasm. It was okay.

Dave picked up his keys and cell phone and was gone.

I grinned at his back as I watched him leave. I was smiling partly from the afterglow of our rolling around in bed, but mostly from him making such an effort for me.

He *had* been thinking of me last night; he just hadn't been with me.

Alone on the bed, I kicked my legs out of pure glee like an eight-year-old. I rolled over and realized that, even though it was late afternoon, I needed more coffee. Dave hated the taste of coffee and was always trying to get me to give it up, but he had bought a little machine that brewed a single cup for when I stayed over.

I got up, went to the kitchen, let the water boil, and leaned against the countertop. I was still totally naked, and being against the counter with pubies everywhere probably wasn't that hygienic.

I could see a stack of phone messages from work, next to where he always put his keys and wallet. I picked up the stack and started leafing through them. It never hurt to check and see if there was one girl who called a bunch of times. Or if the message was from a girl and, instead of leaving her number when she called, an assistant had written, "You know it."

There was nothing at all incriminating; he'd passed the test. "All clear," I said to myself. "No need for any alarm." I carefully put the messages back so he wouldn't know I'd been psycho-snooping.

I spied one small sheet of paper that I had missed, lying facedown. Flipping it over to check the message, I saw that it was a receipt for dinner. It was on Dave's AmEx and it was a big bill, letting me know that it had been dinner for two with a good bottle of wine.

I checked the restaurant: Locanda Veneta. Nice. It was dark and romantic there. When Dave and I would go there, I always saw that guy who used to play Ross on *Friends*. It was weird that Dave never mentioned he had gone out to dinner last week. I squinted at the faint ink for the date.

I froze. The receipt was from last night. Dave had told me he was working last night and couldn't go out with me. But he had gone out, and he'd paid his bill at 10:42 PM. I felt the blood rushing into my face and tears started to gather in my eyes. "Fuck, fuck, fuck!" I yelled out to the empty house. Yellow Alert.

FIVE

I left the receipt and grabbed my clothes. Dave was probably halfway home by now and I didn't know what to do. I wasn't ready to face him and start a fight.

Banging out of his place, I was in my car and heading down the hill within sixty seconds, verging on being totally hysterical. Dialing my friend Ina from my cell, I prayed she would answer. Ina would have some good advice. She was crazy, but she knew about this kind of thing. She picked up on the fourth ring.

"I've got a Yellow Alert with Dave—are you around?"

"What? What's wrong—are you okay?" she asked. "Of course I can meet you. Do you want to go to Alcove?"

"Yes, it's close. I'm on my way," I answered tightly.

"Okay, relax, Dani—I'll see you in a few minutes."

Ina was the only friend I had whose personal situation was even more pathetic than mine. Ina was my Hot Asian Friend, as I liked to call her. I always brought up the Asian part because she didn't drive and I was never sure if it was because she had grown up not driving in Manhattan or if she fit into that stereotype of being a bad

Asian driver. I'd asked her once and she'd looked at me funny and, shruggingly, told me, "Kind of both."

Ina told me over the phone that she had been out running errands with her boyfriend, Larry, who was going to drop her off. I always thought of Larry as a l-o-s-e-r. They had been together for a year and a half and lived in a huge run-down house above Universal Studios. The paint was peeling off the clapboard siding and they couldn't have pets because all the shrubs in the backyard were poisonous, but the place was big. I never knew where the money came from to pay for the house every month, but somehow they came up with it. I knew the two of them didn't have a lot of cash, because last Christmas Larry wouldn't let her get a Christmas tree because he said they couldn't afford the lights.

Larry said he wanted to be a cameraman to make money, but he was studying audio first to learn the ropes, which didn't make sense to me. The cameraman gig would also be temporary because he was *really* going to be an actor. Larry always was "in class" or working out with his personal trainer. I liked to think Ina would have dumped him a long time ago if it weren't for the driving thing, but I wasn't really sure. She put up with a lot from him. Ina was a TV news producer who was currently freelancing. Because she was never at work, I took this to mean she was unemployed. Her parents owned a busy Chinese restaurant in Brooklyn's Sunset Park and I figured they must be helping her out every month.

Ina held her hand up when she spied me at the corner table at Alcove. As she weaved her way toward me through the maze of tables, I felt glad I had called her. I figured Ina was someone I could tell the truth to about what had happened with Dave, and she wouldn't judge me. Ina herself was recovering from what she described as her "freak-out." She had been convinced that Larry was cheating on her. All the signs were there: Class seemed to be always running late; he started wearing cologne; and he was definitely working out more. Also Ina had noticed they weren't having sex as much. The less-sex thing was what had really gotten to her and had led her to snooping through his stuff.

Two months ago, while she'd been moping around the house waiting for Larry to come home again, she'd started nosing through his stuff, and after about twenty minutes of good, solid snooping she'd found his cell-phone bill, sandwiched between some of his sides for acting class, hidden in his backpack. She'd started scrolling down the page, checking each number as she went. Ina recognized their home number, the number for his class, and numbers for a couple of his friends, but there had been a series of long calls to a 310 number she didn't know. One of them had been made at 2 AM and lasted forty minutes.

Ina opened up her day planner and checked the date from a few weeks earlier. Nothing out of the ordinary: It had been just a regular night, which meant she had been at home with him, asleep, and that Larry must have gotten out of bed and gone outside to make the cell-phone call.

So fucking guilty.

To prove her point, Ina dialed the 310 number. Ring, ring, ring. Then finally the machine picked up.

"Hey, it's me, leave a message and don't bore me."

The voice-mail woman had that Demi Moore kind of voice, husky and sexy from too many cigarettes. Ina slammed the phone down, hoping there hadn't been any ambient noise from her end that would identify her to the "don't bore me" woman.

Ina lay around with a stomachache for the rest of that afternoon. Larry had been at class and then was going for drinks with some buddies later. Ina kept running over and over in her head whether there could be any reasonable explanation for the stealth phone calls in the middle of the night, while she'd slept in bed. Maybe it was a friend of his sister's or someone in trouble? It would be just like Larry to try and help someone out. Her ruminating was interrupted by the doorbell.

Normally Ina wouldn't have opened the door, but Larry had mentioned that a script for a project might be dropped off, and she didn't want to blow it by not answering. So Ina opened the door, not to a delivery man but to a striking woman dressed all in black, one of those chicks in their late twenties who had major attitude and smoked and hung out in coffeehouses most of the day.

"Ina, right?"

There it was; *the* voice.

"Yeah, I'm Ina," she replied. Then, wanting to let the girl in black know that she knew about her, Ina folded her arms across her chest. "Larry's not home."

"Yeah, I know. I wanted to come here and tell you something. Just so you know, I'm Larry's wife and he's *never* going to marry you. And I've heard all about you and your lousy blow jobs, which is why Larry has to come to my house twice a week so I can get him off properly."

Ina stood there in stunned silence. She believed every word the girl in black had said. The blow job thing was, literally, a low blow. Ina knew she could use some help in that department, but it wasn't like she wanted to watch a porno and hone her technique.

"I just wanted to let you know what's really going on," the girl said and, as she headed back to the black BMW parked at the curb, she turned around for a parting shot. "And if you're going to call someone to check up on your boyfriend, and you plan on hanging up, you should remember that everyone has caller ID now and it's obvious, okay? It's obvious who's calling."

With that, Miss Size-Four Black Jeans had gotten into her car and peeled away. Ina remained in the open doorway, stunned. She slowly closed the door and turned the deadbolt to lock it into place. Now she really had something to talk to Larry about when he got home.

But, after all this, they were still together two months later. When Ina first unloaded all this drama on me over Ice Blendeds at the Coffee Bean on Larchmont, I'd known to mask my true feelings. I had been down this road before with other friends. When someone told you some horrible story about her boyfriend, you never let her know that you'd always thought the guy was a jerk and it was a huge relief to finally be able to come clean about that time he'd once called you when she was out of town. Saying such a thing was always a mistake, because more often than not they worked it out and went back to pawing each other in front of you and sucking faces.

"Hey," Ina said brightly as she sat down.

"Hey," I answered lifelessly. "I already ordered a salad for us to split."

"That sounds yummy. What happened? You look like you ran into a truck face-first."

"Thanks," I replied, trying to smile. "I kind of did." I was trying to maintain my composure, but I could feel my face crumple up so I knew the ugly-face cry was coming. I told her about the receipt and the Yellow Alert.

"You're never gonna trust him," Ina said. "He's a dog. He's always checking out girls when he thinks you're not looking."

"All guys check out girls—it's *how* guys are," I shot back. "I just don't know—I'm afraid to confront him because I don't want him to know I was going through his stuff."

Ina stared me down. "Look, you've got two choices. You can call him on it or let it go. There could be a lot of explanations for the receipt—maybe something came up last minute and he knew you'd be mad if you knew he changed his plans to accommodate some-one while bailing on you. Which *is* fucked-up in its own way . . ." She perked up even more. "Maybe he was secretly meeting with a jewelry designer to make a ring for you! Maybe this is all about something great for you and you won't want to blow it by ragging on him!"

That was a bit of a stretch even for me. I was so depressed. I re-alized I was not in the mood to hear any more of Ina's Dave theo-ries, so I changed the subject. "Hey, how's Larry? Still married?"

Ina was suddenly distracted, asking the busboy for more iced tea. "Yes, he's still married, but only because that bitch won't give him a divorce."

"I don't get that. If this marriage was some spur-of-the-moment thing in Vegas, like he says it was, why does she want to hang onto a guy like Larry?"

Ina narrowed her eyes. "What do you mean, a guy like Larry?"

"Don't get me wrong, I know Larry is great, but in the future col-umn he's a little lacking. Does he even have a job? Last time we talked, you said something about him not even having a checking account."

"That's just temporary. He needs to use my account because the bank messed up his account so he can't write checks anymore. That's why I put everything into my account now."

"I'm just saying that he's not exactly a candidate for the ideal husband. He's living with you and isn't going to get back with her, right?"

"Right," she replied, but she was gazing down at her place setting and not looking me in the eye.

"They're not in communication at all, are they? I mean, after everything that happened two months ago?"

"No! They're not in communication. I've actually contacted a lawyer about getting the divorce paperwork drawn up."

I froze with my fork halfway to my mouth. "Why are *you* contacting the lawyer, and not Larry?"

"Larry is really busy with class and auditions right now, so I've been doing the research. And also, it's going to cost almost three thousand dollars, and that's a lot of money to us these days."

"You mean, he's not even making an attempt to pay for his own divorce—you're supposed to scrape this together?"

Ina scowled. I knew she would rather be the one asking the questions. She was never in the mood to be interrogated about Larry. "You know," she said, measuring her words, "I would think you, of all people, would be a little more understanding."

I exhaled. Now I felt bad. "Okay, I'll lay off Larry. We'll just beat up on Dave for now. Deal?"

Ina smiled. "Deal."

Driving home from lunch, I wondered if I was predisposed to being slightly whacked when it came to trust issues and men. I had my mom's roomy hips; maybe I'd inherited other unpleasantness from her. I remembered my mom sitting me down in our family room when I was eleven, clenching and unclenching her hands while she carefully tried to explain to me that she and my father were getting divorced.

I had been away at camp for a week, and the two of them, as well as the rest of the family, knew this was happening, but they'd kept it from me because they thought I was too young to handle the news while away from home. My first awkward weekend of visitation with my dad, I sat silently in the car, hoping he would explain what had happened. But Dad could never go that deep. "You know, it's been hard with your mother and me," he began. "We were married just out of high school."

I knew my mother had gotten pregnant with me her senior year and they'd "had" to get married. It was nice knowing you weren't planned. He kept talking, about having worked long hours, spending time apart, and how he tried to make his marriage work over the years. "I guess I'd had enough when I came home and went into the kitchen and there was food on the floor, you know, crumbs from something, and then I put my hand on the counter and it was sticky." I'd been looking at him across the front seat of his car, my preadolescent unibrow a mirror of his own unibrow, while he continued. "It was right then that I realized, you know, I just didn't want to be there. I had to get out of there."

So that was my explanation: He'd left because of a dirty kitchen. Needless to say, wherever I lived, the kitchen was always very clean, no crumbs anywhere.

When I was in high school, I found out through my mother's sly comments that my dad had always messed around on her. Just a year into their marriage, she'd had a feeling that he had something going on with a woman at work. She thought about where he could be hiding clues, things that would betray if he was having an affair. Mom finally thought of the one place she'd never needed to go: the trunk of his car.

She pulled up the carpet in the trunk and found a dozen love letters from the woman at work. He'd put them inside the spare tire, something my mom would never have needed to use. So she was right. I believe in women's intuition. I think what men fail to realize is that we can usually tell because they act totally different when they are leading this other part of their life. The cheaters reveal themselves.

After their separation, life kind of stood still for my mom. She worked long hours and we always had some bill collector calling about something that was past due. The paint peeled from the front of our town house. Our living room carpet was still light-blue shag, a color my mom hated because it was *her* mother's favorite color, which never made sense to me. One summer both our washer and dryer broke down, but we only had the money to get one of them fixed. We fixed the washer; my mom reasoned that our clothes would dry quickly in the Arizona sun. I know the neighbors saw our underwear hanging limply from the clothesline and labeled us white trash.

Mom had no social life after the divorce and never dated, but Dad always had some woman moving in or out of his condo. ("Natasha" was just the latest, with the least legal documentation.) They were usually young, with kids of their own, and arrived with some sad story of having been down and out. Most of them had gotten pregnant young and never obtained high school diplomas. My dad never bothered getting the divorce from my mom finalized. He hated to give all that money to the lawyers.

One weekend he came back to his place with his pickup truck loaded with clothes and furniture. I was hanging out at his condo, and he introduced me to April, a "lovely lady" as he called her. She may have been sweet, but lovely? I didn't know. Her teeth looked like a horse had kicked her in the face. That bothered my dad, and he shuttled her to an orthodontist pronto. April had a fourteen-year-old son, Jeremy. Neither one of them ever spoke much to me. Jeremy had some sort of hearing disability. He wore big hearing aids in both ears, and trying to have a conversation with him was painful. April never talked about her first marriage to "that SOB" as my dad had described him. When my mom would get really mad at me for "smarting off," she'd make me spend the weekends at my dad's house, where April would cook something for dinner that tasted like prison food, and my dad would tell stories about himself in which he was invariably the hero. Jeremy had a room near the laundry, and the guest room where I bunked was right next to his. At night I was lulled to sleep by Jeremy's grunts and cries as he furiously masturbated in bed. With his giant hearing aids sitting on his nightstand, he had no idea how loud he was.

I'd lie in bed, staring up at the ceiling and counting the days until I finished high school and could be someone else and live somewhere else.

SIX

I drove home. I'd left my cell phone off during lunch and saw now that Dave had called twice. It was getting late, and I know he was home preparing for our *Sopranos* dinner and worriedly wondering where I'd run off to. I was thinking of Ina's suggestion that maybe he'd been off doing something nice or even matrimonial last night. I felt stuck because there was no way to confront him with the receipt without letting him know that I'd been looking through his stuff.

As I was stopped in traffic on Franklin, my phone rang again. It was Dave for a third time.

"Hey, baby . . ."

"Heyyy," I answered back.

"Where'd you go? I thought you were going to hang out till tonight."

"I just got really sick to my stomach. Maybe it's some sort of delayed food poisoning thing from last night."

"Tell me again what you ate?" Dave asked.

I wanted to say that I had pasta and wine at Locanda Veneta, but I didn't. "I had some whitefish special. I'm sorry, baby, I'm just not feeling good, and I think I'm just going to go back home to lie down."

"Where are you now?"

"I'm on my way back from the drugstore. I went to pick up some Pepto." Thinking fast.

"That sucks. Are you sure you don't want me to come over?"

"No, it's okay. It's the kind of 'being sick' when you need to be alone, if you know what I mean." Dave had a history of having a sensitive stomach, so I knew he'd be sympathetic, or at least squeamish.

"Okay, let me know if you want or need anything."

"Okay, bye."

He was being so sweet, and I knew there could be a million explanations for the receipt. It *had* been his signature . . . right? Now I wasn't sure. I didn't read the exact signature. After checking out the name of the restaurant and the amount, I guess I figured it was Dave's. I thought I peripherally registered the strong slant of his signature, but now I couldn't be certain. Maybe it wasn't Dave's receipt at all. Maybe it was just something he picked up by accident somewhere.

Trying to convince myself this was the truth, I chose to ignore that the receipt was from late last night and that we'd had brunch together twelve hours later. Maybe the date stamp was wrong from the restaurant. Maybe it had been thrown off by daylight savings time. I didn't know when daylight savings time began, but messing with that kind of stuff could screw up timetables. Computers were sensitive.

Alone at home, I joylessly went through my nighttime routine. I defrosted something low-cal for dinner and opened a bottle of wine—just one glass, I told myself. I leafed through the latest issue of *Angeleno* magazine, tearing out an article on the new cellulite treatments available in town. I didn't really watch *The Sopranos*. I let the show run, with the volume turned down too low to hear clearly and follow.

Every hour I'd leave my perch on the couch and check my e-mail.

There was nothing from Dave. I had told him I was sick; he could have called or e-mailed or *something*. Motherfucker.

I tossed and turned all night, getting practically no sleep. In the morning, to help diffuse the puffiness, I resorted to putting a bag of frozen berries across my eyes. Brushing my teeth, I winced at my reflection in the bathroom mirror. At my age, a night with little sleep could make me look like one of those crazy celebrity mug shots found on smokinggun.com

I was barely in my office before the first crisis hit. Steve rapped on my open door. "Have you seen Haley this morning?"

Placing my bag and Peet's Coffee cup down on my desk, I didn't even sit. "No, I haven't been over to the stage yet. What's up?"

"She's done something to her face," Steve said dryly.

"More Botox?" I asked. "Pretty soon she's going to look more like a corpse than the extras we hire to play dead."

"I don't think it's Botox. It's something different. It looks like she's melting a little bit, like she stood too close to the heat, and the area by the sides of her mouth has started to stream down."

"Restylane," I said with authority. "So it really is that bad?"

"We're shooting a scene where she tells the family that the teenager's body is their daughter. The mother in the scene is holding a three-year-old kid, who's supposed to cry on cue at the news. So, the kid is afraid of Haley's melting face—we can't get her to stop wailing and pointing at Haley's mouth. Her face is literally freaking the kid out."

"Can we lose it? The scene?" I powered on my computer and clicked through the folders to bring up the episode, silently grateful that we had finished shooting last week with Haley for the Marilyn show. Her funny-looking face would be all over Evil Janet's child abduction episode, which was starting to film today.

Steve crossed behind me to read over my shoulder. "Haley's been asking for a dramatic scene like this—she wants to make a run for an Emmy this year, so this was supposed to be her big emotional episode that she could submit for consideration."

"So I guess we can't have her do the scene with her autopsy mask covering her face, right?" I joked.

"Right." He sighed. "I have no idea why you women do stuff like this to yourselves. It's mutilation."

"C'mon, Steve. I doubt you even remember what real breasts feel like. You wonder why we do it? We do *it* because guys like you are dating twenty-year-olds who look like porn stars. Haley's like what, thirty-six? When's the last time you bought a thirty-six-year-old dinner?"

Steve looked down at me and into the top two open buttons on my shirt. "Didn't I buy you dinner recently? We weren't alone— maybe I bought dinner for all the writers, but you were there."

"I am not thirty-six. Not yet." He was unbelievable.

"Don't get so uptight. I like you better when you're the *Cosmopolitan*-magazine-Dani." He laughed. "I don't need the NPR Dani."

"Thanks for that, Steve. Why don't you crawl back in your hole and I'll pull up the scene and try to figure something out. Maybe we can try to shoot it differently, off a reflection in a mirror, or pushing in through a window, something that can help filter out the melting face."

"Okay, great. Thanks, Dani."

He was the boss and this was his problem, which meant it had now become my problem. I turned back to the scene on my computer screen. It was good to be distracted briefly from my Yellow Alert.

Soon I felt much calmer. I tinkered with the scene a bit, but then I pulled a Steve and decided to make it Mick, the show director's, problem. I went over to the soundstage, talked to him, and watched as he got creative, shooting through reflections from the metal gurneys and playing a lot of the scene just through Haley's eyes. Her eyeballs glistened and glowed with emotion; there wouldn't have been much movement in the rest of her face anyway, and I didn't know if it was going to be good enough for an Emmy Nom, but at least the kid cried only on cue.

I was picking through a salad at my desk when Dave called to check in. "Hey, baby. How's it going—are you feeling better?"

"Yeah, I'm okay. Just shit at work, ya know."

"I know how that goes. I wanted to see if you could come by set tomorrow."

"Are you kidding? When? Where?" I was thrilled and instantly high. He never asked me to come to set. This whole Yellow Alert must have been in my head. For him to want to see me when he was working showed that, even though he was so busy shooting, he wanted to make time for me.

That night as I got into bed, I was still giddy with the invite. *The Yellow Alert had been nothing. Nothing was wrong, let it go.* Finally, I slept.

In the morning, I dressed with a little more care than I usually put into my work wardrobe. I wore my new jeans from Fred Segal and a camisole that peeked out from beneath my oxford button-down shirt. In front of the bedroom mirror, putting on mascara, another anomaly, I unbuttoned an extra button. Just because.

After a restless morning at work, I arrived at the set around noon. The security guard guided me to park behind Dave's car in a prime spot on the location where Dave was shooting. The crew had been setting up a wedding scene on the front steps of a church on Lankershim. They were just finishing up a crane shot that I knew Dave had been worried about. I hung back behind the crew, watching everyone. The lead actor, Bob Bradley, had been a mini movie star in the '80s, and, after his career had gone nowhere in the '90s, he found himself on television. Playing Detective Walter Steele on this show, *LA Crime Unit*, had breathed some life into Bob's stale career.

They wrapped the scene and Dave spied me hanging back behind some of the equipment. "Hey, why are you hiding? Get over here."

I'd always felt that being on someone else's set was almost like being in his bedroom. It was a private place where, as a visitor, you wouldn't feel comfortable. But I reminded myself that I had been in Dave's bedroom, a lot. Dave pecked me on the cheek, which was fine—I hadn't expected any huge PDAs while he was on set.

"Hey, Bob, I want to introduce you to someone . . ."

Looking super-rugged and a little more bloated than I remembered, Bob Bradley crushed my hand in his. "Well, it's nice to meet you, finally. I've heard a lot about you from this guy," he said, gesturing toward Dave.

All this attention from an ex-matinee idol seemed to make Dave a little uncomfortable, because he hustled me over to the catering truck to grab lunch. Only a couple of the other actors were seated there, eating.

"Most of them are on the Zone Diet and get their food delivered, so they stay holed up in their trailers," Dave whispered.

I had never watched *LA Crime Unit* before. I was usually too busy writing my own hourlong show. This was Dave's first time directing one of their episodes, but I recognized most of the series regulars from the promo spots that aired around the clock. I spotted a skinny, sullen-faced red-haired girl in the farthest seat at the actors' dining table. I didn't recognize her and was pretty sure she wasn't a regular on the show. Dave called over for her to come join us. Red-Haired Girl picked up her salad plate and walked over to our table. Even though there were plenty of seats, she planted herself right next to Dave so the three of us were like a ladyfinger cookie, with Dave the cream center. She was English, and kind of cold and aloof in that English way. She didn't say hello and no one introduced us, so I covertly gave her my usual once-over, in that way all women assess each other, and dismissed her as no competition: too many freckles and no ass.

The lunch chatter involved what I'd gotten used to around actors. I used to feel self-conscious around them, trying to suck my cheeks in and not stare at their zits and enlarged pores (you never saw those in an airbrushed publicity photo). But after being around the cast of *Flesh and Bone* for most of the season, I'd realized they were concerned only with themselves and were paying no attention to me. Bob Bradley was talking about his new Prius, which he drove to set during the day, "to do my part for the Green movement." Bob said he still drove his Range Rover, but only when he was going "out at night."

Dave told Bob I was writing this season on *Flesh and Bone,* and he seemed impressed.

"I love that Haley Caldwell—that girl is built on top!" he added with gusto.

"You're the audience we're aiming for. They say people love seeing her on the show wearing a tight tank top under a fitted leather jacket."

Dave and Bob laughed hard in that dumb way straight guys do when they start thinking about boobies. Red-Haired Girl let out a dramatic sigh and left the table without another word. Because she never said hello, I guess I shouldn't have been bothered that she didn't say good-bye. What a bitch.

A production assistant wearing a headset gave a hand signal to Dave indicating lunch was over. Shooting on location meant that production was always fighting the sun to get the last bit of work out of the shooting day.

"You okay to get yourself back to your car?" Dave asked.

"Sure. I've got to get back to work too. Steve is probably looking for me."

Dave smiled at the notion of Steve being stressed. He leaned in to kiss me good-bye. "Well, then, fuck Steve." Dave smiled.

"You're terrible! I'll see you later for pizza right?"

"Yeah, we should wrap around seven thirty." Dave turned to head back to set.

"Okay, bye," I said to his retreating back.

The whole good-bye thing had been so brief that I felt a little like I'd been dismissed. I hated being given the signal that it was time for me to go. Oh well, he was working, I reasoned to myself.

Checking the clock in my car, I was stunned to see that it was almost three. I had been out of the office for way too long. I charged back over the hill weaving in and out of traffic as I made my way over to Barham. I usually didn't go to lunch, let alone disappear from the office for nearly three hours. At the office, I tried to slip unnoticed through the cubicles toward my office door, keeping my head bowed. All I needed was to be apprehended coming back late from lunch by Evil Janet.

"Hey Dani, where've you been?" Steve called from the doorway to the kitchen.

Turning around, I knew I looked guilty, with my purse over my shoulder and car keys still my hand.

"You look like you've been caught, my dear," Steve teased. "Were you trying to sneak back to your office after taking a two-hour lunch?"

"I am running late. I'm sorry . . . I had a doctor's appointment."

Steve savored my excuse, enjoying my flushed face and sweaty forehead. It wasn't even May and it was approaching ninety degrees outside in the Valley.

"Doctor's appointment?"

"I had a doctor's appointment about a 'female matter,'" I answered soberly. I dared him to challenge that one.

Steve was instantly uncomfortable. "Oh, okay . . . I hope every-thing's all right."

I smiled back mysteriously. A doctor's appointment about a "fe-male matter" always shut guys up good.

"I was just looking for you over lunch," Steve said, "and I left you a voice mail and you didn't respond. We just need you to make an-other pass at the scene in the woods when we find the teenager's body. It could use a bit more punch in the dialogue."

"Sorry, I didn't get the message, but I'll get right on the pages." I ducked away like a truant kid at school. Caught up in my Dave Delir-ium, I hadn't checked my phone. I didn't want Steve to feel I was let-ting him down, and I was sure he only half bought the doctor's appointment excuse.

I tried to focus on work. Enough with Dave.

I managed to make it through the scene, but I'd found it hard to slip back into my groove. I worked until a little after eight, hoping Steve noticed. When I got to Dave's, a little late, he was already cleaned up and on his second slice of pizza, scanning through dailies on the DVD player. I grabbed a slice and beer and settled next to Dave on the couch, ready for the two of us to finally be alone and relax a lit-tle. I knew that "our" time wouldn't start until he was done with dailies, so I munched my pizza and watched somewhat disinterestedly. There on the screen was the freckly face of Red-Haired Girl. Dave had shot her tightly framed, so the shot was an intense close-up.

"What's her name?" I asked.

"Chloe Johnson." He concentrated on the scene playing out on the screen. "She has great eyes. I'm trying to shoot her so that you can see the whole scene in her eyes."

In an attempt to take the high road, I said, "She seemed nice." (Not.)

"We're really lucky to have her. She worked with Soderbergh in *Traffic* and had a role in Scorsese's last film."

"Really?"

He was acting as if this was something that should have impressed me, but it left me feeling nonplussed. "Well, if she has such an illustrious pedigree, why is she doing a supporting part in an episode of *LA Crime Unit?*"

"I actually got them to flesh out her character a bit. Having her on the show is a big plus for us. I even suggested to the producers that they should consider having her character come back."

"Oh," was all I could think of to say.

Dave wouldn't let it die. "Think about it—Chloe's worked with two of the best directors in the world. They chose her for both of their films when they could have cast anyone."

"Yeah, you're right," I mumbled back.

"She told me that Soderbergh likes to shoot really quick—he operates the camera himself and is so close to the actors in a scene that he can lean in and whisper in their ear."

"Wow."

"Scorsese is just the opposite. He could spend up to a week just shooting one scene. He sometimes asks the actors to do twenty or thirty takes of a single scene. Chloe told me that working like that just takes you to a totally different place as an actor. You *become* the character."

"You guys sure had a lot of time to talk between scenes," I said in my best evenhanded journalist voice.

"Well, actually," he said very carefully, stacking his DVDs neatly on the edge of the table, "we grabbed a quick dinner last Wednesday at Barney's Beanery. It was after shooting wrapped for the day and we were down the street. That's when she gave me the 411 on everything."

"You guys had dinner?" This was shocking to me. I'd never known Dave to hang with any of the actors on his shows. "Where was I? Was I still gone?"

"Yeah, you were still on your research trip to the Coroner's Hall of Fame."

"I wasn't at the Coroner's Hall of Fame," I shot back. "I was meeting with some of the country's top criminal profilers at Quantico. We're really lucky the FBI is giving the show this kind of access. It's almost unprecedented."

"Yeah, you get access, and so does every other forensic show on television."

"Well, that's not true, and what exactly do you mean?" Sometimes Dave could be a total dick.

"I'm just saying, the way you talk about your 'research,' you act like you're curing cancer or something. Just to set you straight, Dani, you ain't no doctor." He swallowed the rest of his beer.

I worked hard to keep myself from shoving one of his DVDs down his throat. "Well, just to set the record straight with you, these trips have really helped me flesh out some of the characters and given me great ideas for upcoming episodes."

"Well, then, all the travel has been worth it," Dave remarked.

"Yes, it has."

I realized that, at some point, I had folded my arms across my chest in a defensive posture. I wanted to fire a few shots of my own. "So how was your dinner at Barney's Beanery?"

"What's that supposed to mean? I can feel a trap coming."

"I'm not setting you up for any trick question. I was just curious." I was trying hard to act like I didn't care, but I was observing him very closely. "The two of you seemed to have had an interesting conversation."

"Is this you putting a guilt trip on me?"

"No. I'm just a little surprised. I've never known you to get dinner with one of the actresses on your show."

Dave sat back on the couch. "Okay, you're putting me behind the eight ball here. We're just friends—why don't you get that?" He set his mouth. "I am allowed to have female friends."

"I know you are. I just wouldn't go out for dinner with some guy I worked with, while you were out of town."

"Well, I guess that's you then."

"No, it's because I can't go out with a guy in a platonic situation without him getting the wrong idea. It just makes me uncomfortable, and I *know* you wouldn't dig me telling you about it after the fact."

He drew back a little and I could tell he was about to really lash into me. But he held himself back and started running his hands through his unruly hair. "Baby, stop being so crazy." He reached across the couch for my hand. "She's just a friend, and I don't know why you're so insecure about other women. Look, she has a boyfriend, okay? She's dating Colin Farrell, but she doesn't like anyone to know."

"She's dating Colin Farrell? I think I would have read about that on PerezHilton.com or something if it were true. Was she the one in the sex video?"

"No, that sex video is ancient history. Chloe is in that new western he has coming out. She told me that, between takes, they got to know each other, and that one thing led to another and she found herself making out with him in his trailer. She said he was so rough with her that his jeans rubbed her thighs raw—that's how intense they are. Believe me, she's totally into him. Chloe had another boyfriend before shooting started and said she felt so bad about all the Colin stuff that she had to break it off with the guy back in England. Okay?"

"Okay what?" I asked. "Is this conversation about Chloe's roughed-up thighs supposed to make me feel better?"

Dave squeezed my hand and focused his eyes directly into mine. "You know how crazy I am about you. You take my breath away, Dani. When I saw you for the first time at the airport, I thought you were the most beautiful woman I'd ever seen."

This perked me up, but I was still going to make him earn this. "Really?"

"Really. So will you please stop being crazy like this?"

"I thought you liked it when I was crazy."

"I do, but when you're crazy-sexy and not really crazy."

I thought about this for a second and then tilted my head toward him. I could feel his breath on my face, and I whispered into his lips, "I'll stop being crazy."

I closed my eyes and we kissed. I went over everything in my mind. He should be allowed to have female friends; I couldn't strangle him like this. I reminded myself of that poem about a caged bird: If you open the cage door and it flies away, it was never really yours. I had to leave the cage door open. The show would finish taping the following week and Chloe Johnson and all those freckles would be history.

SEVEN

The next few days at work were a blur as we put the finishing postproduction touches on the Marilyn episode.

On Friday, I lingered in the back of the edit bay watching the postproduction team lay in the last couple of scenes we'd shot just days ago. Relieved and tired, I left the guys to their work and made my way back to my office. It all ended up coming together and I could tell the show was going to be great.

After lunch I lay low and went through a couple of new books that research had ordered for me. I loved poring over the forensic books. Most people thought it was gross, but I loved all the gruesome details.

I collected my things and left early for an appointment downtown with one of the consulting coroners on *Flesh and Bone*. Bobby Kucerak was a senior coroner for LA County. Having Bobby on call was great for us, because we could run anything by him and he'd let us know if it was plausible or just TV mumbo jumbo. Bobby and I shared an interest in all this stuff, and he loved explaining the science to me, as if I were one of the dumb investigators Maggie always had to explain things to, so that the viewers would understand the technical info.

The examination room downtown was adjacent to the LA County Morgue. This was where they brought Marilyn the day she died. Dr. Thomas Noguchi had performed her autopsy. Back in the day, Dr. Noguchi had been the "coroner to the stars." His memoir in the '70s had inspired the show *Quincy*. If it hadn't been for Marilyn and Dr. Noguchi, I probably wouldn't have had a job.

The building was a typically antiseptic but serviceable beige-and-gray government space. I pushed the elevator button and waited. My eyes drifted across the hallway to a small storefront, where a sign read, "This is not an urban legend." This was the LA County Morgue's very own gift shop. Skeletons in the Closet sold all kinds of trinkets: garment bags shaped like body bags, coffee mugs, sweatshirts, and even boxer shorts called Undertakers. Whenever I came down here, I wondered how grieving families, summoned here to identify a loved one, reacted to all this commercialization of death. Over a decade ago, the coroner's office had created its own coffee mugs and T-shirts for the staff to take to conventions. Demand became so great that the gift shop was opened.

Exiting the elevator, I was met by a long, linoleum-lined hallway that dead-ended at a wooden door plainly labeled "Los Angeles County Morgue." The morgue took in around two dozen bodies a day and had to determine a cause of death for each. There were classifications like "natural causes," "murder," and "LA natural," which was their slang for death by gunshot.

The air-conditioning kept the room icebox cold. Bobby greeted me with his usual lab-geek awkwardness. He looked a little like Matthew Perry if I squinted hard enough. Sure, he was cute, but he had an unfortunate chin. I donned scrubs and gloves, and covered my mouth with a surgical mask in an attempt to keep out the smell of death. It wasn't working.

Bobby handed me a smooth, cleaned skull, which had been waiting for us in a steel tray. I was surprised that holding someone's skull in my hands didn't freak me out, but I figured that when you'd been around this stuff long enough, you just became accustomed to it. You built up immunity to the shock value of everything.

"What do you think?" Bobby asked.

I weighed the skull in my hands for a moment. "Well, this person obviously died of a gunshot wound to the head." I turned the skull so that the two round holes were visible.

"And what about the entry wound?"

"The hole in the back of the skull is smaller than the hole in the front of the skull, so I would say this person was shot in the head from behind. He was off guard and the bullet exited through the forehead."

Bobby peered at the skull. "Right. That's how this gunshot wound happened. But the problem with this case is the wife. She found the body, and she's been claiming that her husband committed suicide. She says he'd been depressed for months. But for someone to commit suicide by shooting himself in the back of the head is almost impossible."

Bobby reached his hand around his own head, making his finger and thumb into a mock gun. "See? Who could reach around like that? Why reach around like that? Why not just shoot yourself in the side of the head?" Again he pointed around with his finger-gun.

"Did the police on the scene test for gunshot residue? Did they swab the wife's hands?" I asked.

"No, she was hysterical over the suicide and they didn't push it." He motioned for me to come over to the side lab table. "But check this out."

He opened up a labeled folder and flipped through to the actual autopsy photos of the body. It was weird: I was holding the skull of the man in the photos. The coroner had had to shave the victim's hair off to get a better look at the wounds. Bobby pointed to dark marks in the photos.

"The dark shadows are definitely gunshot residue and, if you look closely, the barrel of the gun left an indentation where it was pressed against the back of his skull." His finger moved across the picture. "There's no way he could have reached around or pressed the gun that hard into his own skull."

He flipped through the file, pulling out more photos. "And look here," he said, pointing to an image of the dead body stretched out on a bed. "Look where his arms are positioned. If he had shot himself, his right arm would be down by his side, not in front of his stomach."

I thought of Marilyn and her soldier's position, no arms clawing at the air the way they should have been. None of this stuff bothered me. I'd been watching shows on TV that dealt with this kind of stuff since I was a little girl. I had sat in on an actual autopsy before, although that had been a bit much even for me.

I was leaning toward Bobby as he continued his analysis, and all of a sudden I realized how close we were. I was very aware of him as a man. I glanced up at his face and caught him studying me intently. Now I wondered if he had drawn this whole procedure out, to spend a bit more time with me. Bobby was attractive enough. I'd always wondered why someone like him would want to do this, work with dead people. But I'd never asked him; I hadn't wanted to get too personal. No matter how sick I might be, all that talk of skulls and autopsy photos wasn't my idea of foreplay. If Bobby had come in for a kiss right then, that would have been just way too creepy. Creepier than handling skulls. I hoped he wouldn't make a pass at me. I didn't want to have to rebuff him.

Moving away from him, I scanned the disinfected tools lying neatly on the stainless tray. "Bobby, I've never asked you what you thought of the Marilyn rumors—not about the necrophilia stuff, but if you thought she committed suicide or was murdered."

Bobby closed the file and turned to tidy his tray of examination tools. "Dr. Noguchi performed the autopsy and ruled Marilyn's cause of death a suicide."

"I know what Dr. Noguchi said in his report, but what do *you* think?"

Bobby brought the skull back to the examination table and carefully placed it back into position. "Marilyn died because of an overdose of sleeping pills in her system."

"Yeah, I've read the report. So?"

"There were no pills found in her stomach, and Noguchi did a thorough exam of her body looking for needle marks and found none, but he did note that there was an unusual purplish substance found in Marilyn's colon, suggesting that Marilyn may have received the lethal dose of narcotics that way."

"That way?" I asked.

Bobby smiled. "Yes, *that* way. So think about it. If you were going to kill yourself, you could think of easier and more efficient ways to do it than with a barbiturate enema."

"Yeah, you're right, I guess." I sighed. "I guess we'll never really know how she died." Thinking of Marilyn made me sad. I gave Bobby a quick good-bye, turning at the door to give him a half-salute. I knew he'd stare at the door long after I left.

That night I settled into the sofa and automatically reached for the remote and turned on the television. There had been no voice mail on my cell or at home from Dave. He was shooting nights and busy, and while it only took ten seconds to leave a voice-mail message, I figured he'd call me later. I was giving him some slack because he was being great about going with me to see my mom tomorrow, and I knew we'd have tomorrow night together to watch the "Marilyn" show.

Robotically, I flicked through the channels, never staying on any show for longer than a few seconds. This was how I unwound at the end of the day. The room was dark except for the illumination from the television set as I scoured through the channels. Sipping my cold beer, I thought about what Bobby had said about Marilyn. He had a point: a barbiturate enema is a strange way to commit suicide.

Lucy woke me up the next morning, purring close to my face. That wasn't a sign of affection; it meant the food bowl was empty. I'd fallen asleep on the couch. Cursing myself for not moving into the bedroom to sleep, I made my way to the kitchen to make coffee. I was joyless because today was the day my mom was in town and I had to meet her for brunch.

She wasn't *in* LA. She was in the "Los Angeles area" as she liked to call it. Mom thought LA was ugly; she preferred San Diego, like every other person with an Arizona license plate driving up and down Balboa Boulevard in Pacific Beach. Fortunately, her preference kept her out of my zip code most of the time, but there was no getting out of seeing her today. Mom was in Anaheim at some sort of annual conference held by Crate and Barrel Furniture, a meeting of the laminate-wood sales force to bolster morale. Even though she was working, Mom had made time on Saturday to come up and see me, and she was going to be bringing a friend from work, Carolyn. She probably thought she needed the support to sit through a lunch with me.

Amid the craziness of getting the final edit of the "Marilyn" show complete, I had to come up with a sort of a plan for getting together. I knew not to have her come to my place again. The last time Mom was in town, I excitedly had her over to check out my new house. My Spanish classic bungalow rental was lost on her. She took in the slightly worn hardwood floors and original tile and made a little grimace. I thought she'd be impressed with the moss green corduroy couch from Shabby Chic on Montana. It had set me back almost four thousand dollars and was the best place ever to fall asleep while watching TV.

"Here, check out my new sofa. It's filled with down," I'd prodded. Mom placed herself on the edge of the green marshmallow and ran her hand over the arm of the couch, feeling the richness of the corduroy.

"Isn't it amazing?" I pressed.

"It's gorgeous," Mom admitted. "You know, it's just like the Shelter Island sofa that we have on the floor now. We're trying to be a bit more cosmopolitan with our new designs."

I knew there was no way Crate and Barrel had a sofa to compare to the green marshmallow. I let her tell me about the rest of the new line and box spring sets that had just come in. I ached for the time, later that night, when she would be back in her hotel room in Anaheim and I would be curled up in the fetal position in the dark on the green marshmallow. Oprah said we couldn't change people, just our reaction to them; I needed to work on changing my reactions to Mom, I'd told myself.

She'd ignored my silence and moved into the kitchen to examine the slightly dirty dishtowel that I'd folded over the faucet. "You sure don't get much for your real estate dollar in California," she said. And then, "You know what I see here, Dani?" She took a deep breath. "I see po-ten-tial . . . potential!"

Thanks, Mom.

So this morning I was totally justified in popping one of my pilfered Xanax pills from the Outpost open house into my mouth before brunch with my mother. I contemplated biting the pill in half, but then just took the whole thing. Very Judy Garland of me. Within thirty minutes, I sensed the warmth of the pill flow through me and felt pretty good sitting next to Dave as he maneuvered through West Hollywood traffic. Despite the Yellow Alert and weirdness with Dave he was being a trouper by being my date.

The paparazzi were in position as we turned left onto Robertson. Nowadays they were omnipresent, their hulking black SUVs with blacked-out windows lying in wait for their prey. The vehicles were so imposing you'd have thought *they* housed the celebrities. Instead, they lurked like giant shiny beetles waiting for some skankbait young fame-ho to walk by. There used to be a hot dog cart directly across from the valet stand at the Ivy, but some new swanky store had opened nearby and petitioned the Beverly Hills City Council to get the guy kicked out. The store owner claimed the long line at lunch prevented customers from accessing her store. I had a feeling maybe money had changed hands. No more hot dogs on Robertson.

We pulled up and gave the keys to the valet. A gaggle of Ladies Who Lunch waited for their leased luxury cars paid for by their Vaginamony. All you needed was one rich ex and you were set for life with a Mercedes and yoga retreats with your girlfriends.

Today was a perfect, sunny California Saturday afternoon. I'd used the good Greek sunscreen you had to buy on eBay from Canada because it wasn't FDA approved. My hair looked good and I was wearing my new Sama sunglasses. These were featherlight and the lenses were lightly tinted. I planned this so I wouldn't have to remove them during the entire lunch.

I saw my mother and her friend at a table directly to the left of the hostess stand, the worst place to sit ever. Not only did everyone who was waiting to be seated stand over you the entire meal and eye your food, but the purses on the tight and tanned shoulders occasionally would knock you good in the head. Shit, I wished we'd gotten here first.

Mom looked good, with lots of makeup, a persistent cloud of perfume, and a fuchsia print ensemble with no beginning, middle, or end. When my mom decided to become invisible to men, she'd given up worrying about calories.

I thought the Ivy was a good choice. Mom just wanted the story of a Beverly Hills brunch to tell her girlfriends at home about. If we had any chance of seeing a celebrity, it was here, but I hoped it would get better than Pam Dawber of *Mork and Mindy* fame, whom we passed on the way in.

Dave looked handsome in his open-neck white shirt with his gold cross glistening against his dark skin. Mom liked Dave, as far as I could tell. He wasn't Jack, my old college boyfriend whom Mom hadn't appreciated. I was sure she figured that at least Dave had a job and, given the way her mind worked, if Dave was financially solvent and I was with Dave, that somehow ensured that *she* would be financially solvent. Money had always been a problem with Mom. Once when I asked her why she never saved any money, she was unflinching in her response. "I have a family who loves me and I will never be homeless."

My mom hated her friend Carolyn. I was always hearing about how competitive Carolyn was when it came to sales at work. To hear my mom tell it, Carolyn was diabolical and always out to steal a sale from her. When I looked at Carolyn, I just saw a timid Mormon mother of four who wore ugly shoes. How these two women had come together was a mystery.

"So how's work, Dani?" Carolyn asked.

"Oh it's been good, but crazy." I told them a bit about Haley's face always being a work-in-progress, thanks to her dermatologist. "On TV you never really get to see the actors close up, so you don't ever get a real idea of what they look like. That's why a lot of TV people can't make the transition to movies. They don't look that good all blown up on that big screen."

"George Clooney does!" Mom exclaimed. "He's the biggest movie star there is and he used to be TV's top doc." She recited this as if she were reading from a *TV Guide* cover from 1995.

"Well, George Clooney is a genetic freak, Mom. I mean, he's a very handsome man. I used to see him on the lot when he would come play basketball with his buddies even after he'd left *ER*."

"You've met George Clooney?" my mom asked, incredulous.

"I didn't say I *met* him. I saw him."

"I've met him," Dave interjected.

"You have?" Mom asked.

Dave had our full attention now. "I didn't know you'd met George," I said. This was news to me.

"Well, I was at the Arclight once and we were leaving the theater at the same time. I was right behind him and he waited a beat to hold the door open for me. I said, 'Thanks, man,' and he said, 'No problem.'"

"That's not meeting him," I said.

"It's meeting him," Dave insisted. "We talked, we spoke—that's practically a conversation." Mom and Carolyn were impressed. I knew the Clooney story would be repeated back in Arizona with the emphasis on "met and had a conversation" and no mention of the "door holding" extent of the encounter.

Luckily, the waiter interrupted to take our order. "I'll have that champagne drink to start." I piped up. Best to get the liquor to the table quickly.

Mom ordered a rum and Coke. "Mom," I said, "you should try this champagne cocktail drink they make. It's with pureed raspberries and it's so good—it's what they're famous for."

Mom made a face. "I can't take that sweet stuff. I'll just have my rum and Coke."

Carolyn had the same and Dave stuck with water. I was so glad he was choosing to be sober for the entire afternoon.

The drinks arrived and Mom got in her groove, sipping on her rum and Coke, craning her neck to stare at each arriving brunch guest, and giving us her take on the movie business. "Anyway, back to the actor thing," she declared, "I was on an airplane and some movie came on with that woman from *Will & Grace* and she sure did look funny. Her nose is very big. I just don't think her face is made for the big screen.

It wasn't even made for the very small screen on the airplane." Mom cackled a bit and slapped Carolyn's forearm. "But I guess it didn't stop her from being successful," Mom continued. The rum and Coke was drained from the glass and now she was gnawing on the straw. She got the waiter's attention and ordered just a plain Coke, for which I was grateful. I could tell she was feeling very relaxed.

"What I'm saying, Dave," my mother announced, "is that some people who choose to keep their features *can* be successful to some extent."

She's not doing this. My heart started to beat out of my linen Trina Turk top. *I can't believe she's going to do this.* Mom caught herself, but then shot me a look letting me know that, yes, she was going to do this.

"I mean, Dani chose to change the only feature she got from me." Mom ran a French-tipped finger along the bridge of her nose. She opened her mouth to continue, but I cut her off.

"Okay, I know where this is going." Glancing at Dave, I took a deep breath. "I had a deviated septum problem and decided to have surgery to fix it. It was a medical condition." I said this last part firmly, glaring at Mom to keep her trap shut.

"She snored," Mom interrupted, chuckling to Carolyn, and giving Dave a knowing look. Dave looked totally absorbed in this story, which worried me. He took his left hand from my thigh, where he had placed it for moral support when we sat down, and reached for his ice water.

"Really?" he asked.

"Yes, I snored," I echoed patiently. "And the doctor told me that was because my nasal passage was as curvy as Mulholland Drive. It was a *deviated septum*. He didn't break my nose, but there ended up being a slight cosmetic change because of the procedure."

"You had a nose job?" Dave asked.

"I *told* you, it wasn't a 'nose job.' It was a deviated septum procedure." I enunciated the medical term carefully. I had long ago gotten this story down.

"You never told me you had any plastic surgery." Dave looked very concerned, although I didn't know why he was worried—we weren't having lunch with *his* mom, and she hadn't just spilled the beans about any elective surgery *he* might have had.

So ended the fun part of our brunch. Mom took over the conversation, talking about Jenny from work and her manager who was married but who she was sure was gay. I nodded and smiled at what felt like appropriate times. I was glad for the stolen Xanax and the semi-sunglasses that I'd kept on through lunch. I could covertly keep my eyes on Dave. His hand stayed on the arm of his white wicker chair. The waiter cleared away the plates and brought the coffee and plate of home-baked cookies. The check came and Mom fought to grab it out of the waiter's hand. Luckily, Dave won out, but not before the table of chicks celebrating a bridal shower noticed and mocked Mom's efforts. People with money and class don't worry about checks; they didn't care who paid because the Company always paid, so it wasn't a big gesture to pick up a tab. Universal and Paramount probably paid for seventy percent of all meals consumed in Hollywood.

There was a hug good-bye and more perfume. Mom seemed a little loose. I was glad Carolyn was going to drive the rental car back to Anaheim. I reminded her to watch the "Marilyn" episode of *Flesh and Bone* tonight—hoping she wouldn't ask to watch it with me, because I planned to do that alone with Dave.

"You're just so pretty, so pretty—you're very lucky, Danielle," she told me.

"Thanks, Mom, I love you." But I said the words while we were embracing, looking over her shoulder to where the hot dog cart used to be.

• • •

Dave and I drove in silence up to Sunset. After ten minutes, he finally spoke. "They charged me for six rum and Cokes."

"What?"

"Your mom and her friend were spiking their drinks. The management must have seen them with their little bottle under the table and they charged me."

"I didn't see her spike her drink," I said. "You saw her? You're sure? That's crazy."

"I guess you were distracted with trying to cover your ass about your nose job." His hands were on the steering wheel and his eyes straight ahead.

"I wasn't trying to 'cover my ass.' It was no big deal. It wasn't a nose job—it was for my breathing problem."

"Well, he didn't do that great of a job. Your nose may look fine, but you still snore."

"I know I don't snore like I used to."

Dave gunned his VW through a yellow light.

I was tired of being defensive, and I didn't want to start crying. I focused my attention on looking out the window.

After a few more traffic lights, Dave broke the silence. "So did all the guys you used to sleep with tell you that you snored? Is that why you decided to get the surgery?"

Deep breath in, then out. Guys and their madonna/whore complexes. Now, because he knew I used to snore a lot, I was a slut. I stayed silent and kept looking out the window.

"Anything else?" he prodded.

"I think I've said all I need to on the subject."

"No, is there anything else you've had done? Any more surgeries?" He reached across the seat to touch my face. "Those beautiful lips? Are those yours, or did you pay to get them plumped up?" His hand left my face and started to wander down my woven seatbelt. "How 'bout these? Did you pay for these too?"

I swatted his hand away. "I think that's enough, okay? I don't need this shit from you, Dave."

"Hey, baby, you've got to understand why I'm so upset. I would always tell the guys that you were 100 percent 'factory'—as in, this is how you came. All your equipment was standard, not like you were *made* in a factory."

This was the meanest he'd ever been. As I tried to figure out how to tell him exactly in which manner he could go fuck himself, I was mortified to feel my eyes start to well with tears.

"You can just fucking back off with all this shit, okay?" I stammered out. "It's not fair—I *am* 'all factory' as you put it. You know that seeing my mom is tough enough for me—now I have to deal with you in addition to all of her shit? That's so not fair! You should be on my side when it comes to me and my mom. The two of you aren't allowed to joke about me like that. So fuck off!"

EIGHT

Dave dropped me off at my house without another word.

I slammed the door of his car so hard he winced, not out of concern for me but worry over the sheet metal of his precious VW Beetle. I didn't look back as he roared off. I couldn't get away from him fast enough. I couldn't believe my mom had screwed up my weekend plans so totally.

Staring at my front door, I felt restless. Instead of going inside, I hopped into my BMW. I didn't have a plan for where I was going, but I just didn't feel like being home alone.

Heading back to Sunset, I made a right, toward Beverly Hills. Catching sight of myself in my rearview mirror, I saw my overgrown eyebrows, desperately threatening to become a unibrow. With work so insane, I hadn't had them done in a long time. I headed to Anastasia's for a little maintenance. I didn't have an appointment, so I plowed through fashion magazines with the dozen or so other women in the lobby of the salon. We all slyly checked out each other's jewelry, shoes, and bags between flipping pages of last month's *Vogue*. I was the only woman waiting who didn't have a ring on her ring finger.

I checked my phone to see if Dave had called. There was nothing, but I didn't want to talk to him anyway. I turned my cell phone off, so if Dave tried to reach me it would go straight to voice mail. My own little punishment for his nasty attitude at brunch.

The actual waxing of brows took a total of six minutes. Then the girl tried to sell me a highlight stick for the brow bone, a setting gel for my eyebrows, "to keep them in place," and a pencil to fill in the little bald spots. I bought everything and left having dropped $140 with tip.

I walked around the corner and tried on a couple of pairs of shoes at Madison, but bought nothing. I checked my phone and Dave hadn't called. Sure, it had only been a couple of hours, but it was weird for him to have not left me a message about our plans tonight. He'd been a dick, but now that I'd cooled down a bit from the whole thing, I could partly understand why he'd been so pissed. He'd discovered a secret that I'd kept from him. I felt bad, even a little teary; I could understand why he felt betrayed. I tried him on his cell. On the fourth ring he picked up.

"Hey, baby," I purred, trying to forget the anger of lunch.

"Hey," he replied flatly.

"So when are you coming over later?" I asked.

"For what?" he answered.

I thought he was joking. "You know. The Marilyn show is premiering tonight. We're going to hang out and watch it together."

"Oh, wow," he said, "I totally forgot that was tonight. Did we make an actual plan to watch it together?"

This wasn't something I was assuming—we *had* spoken about it. I'd even mentioned it to my mother in his earshot not four hours ago. Dave knew how excited I was to see my name all alone on the screen. He was going to come over and we were going to watch the show together. I was going to grill up some steaks outside and make his favorite twice-baked potatoes.

"Well, I don't know if we actually made a 'plan' as you call it, but I've been talking about this for weeks. You knew it was tonight—the show is airing special during sweeps and we're on Saturday nights all May. You know what a big deal this is for me. It's *my* show. Is this about brunch with Mom?"

"No, it's not about brunch," Dave said, too fast. "I'm so sorry, baby—my buddy Isaac is having a bad time and asked me if he could come over and hang with me. I think he wants a shoulder to lean on. His writing career is going nowhere and he's really down."

I tried to gulp down my hurt feelings. "I just thought we were going to be together. It's a big night for me."

"I know, but not everyone is lucky enough to be able to write on a prime-time show. Don't you remember what it was like when you were just starting out and would get so down about not having any work?"

I actually didn't remember, because I'd always been working. I'd had to work to survive. I didn't know how all these struggling writers came to LA to write but didn't have jobs. I mean, how did they live?

"I don't really feel it would be cool to cancel on him, do you?" Dave sounded so reasonable, but still, this was the second Saturday night in a row he had left me on my own. And last Saturday he had ended up at Locanda Veneta. "Baby, remember that we have a lifetime of Saturday nights ahead of us. This is just one night." Dave could be so smooth when he wanted to, and he'd said the magic word, "lifetime."

"Well, I guess if Isaac is having a tough time and needs to talk, you should be there for him," I stammered out. I was looking down at my fingernails, which I had again gnawed to nothing.

"I don't know why you didn't plan to have your mom come over and watch the show with you. You should call her."

"Are you kidding me? This is something I want to celebrate. She'd just ruin it somehow." I couldn't think of anything worse.

"Hey, why don't you TiVo the show, and I can come over tomorrow night and we can watch it then?"

I considered his suggestion. "Yeah, I guess I can do that." I answered, shrugging.

"So don't watch it tonight, okay? We'll make it special tomorrow and see the show for the first time together."

Now he sounded cheered up, and I guessed I should cheer up too. "Okay."

"That's my girl. C'mon, don't be like that. I can tell you're frowning through the phone, so be sure to not watch the show tonight."

"Okay," I said glumly, and hung up.

I headed to Whole Foods to pick up the steaks I'd planned on making tonight, but which we were now grilling tomorrow night. I wandered over to the salad bar and made myself a salad to have later. Driving home, I thought about calling Lauren or Ina to see if they wanted to get together, but I was too embarrassed to let them know that Dave wasn't spending my big evening with me. Lauren would have something bitchy to say.

The light in the living room was fading, letting me know the day was almost over. I'd spent the late afternoon going over the plotlines for the show we would shoot that week. There was always the A story line, the major story of the show, and the B story line. Sometimes there would even be a C, and we also followed some larger plotlines and character stories that passed from show to show. The most important thing for me to remember when writing the show was there always had to be one dumb investigator. Well, he or she could either be dumb or just a new recruit, but having a dummy there enabled us to explain stuff to the viewers. The smart investigator was always elucidating the science of the show to the know-nothing. The audiences at home were really the dummies.

I glanced at the clock: ten minutes until showtime. I pulled my salad out of the fridge and scraped it onto a plate. A beer was also in order, and I carried both into the living room.

I didn't turn any of the lights on. It was growing dark outside and I liked the light dimming around me. I munched on my salad. Whenever I found myself home alone like this, having a salad for dinner, I thought of it as the single girl's dinner, high in fiber and loneliness. I shoved another forkful of arugula into my mouth and tried to convince myself that it was satisfying. The beer was nice and cold, and I was about halfway through the bottle when I started to get angry. I mean really, fucking angry.

It was totally out of line that Dave had bailed on getting together tonight, no matter how many times I'd told myself that he was allowed to hang out with his friends, especially when they were depressed. He knew what a big night this was for me. And besides, it was a Saturday night.

But the main reason I was so mad was that I was sitting here in the dark and not watching *my* show, because Dave had told me not to. Just because he had other plans didn't mean that I shouldn't enjoy my big night. This was special to me. Lord knows, I had watched every episode of *Militia Man* he'd directed.

I set my beer down and reached for the remote. The TV came alive in front of me, and I caught the end of a promo for the episode designed to persuade audiences not to change the channel but stay instead and catch "A whole new recipe for murder!" as the announcer boomed.

I turned the set off. I didn't know what to do. I felt like I would be cheating on him if I watched the show on my own. Dave was ruining the whole experience for me.

This whole mess had me conflicted. One side of my head was trying to tell me that he was with his friend, who was broke and out of work, and that I shouldn't be so selfish. The other side thought I was justified in being mad. I thought about both sides, and then said out loud, "Fuck him."

I decided to do a drive-by, just to be sure that his friend Isaac was there. I jumped in my car and headed down the hill to Highland. Taking a right, I drove south on Highland, making a left onto Franklin. Traffic was all backed up, because of that stupid Kodak Theatre outdoor mall. This time of year, you couldn't even get near this intersection, because *American Idol* taped some of their big performance shows at the theater. At a dead stop, I yelled out the window, "Damn you, Ryan Seacrest!"

Finally reaching Beachwood Canyon, I stopped at the bottom. I didn't want to drive by and have Dave and his friend come out front and bust me. I couldn't see anyone, so I slowly started down Dave's street. I didn't want to appear to be stopping and looking if anyone glanced out the window. As I pulled closer, I could see another car in his driveway. Dave's classic VW could fit inside the garage, but Dave never wanted to risk scraping one of the wide-swinging car doors, so he always parked in the covered driveway.

Even though I had promised myself to cruise by and not stop, I felt myself braking when I got directly in front of his house. There was another car in the driveway in front of Dave's car: a cherry-red convertible Mercedes.

This wasn't the car of a buddy who was "down and out" and looking for his big break in television. This was a chick car. I couldn't believe it.

But maybe I could.

Why had I felt the need to do a drive-by? I drove halfway down the block and then stopped. My hands gripped the wheel. Should I go back and pound on the door and confront Dave and his guest, perhaps interrupting some sort of intimate clinch? Probably not, I told myself—there was no dignity in embarrassing myself. And what if Isaac was really in there and he'd just borrowed the Mercedes from a friend? Also, how could I explain to Dave why, instead of being home alone not watching the show I had written, I had been driving by his house?

I slowly drove back to my place, letting my mind go wild with the possibilities.

Missing the turn from Franklin onto Highland, I found myself driving toward Beverly Hills. I don't know why, but I just drove and thought about the conversation Dave and I had had about tonight: Isaac needed him; I should be less selfish. I passed the Beverly Center and idled at the red light. Through the intersection I saw the sign for Locanda Veneta on the corner. Because it was Saturday night, they were busy, the valet running to grab keys and give out claim tickets to impatient drivers. I flipped a quick left and slid into the small parking lot. The valet waited by my car door for me to get out.

"Hi, how are you?" I began. "I'm not parking the car, but I have a question. Do you work every Saturday night?"

"Sí, miss, I work here every weekend."

"I was here last Saturday night with my husband, and we just discovered a dent in our car, and we're trying to retrace our steps about when it happened . . . I'm not accusing you or anything, but do you remember? It was a special car, a cream-colored older VW Bug? Do you remember the car?"

My valet guy smiled. "Sí, señora, I remember the car. It's a beautiful car. But when we take a car we walk around once to see if there is any damage. People like to blame the valet. It happens a lot in this neighborhood."

He held up a claim ticket with an outline of a car on one side. I'd never noticed the drawing before. "We make an X on the picture where the dent is. If there was a dent, I'd remember. A car like that shouldn't have anything wrong—it's a thoroughbred, like a horse, sí?"

"Sí. You're right. I'm sorry to bother you, and like I said, I was just driving by and remembered we had been here. You remember cars more than the faces?"

"Everyone comes here from Beverly Hills, *señora*. All the women's faces look the same."

He smiled and I thanked him again.

Fucking Yellow Alert. Dave *had* been here, maybe with Cherry Red Mercedes. I drove home.

Inside my apartment, I checked the TiVo box. The red light was lit, letting me know it was still recording my show. I felt totally deflated. We should have been here, together, watching my show and getting ready for dessert when it was over.

I lay on the couch with a giant stomachache. When the show ended, I waited a few minutes and then went online. In my AOL inbox were messages from several friends who had watched the show. "MARILYN ROCKS!" and "I'm so proud of you" were the subject lines. But there was no e-mail from Dave. Earlier in the evening I'd sent him an e-mail saying I would miss waking up with him. We always stayed with each other on Saturday nights—except these last two. I checked to see if he had opened my e-mail. He had, at 6:20 PM. He had opened my e-mail, and he hadn't responded. Maybe he thought I was trying to pressure him into canceling his plans and guilt him into coming over. I logged off.

I knew there was no way I could get to sleep, so I rummaged through my makeup drawer for my precious bottle of Ambien. My ear-nose-and-throat doctor had given me a prescription for ten pills back when I started traveling a lot, doing research. I had four left. I shook one pill into my hand and swallowed it dry. Then I remembered something about always taking pills with water or else they don't run through your system, so I cupped my hand under the faucet and scooped water into my mouth like a kid. I was too lazy and depressed to walk into the kitchen and get a glass.

Just in case there was something wrong with my phone, I dialed in to check the messages. In addition to their e-mails, Lauren and Ina had called to tell me how much they'd liked the show. They'd left a joint voice mail, and it sounded as though they'd been drinking since noon.

"That mutilation murder scene at the top of the show is so *you!*"

"You're the creepiest person we know!" Ina yelled in the background. "We love you!"

Before the two clicked off, Lauren added, "We're sure you and Dave are having your own private celebration. Have fun!"

There had been no voice mail from Dave. I checked my cell phone, to make sure it was working, and there were no messages there either.

I took both phones and walked back to my bedroom, placing them carefully on my nightstand, right next to a picture of Dave and me, taken out on my patio.

I folded myself onto the bed and curled into the fetal position. I felt the bed gently shake as Lucy jumped up to take her usual position near my feet. She was excited that we were going to bed so early. I closed my eyes and waited for the Ambien to kick in and soothe me to sleep.

I dreamt of a cherry-red Mercedes. I was behind the wheel of my car but it wouldn't move, and the Mercedes blew past me, leaving me in its fumes. I woke up with a start: I had been falling and flailing my arms as I was being sucked down to some terrible unknown fate. It was still dark outside. I looked at the digital clock and saw it was a little before 6 AM. At this point I also realized that I was fully clothed. I'd been in such a daze after getting home from the drive-by that I hadn't even remembered to get undressed. Oy.

I padded into the living room and turned on my laptop. I knew there would be an e-mail or something to wake me up, a "Hey, baby" e-mail telling me I was being missed. But when I logged on, I found no message from Dave. I looked outside and the sky was just beginning to lighten. I grabbed my keys and banged out of the house. I just needed to check.

I pulled onto Dave's street and drove at a regular pace toward his bungalow. I didn't need to be careful driving down his street this time; it was too early for anyone to be up and notice me. There it was, the cherry-red Mercedes, still parked in the driveway with Dave's Beetle behind it. It was almost like the Beetle was taking care of the Mercedes, protecting it from the evils of the world.

The effects of the Ambien were totally gone now, pushed aside by adrenaline.

I grabbed a napkin from the passenger seat and scrawled down the six-digit plate number. I had a friend to call.

NINE

It was before ten on a Sunday morning, and that was usually a no-call zone, but I couldn't control myself.

I banged through my desk drawers and finally found the cast and crew phone list under a messy stack of bloody-crime-scene photos. Flipping through the pages, I dragged my finger down the list of last names, praying he would be there, even though he was a consultant. Cast and crew lists were confidential, and handed out with care, because they listed everyone's home addresses and cell phone numbers.

Halfway down the fourth page I found it. Rich Pisani. Punching in his cell number, I prayed he'd pick up.

Hearing the first ring, I closed my eyes, hoping it wouldn't go to voice mail. "C'mon, c'mon, pick up." I breathed into the phone.

After six rings he picked up. "Hello?"

"Hey, Rich, it's Dani, Dani Hale from *Flesh and Bone*."

"Dani, you don't have to say your last name with me. I only know one Dani who's a woman."

This made me happy for some reason and I lingered over it for a second. Then I pressed on, realizing I didn't need to play footsie on the phone with some ex-cop. "Listen, I've got a problem. I feel like

I've been followed home from the office the last couple of nights. I just spied the car in front of my house a few minutes ago—that's why I'm bothering you on a Sunday morning. I'm just a little nervous and was wondering—could you run the license plate for me?"

There was a long pause while Rich thought over what I was asking. I held my breath.

"Are you okay? Do you have a description of the guy?" He sounded a little alarmed.

"No, no description. It's probably nothing. I mean, this is a one-time thing, Rich. I won't ever ask you again to do something like this for me."

"Mmm . . . okay, I can help you out," he said. "But you can't tell anyone I'm doing this for you, obviously."

"Of course. I won't breathe a word to anyone about your helping me. This whole phone call will be our secret," I assured him.

"Give me the plate number. I have a guy I can call. He should be able to give me a name to go with the plate while I wait on the phone."

"Okay." I didn't want to say any more, in case my voice betrayed me for the crazy drive-by stalker I was.

I gave him the number and felt my pulse pounding in my ears. Maybe this was nothing, I thought to myself. Maybe Isaac had just borrowed a friend's fancy car. And then stayed all night.

"Okay, just hold a sec, I'm calling him on my other line."

I could make out his voice as he called on the other phone, but I couldn't quite discern what he was asking. I wondered where Rich was on a Sunday morning. Was he staying over at a girlfriend's house? Was he in bed, naked under the sheet while making the phone call to get me the plate information? I'd never thought about Rich being naked before; it was a little scary because he was so big. Maybe it was safer and easier to picture him in his navy jacket at the office.

As promised, he was back on the line with me in less than a minute.

"Okay, Dani, the Mercedes is registered to a Chloe Johnson. Does that ring a bell?"

I froze. *Fucker.*

"The name doesn't ring a bell, but thanks, Rich."

"No problem, Dani, anytime. And if you need anything, call me. I want to be sure you're okay."

"Yeah, thanks, Rich. I'll remember that."

I looked at the phone resting in the charger. I reached down and picked it up and slammed it down hard. For some reason I blamed the phone for being the messenger of this bad news.

He was fucking Chloe. All that talk of being "just friends" and how "women are interesting" was just a smoke screen for his cheating. I imagined the two of them in bed, on the Donna Karan sheets I had given Dave over Christmas . . . laughing about it. Laughing about me.

I thought of Chloe's thighs, all rubbed raw from Colin Farrell. Was that even true, or just some bullshit line Dave gave me? Maybe it was some bullshit line Chloe gave *him*, to get Dave thinking about her thighs.

I drifted around my apartment in a total fog, trying to figure if there could be any reasonable explanation for her car being in his driveway all night, but I came up with nothing. I sat down and stared. The light was streaming brightly through the windows and I realized how much time had passed with me moping around. Thank God it was a Sunday and I didn't have to go to work. But I also didn't have anyone to go to Viktor's with for Sunday brunch. When the phone rang I almost fell off my couch.

The caller ID told me it was Dave. I wanted to let it go to voice mail and not call him back all day to punish him. I wanted him to worry, to think about me and why I wasn't calling him back. Let him sweat. But on the fifth ring I grabbed the phone. I was going to dive into this one headfirst.

"Hello."

"Hey, baby . . . how are you?"

"I'm fine," I said tightly. "How are you?"

"Good. Thanks for being so understanding last night, about postponing the show and everything."

"Yeah, I'm glad I could be so understanding with you fucking Chloe Johnson!"

I had totally busted him, and just by the gasping sound he made, I could tell he was completely taken aback.

"What did you do?" he demanded.

"What do you mean, what did I do? You're the one who has some explaining to do to me about last night."

"I . . . uh . . . ." I could tell he was shitting his pants about now. "You obviously think you've got something on me—so why don't you just let me have it?"

"I know you were with *her* last night! You weren't with Isaac. You fucking lied to me about everything! On one of my biggest nights, you were with Chloe!"

"No, that wasn't the way it was, Dani . . . please let me come over and explain . . ."

"There's nothing to explain. I think I really get it."

With that I slammed the phone down. I waited a second and then left it off the hook. Let him call back as many times as he wants, I said to myself—it's just going to go straight to voice mail. I knew how crazy that would make him. But as I sat down on my green marshmallow sofa, I felt my face crumple up. It was over.

I was still sitting on the couch when he pounded on my security gate. I had opened the front door earlier, but kept the metal security screen door locked. Through the window I could see he was holding a bouquet of daisies, my favorite.

I got up and walked over to the locked screen door. "I don't know why you bothered coming over. I think you should get the fuck out of here!"

"Dani, let me in, I can explain," he pleaded.

"Well, I don't want to talk. I really don't want to see you. What did you think you were going to accomplish by coming here?"

I almost always kept my front door open; the security screen bolted shut from the inside. Now, with Dave breathing through the screen, I felt way too vulnerable. I grabbed the front door to close it. At least then I wouldn't feel so exposed to him. "Please leave. There's nothing to discuss."

He looked tired. His eyes were bloodshot and it looked like he had been crying. I shut the door on him.

"Please don't do this, baby! Do you know what I have in my car?" He was pleading with me now. "I picked up Christmas lights. I was going to decorate your place so it would be special tonight when we watched your show."

He was practically yelling to be heard through the screen and closed door. The neighbors were going to get an earful.

I watched through the glass in the door as he pulled his hand out of his pocket holding the key to my door. I forgot he had that.

Dave unlocked both doors and stepped inside.

"Don't, baby. Don't throw this away," he said gently.

"You're the one that threw this away. By fucking that whore."

"I didn't fuck her!"

I couldn't believe he was even trying to deny this. He was so caught.

"I'm so sorry. I was so stupid—yes, Chloe and I hung out. I was just feeling insecure."

"You were *insecure?*"

"Well, yeah." Dave cocked his head and choked a little. "And upset. Chloe told me you were cheating on me. She said that when you were on the road, she heard you were messing around with someone."

"What? She said that and you *believed* her, without asking me if it was true?"

Dave dug his hands deep into his pockets and walked toward the bay window, staring at the trees in the courtyard.

"A lot of things are changing." Turning toward me, he exhaled deeply. "You've really changed just in the two years I've known you. Now that you've landed the big gig on the show, you're like a different person."

"What do you mean? I'm just the same!"

"No, no you're not. You're working all the time. You're at the studio practically around the clock. You spent a whole week away, for that trip to Quantico. When we do hang out, you're totally preoccupied all the time." Now he did seem insecure, as if I were the one hurting him. "How could I not think you were going to bail on me?"

I felt helpless as I recognized what he was doing—he was shifting gears from acting forlorn and wounded to gaining steam for his own accusations. "I can't even get through to you when I call," he went on. "You're always in a meeting with Steve Jacobs. Or as that bitch assistant Azita puts it"—he mimicked quotation marks with his fingers—"behind closed doors."

"He's my boss," I said. "We have a lot of meetings. And usually when we meet the other writers are there too. It's not like we're alone."

Dave scowled. "You know that guy is dying to get into your pants."

"Stop it with this. You're trying to put this on me, and it's not going to work! I wasn't cheating on you—you know that! Even when I was out of town, you were my last call before going to bed every night. Do you really think I'd call you at midnight and talk for twenty minutes and then slink off to bed with someone else?" I couldn't believe the words coming out of my mouth. Why was I trying to force him to believe me?

Dave straightened up and folded his arms defensively across his chest. "Well, you could see how I have my doubts. Plus I had to hear about your plastic surgery from your mom. What was I supposed to think of that? You've been deceiving me this whole time. I thought you were factory!"

I rolled my eyes.

"You've been changing big time. It made sense when Chloe said you were hooking up with someone else."

I reeled at his mention of Chloe, then tried to ground myself and cycle through what he was saying. I had been really consumed with work, but Dave was often shooting at night and I really didn't think he'd noticed. This show was my big break, and I had to make it work. My job wasn't making me any busier than he was, though. Dave was just used to my always being around for a text message or a phone call. The trip to Quantico had been only for four days. Since I'd returned from Quantico we'd stayed over at each other's houses several times, but that still left him with a lot of nights on his own.

Standing there in front of Dave, running my hands through my hair, I thought of that bitch Chloe. She must have planned this whole thing out. She had targeted Dave, even after he said he had a long-time girlfriend. Then she waited until I was out of town to seduce my boyfriend with tales of A-list directors and stories about her raw thighs. Then she delivered the final blow by telling him I was cheating on him.

Suddenly I was furious again. "You couldn't get it up with me the other night because you'd been fucking her! You were tired. Did you even wipe your dick off before you *tried* to slide it inside me?"

"Holy shit, can you just calm down? None of that's true. I've just had a lot on my mind. I told you I didn't fuck her. I swear I didn't fuck her."

I don't know why, but when he stepped toward me and put his

arms around me, I didn't push him away. I let myself melt into him and sobbed into his shirt. He leaned his head into mine and I could feel his damp face. He wouldn't be over here this upset if he cared about her and not me.

"I'm sorry, sweetie. It'll never happen again. I'll never let someone or something come between us."

His hands held my head close, and he started caressing my hair. This made me cry harder.

"Do you know what I want to do today?" he whispered into my hair.

"What?"

"I want us to go to St. Monica's Church and pray. I want us to pray for some sort of guidance, some way to right all this wrong between us. I don't want to give up on us."

Dave kept his arms wrapped around me and walked me backward down the hall to the bed, easing us both down onto the duvet. I held on to him, closing my eyes against his neck and smelling his familiar smell. Behind his ear his hair was wet from my tears. I closed my eyes as he trailed his fingers over my lips and kissed my forehead. I remember at some point hearing him whisper into my ear that he was going to make everything okay. I was emotionally drained and was still nursing my Ambien hangover. Exhausted, I slept.

When I woke up, I could see the daisies on the counter in the kitchen in a beautiful crystal vase. It wasn't mine; Dave must have run out to the store and picked it up. I looked at the clock—it was three. I closed my eyes and drifted off some more. Keeping my eyes open was too exhausting. I dozed again, and when I woke up it was dark outside. From my bed I could stare down the hall and see twinkling Christmas lights strung across the ceiling, looping around my furniture and houseplants, casting bits of flickering light on the ceilings and walls.

Dave came into the room, walking slowly, as if he thought if he made any sudden movements I'd bolt. He had shaved and was dressed in the kind of blazer and shirt I'd seen him wear to church.

"Hey, baby. You slept for a long time." He looked at me. "You're so beautiful. You're the most beautiful woman in the world to me."

His hazel eyes held mine, and he made his way to my side of the bed and sat down. Lucy immediately jumped up on the wooden nightstand and hopped over onto his lap. She was such a traitor. He started stroking her and I could hear her purring. We sat there for a couple of minutes while he stroked her. At some point he took my hand, and I felt the pressure of his thumb stroking the inside of my palm.

He gave me a little squeeze. "Please don't ruin this with your crazy thoughts. I love you, Dani."

I wanted to believe him. I remembered the way his face looked when he pulled me toward him to kiss him for the first time. I loved that look. I loved the love notes, the e-mails he tossed off saying he was thinking about me. I remembered how, after I vaguely mentioned I loved Paul Auster, he'd surprised me with an early copy of his new novel. The daisies, the twinkling lights, the prayers he promised for us at St. Monica's—he did so many things to make me feel special.

"I'm thirsty. I'll be right back," I told him, extricating myself from his arms and walking slowly into the kitchen.

"I would have brought you something to drink," he called after me.

"It's okay."

I poured myself some water and stood at the kitchen counter thinking of Dave and his prayers. Just a few inches from my glass I spied Dave's cell phone, a black Razr. He'd set it down next to his keys when he came back from praying for us at church. Instantly I was mesmerized by the phone. I could just make out the time in the slick black screen, letting me know the phone was on.

"So where else did you go while I was napping?" I called back to him in the bedroom.

"Just home and then to church. I wanted to get back here to my sweetheart," Dave yelled.

My hand lay on the counter next to my glass, just inches from his phone. My heart was pounding ferociously. Staring at the phone, I thought that I just wanted to know; I just wanted to be sure. Moving quickly, I picked up the phone and flipped it open, cringing in anticipation of some sort of cell phone warning jingle.

But the phone didn't make a peep. Fingering the smooth buttons, I quickly pressed the button labeled "calls," which spitted me into the menu asking me for "received calls" or "dialed calls." My thumb pressed the button for "dialed calls." The screen quickly filled with a uniform column of the same name that had been dialed over and over: "CLO."

"CLO" was pretty self-explanatory. Scrolling down the list, I saw he'd dialed me three times and CLO seven times.

That was like the score from a really boring football game, and I'd lost. Clicking the last time he'd called CLO, I could see it was today at 3:44, lasting for thirty-five minutes. Mapquesting the drive time to St. Monica's Church in my head, I grimaced: It just didn't add up that he would have been able to be on the phone that long and go to church.

"Baby, come back in here, and lie down with me," Dave called out from the bedroom.

Still holding his phone, I thought of the red Mercedes. I saw myself looking through his receipts and address book log. I thought about how Dave had said that he'd just "hung out with Chloe," but the red Mercedes had stayed in his driveway *all night.*

I couldn't do this. I couldn't end up like Mom, checking in the car trunk by the spare tire.

"Dave, can you come here a sec?"

"Sure." I heard the bed springs bounce under him as he got up and quickly shuffled toward the kitchen.

"I love you, I love you," he singsonged. As he got closer, his smile faded when he saw me holding his phone.

"Hey, what's Chloe's number?" I asked, making his phone dance a little jig with my hand. "I'd love to call her right now and have her come over so the three of us could talk."

Dave seemed stunned that I would trump him this way. He started to say something, but the sight of me holding his phone made him shut his mouth.

"You are such a fucking liar," I shrieked.

"Dani, don't do this," he begged, moving my way, "I can explain."

I threw the phone at him hard. It bounced off his shoulder, then skidded across the hardwood floor. "I'd love to hear another explanation from you about this!" I screamed, surprising myself with my shriek.

"Why did you have to get all Five-O on me about this?" Dave screamed back. "This is your work shit—all this spying and sneaking around. You're a crazy bitch!"

"*All Five-O on you?*" I yelled. "Is that some sort of hipster slang for *Hawaii Five-0?*"

"Yeah, it is," he answered. "Half my friends don't know how I put up with your crazy shit for this long!"

"Oh fine, that's great, Dave," I shouted back. "You're full of shit. You fucked her. Of course you did. You're trying to put this on me— and for once, I'm standing up to your bullshit. So get out of here— you're a liar."

I was surprised how strong I sounded, because I was a mess.

Picking up his phone from the floor, he brushed by me toward the front door. Giving me one last look, he pointed his finger at me and gritted, "You are psycho."

"Get out of here, I hate you!" I screamed.

But he was already out the door and gone.

• • •

Throwing myself across the green marshmallow couch, I let myself fall apart. The hot tears rolled down my face. I wrapped my arms tightly around myself and just let them flow. My mom used to tell me if I didn't stop crying when I was horizontal I would have "tears in my ears."

Lucy knew it was a crisis. She rubbed up against my leg and held her head up toward me so I would pet her.

"Hey, pretty girl," I cooed, scratching her neck the way she liked. Lucy purred back appreciatively. I really loved her so much, and for a brief second I didn't feel so lonely. Then I started crying, because a woman in her thirties home alone with her cat is just pathetic.

Getting myself together, I strained to hear something . . . anything. My eyes darted around my living room, taking in my apartment. Hardwood floors, flat screen TV, overflowing desk. Everything seemed in order, but I still sought to discern any noise at all. The house was still and quiet. It finally dawned on me what I was hearing.

I heard nothing, and I knew it was the sound of being single.

My head was heavy and my face was starting to turn red. There was no moaning or rocking back and forth this time. I had cried on this couch a lot about Dave, but I knew this time he wouldn't be coming over later with flowers. Lucy started creeping toward my chest. She was obviously very worried about what was going on with me. I scratched her head and she started to drool a little bit. I felt wetness on my hand, but I wasn't sure if it was my fresh tears or her drooling. She was like a faucet. She stretched herself out across my stomach as if she were holding on tight. I imagined this was her thinking she was giving me a hug to make everything all right. I felt even more pathetic, and I squeezed my eyes tight and settled in for an ugly-face cry.

Maybe I should call him, I thought, maybe we *can* work through this. I was starting to feel panicked and regretful. The phone hadn't rung; I clicked it on to make sure it wasn't out of order, but I heard the expected dial tone. I scrambled up from the couch, dislodging Lucy, and dashed to the desk. After powering on my computer, I logged on to AOL to see if there was an e-mail from Dave. First I had to discard the usual porn spam that filled my inbox. Ever since I bought a vibrator online for a friend as a wedding shower gift, I'd been getting a dozen lewd e-mails every morning to get my day started. There was nothing from Dave. He had just left an hour ago—I didn't know why'd I expected him to draft me something in so short a time.

My house was a virtual shrine of photos of us. I was always smiling big and he was always taking the photos. He loved documenting everything, and then giving me special black-and-white photos he had a lab print up special. I could have done with a little less picture taking, but I knew he did it because he loved me. Or did.

I took down the Christmas lights and slowly collected the framed pictures from their places of honor on the coffee table and the small table where I put my purse and keys when I came home. Everything went into a shoebox that I placed far back in my bedroom closet.

Back at the computer, I deleted my user name and punched in his. I hadn't had much luck since the last time he changed his password, but I gave it a shot. The computer screen denied me access. AOL dumped me back to the welcome page and I tried again. I entered "secret"—that didn't work. I gave "davegallagher" a shot. Nothing. I even tried "DaniHale," to see if he paid some sort of tribute to me by having my name as his password . . . but no access.

Dave was careful and changed his password frequently. It hadn't been hard to get his password originally; I just waited until his computer was left on after he had been working on it. Whenever he jumped into the shower, all I had to do was go into the hard drive and click on Keychains, and all the passwords stored on the computer popped up. The computer just had to be on and Dave would have had to log in when he first powered it up. People never log off after each time they use their computer.

I hadn't been able to get on and check his account for the past month. Having no e-mail access to Dave's account had actually made it pretty peaceful for me. I hadn't checked his e-mail four or five times a day the way I usually did. But I did have the sour satisfaction of knowing he couldn't dial up Amy Robbins.

I turned off the computer and picked up the phone. I dialed Verizon voice mail and punched in his voice mail number, then his voice mail password, which hadn't been hard to get. I had just waited until he checked his messages and then when he went to the bathroom I hit "redial." The LCD readout on the phone showed his code, complete with all the pound signs.

He'd changed the code. I couldn't get it.

Shit.

TEN

The cat box smell woke me up. Wrinkling my nose, I opened one eye and could see Lucy sitting inches from my head purring contentedly. Of course she was purring and very content—she'd just done something horrendous in the litter box.

"Jesus, Lucy." She flicked her tail in response. I could smell the flowery perfume of the litter on her tail. The combination curdled my stomach.

Lying immobilized, I stared up at the ceiling, my eyelids like sandpaper raking across my corneas with every blink. *I'm single and alone, I thought. I have no emergency contact person for when I go to the doctor.* Dave had been my emergency person. Now I'd have to correct that. The nurses would know that Dave had cheated on me. They'd talk about me behind their glass partition.

Fighting tears, I knew I had to drag myself out of bed and go through the motions of being a real living, breathing person. I'd have to pretend to be human when I really felt like a pod person dropped out of a flying spacecraft.

Making my way into the bathroom, I splashed water on my face and stared at my reflection closely. Not good enough, not pretty enough, not smart enough or thin enough. Sure, I was a good person on the inside, but all that had gotten me was cheated on.

I tugged on some jeans, thinking about my Weight Watchers points. I had to start doing lunges every morning to tighten my rear view. I knew that if I'd had a candy apple ass, Dave wouldn't have cheated with Chloe. No one would leave a rock-hard ass; it was something to keep a guy warm at night. My jeans were snug, but not in the good, JLo kind of way. They were snug more in the I-will-always-have-my-mother's-ass kind of way.

If I'd been obsessive about Dave before, this morning my obsession was totally consuming me. As I made my coffee and toasted my English muffin, I wondered where he was. Was he waking up alone? Was he with Chloe? Were they making fun of me right now? He often didn't like to stay over with me on what he called "school nights." Would his passion for Chloe push all the work priorities aside?

Leaving the house, I had to summon all my strength and willpower not to drive by Dave's house to see if Chloe's red Mercedes was there this early in the morning. I took a left on Highland, the road to work, instead of the right turn that would have led me on the quick drive to Dave's. I could do this, I told myself. Gripping the wheel and trying to hold back a sob, I repeated, "I can get through a Monday at work."

The next few days at the office, I tried not to think about Dave or Chloe. When Steve Jacobs told me the Marilyn show had scored the highest ratings ever for the series, I just smiled numbly and gave him a big "thumbs up" sign from my desk. I even endured an awkward embrace of congratulations from Haley. Awkward in that the hug was a first between us, and also that her breast implants felt like concrete bricks through her thin T-shirt.

"You just get me like no one else on the writing staff," she told me intently.

"Are you kidding me? You're a breeze to write for," I bullshitted back.

"I love the final shot, where they push in tight to the photo of Marilyn on the desk."

"Me too," I replied, covering. After everything with Dave, I had never ended up watching the show.

I threw myself into writing. I wasn't working on a stand-alone show, but I'd been on fire when it came to coming up with crazy ideas in the writers' room meetings. Steve was ecstatic. "This is the kind of shit we need to be putting out on a weekly basis to compete with the other shows—you've really stepped up," he told me.

"Thanks, I try," I mumbled back. I didn't want Steve to know how much of a mess I was when I wasn't in the office for my fourteen-hour workday.

"You've been doing such a great job in the writers' room that from now on I want you to take a more active role in the running of meetings," Steve told me.

"Really? Are you serious?" I asked.

"I'm very serious. I can't sit in on every meeting, and knowing you're helping to move ideas forward is a relief."

This was totally unexpected, and showed Steve's confidence in my work. But there was definitely going to be some nuclear reactor–sized fallout from the other members of the writing staff. I pointed this out to Steve.

"Let me worry about them. You just keep doing what you're doing."

"I don't know what to say," I replied, truly grateful.

"Say 'thank you, Steve.'" He grinned.

"Thank you, Steve!" I answered brightly.

At least something was going right. I was still smiling an hour later as I scanned through my mail, which Azita had dropped off. I was thinking how mad Evil Janet was going to be when she heard about my new duties . . . hee, hee, hee.

Shuffling through the usual junk, I hesitated over a cream envelope with no return address. It definitely looked like an invite of some type, probably for some sort of lame Hollywood PR event. Sliding my finger under the flap, I ripped open the envelope, a little curious, thinking that whatever it was inviting me to attend, no matter how lame, I was going to go to. I needed to do *everything* I could to meet a man *pronto*.

But it wasn't an invitation.

The envelope contained a single four- by six-inch photograph of a woman's breast. The photo was printed in black and white with the dark border from the negative included. This was how Dave printed all the photos he'd always given me. Scrutinizing the envelope carefully, I double-checked to make sure I wasn't missing any kind of additional note. Nothing.

Dave had very distinctive, angular handwriting. Judging by the feminine script on the front of the envelope, I knew a woman had addressed the picture to me.

The breast was lightly covered in freckles, and I knew it was a photo of Chloe.

My face instantly flushed. I glared at the picture, thinking of Dave's hand with his own freckles, caressing the curve of her breast and lingering near her small nipple. She did this—she had sent this to me at work to fuck with me. Right after I'd gotten this great news from Steve.

Shaking, I began unconsciously shredding the picture with my fingers.

"Bitch, bitch, bitch," I said aloud between gritted teeth.

When there was nothing left of the photo and envelope but a soft pile of white fragments on my desk, I flung the pieces toward the wall, letting the tiny bits lightly float to the floor. Chloe Johnson had just ruined another good thing.

I moved like a zombie in quicksand through the first couple of weeks post-breakup.

Staying late wasn't a problem now, and being around people made me feel just slightly better than I did at home alone drinking Amstel Light on the green marshmallow couch. My only male companionship was Jon Stewart on TiVo.

I survived on a selection of Lean Cuisines for dinner, and I just told Ina, Lauren, and my other friends that things were really busy at work and I couldn't meet up. All I wanted was to curl into the fetal position and cry in the dark.

Every time the phone rang, I'd fumble to check the caller ID, hoping it was Dave. I had no idea why I was wishing he'd call. He'd been lying and cheating on me. But some part of me wanted him to feel like he'd made a mistake. I wanted him to regret screwing "us" up.

But there were no calls or e-mails. He didn't regret anything.

I told no one at work about our breaking up. I wanted to keep it private and separate from office drama . . . I just didn't want to deal with the office gossip and the pickup lines that were sure to follow.

Hunkered over my computer one afternoon, I squinted at my screen, trying to make sense of some dialogue for the show we were prepping to shoot. I always got a little frustrated in the "playing it blond" scenes. That was the sexist description we gave to scenes where we had to explain everything in very simple language for the viewers to understand.

"Hey, Dani, you got a sec?"

"Sure, Steve," I answered, hitting "save" on my computer. "I'm just working on the revised draft for next week's show—the scene where Haley realizes the 'evil twin' has murdered her sister, so she can assume her life."

"Fantastic, that's a great one," Steve said distractedly. "I just wanted to let you know a lot of eyes are on the show right now. Your buddy Les Moonves is watching the show very closely."

"He's not my buddy," I said. "I'm sure he'd have no idea who I was if he met me."

Les Moonves was not only president of CBS, but he also presided over all the cable channels that CBS owned. He was a very important and busy man, the guiding force that brought the network from the bottom of the ratings to number one.

One of my first jobs as a temp was addressing Christmas cards for Les over the holidays when he was at Lorimar, which was fun. I also got to help send out the gifts to the stars of the Lorimar TV shows and their creative teams. For the people on *Knots Landing*, there were small portable TVs, back when they were new and that was a good gift. There were fruit baskets for the vegans, giant smoked salmon for the Jewish people (I had to be careful to send them the blue holiday card), and Tiffany clocks for the people lowest in the pecking order. The Tiffany clocks seemed like a good gift, but the studio got a huge discount because they bought so much stuff in bulk all year. My job was scheduled to last only a few weeks, but it was a blast, and I'd hoped it might turn into something more permanent. Maybe I could be the temp who got to stay on, the ultimate success story! But at the end of the third week, they asked me to hand back my temporary key card. When that job was over, I filled in the time during my unemployed afternoons by driving past the houses of the stars of *Knots Landing*. I had copied down all of their addresses and phone numbers, and would call Nicolette Sheridan just to hear her pick up and say "Hello?" and then I'd hang up. That was before caller ID. Things were so much fun before caller ID.

But that was years ago, and Les left Lorimar and went to run CBS. The network languished in last place for years before Les green-lit *CSI* and *Survivor*. Now he was one of the most powerful men in Hollywood.

Steve smiled across the desk at me. "Well, we'll just call him 'your buddy' between the two of us, knowing that he's loving what we've done lately. The network is giving us ten extra promo spots during the week all summer to help boost ratings against all that reality crap that's on this fall."

"Do we need the extra promos?" I asked. "I thought the numbers have been great."

"They have. So much so that Les is thinking there may be a spin-off or franchise for the show. Every episode we put on the air now is being looked at closely to see if we can spin off something into another hour."

"Wow, that is huge news. Good for you, I mean. How many different *CSI*s and *Law and Order*s are on the air now? That's big money."

We both contemplated the big money possibilities. Steve finally broke our silence. "I've been meaning to ask you—have you and Dave split up?"

I hit "save" again on my computer, just for something to do. As comfortable as I felt around Steve, he never asked me anything personal; we just didn't go there. I knew he was not a fan of Dave's, so it seemed weird for him to put me on the spot like this. Running my finger over the titanium keypad, I flicked away the lint and crumbs left from my low-fat Starbucks muffin. I knew I had to be straight with Steve; there was no use in trying to avoid his direct question. I practically gulped out the words. "Yeah, we did. Who told you?"

"Oh, I just heard it around, ya know. You hadn't brought anything up and I just wanted to see if it was true."

Meeting his gaze, I said, "Yeah, it is. Love is hard." This seemed like a blanket answer Doctor Robin would approve of on *Oprah*.

Steve looked away. Now he was the one who was feeling a bit awkward. "I know you've been really putting in the hours here, so I was wondering if the show contributed to what was going on with you two. You're pretty dedicated, and as much as I love the amount of work you can output, I do have a heart, and I'd hate to think that you're so married to your job that it would mess up your love life."

I eyed Steve. What was he up to, suddenly caring about my personal life? "Okay, Steve, this is getting weird. You never liked Dave, and it wasn't any secret that he wasn't crazy about you, and I'm putting out more pages here than ever. So what's the problem?"

"There's no problem. I just want you to be happy and have a life. I just wanted to ask because I know you guys were serious."

"We were and now we aren't, and I'm fine. No bad feelings. He's going to have a great career directing shows like *Militia Man*, and I'm here." I knew that sounded a bit bitter, but I really didn't need an interrogation from Steve. "How's *your* love life?"

Steve grinned, his suntanned cheeks crinkling into the creases around his eyes. It was so unfair how wrinkles could look good on guys. He stepped away from my desk and moved to leave. "I get it, Dani. Happy writing. No more personal questions."

"Deal, boss," I said to his back. But he was already out of my office.

I guess my news was public knowledge. Fuck.

There was nothing from Dave. Not an e-mail or a message on my cell. I kept checking my voice mail for messages on the hour every hour. Without even glancing at the keypad, I could punch in my secret code.

"You have no messages."

Coming home from work after 10 PM on my second Friday night

as a thirtysomething single woman, I felt sad and heavy, entering the courtyard and making my way across the garden to my front door. I'd forgotten to leave the light on that morning when I left for work. As I slid my key into the lock, my leg hit something on the ground resting against the door. When I bent down, my hand hit a large paper shopping bag with woven handles. My heart skipped faster. Maybe it was a present or flowers. Maybe Dave did feel regret. I was surprised by the weight of the bag as I opened the door and carried it inside.

Lucy watched me in the dark as I fumbled for the light switch and eagerly reached into the bag's contents. I peered in, and I could feel my face fall.

Snorkel fins from our vacation in Hawaii last year. Some underwear and two bras. I fumbled around and then just dumped the whole thing upside down onto the hardwood floor.

My stuff.

A small bottle of my favorite body wash, a pink toothbrush, and a few stray tampons. The tampons seemed like a low blow. He didn't need to give me *those* back.

Separating all the items, I looked for a note or a card.

There was nothing.

I checked the outside of the bag but there wasn't even a Post-it on it. Dave had just dropped everything off and bailed. It all seemed like a big "screw you."

Happy Friday.

Lucy lay down next to me and started to clean herself. She probably thought I was cleaning *myself*, thanks to my weird position on the floor. She rolled over to get my attention and I absentmindedly rubbed her tummy. She purred loudly. Dave was ready to clear out all reminders of me after two weeks.

Leaving the pile of stuff on the floor, I went to the kitchen to make myself something to eat. When I opened the fridge door, the first thing I saw were two cans of Dr Pepper that I always kept around for Dave. Dr Pepper was the only soda he'd drink. I grabbed the cans and threw them with a big thud into the trash. That felt good. I stared across to the pile of stuff. I couldn't believe he would bring all that over here on a Friday night. Growing more agitated, I left the kitchen and headed for the bathroom to do my own cleaning out.

His toothbrush, his Avacor (for that little spot in the back that was getting thin but we never talked about), his toenail clippers that I once saw him use while sitting on the couch, letting toenail shrapnel fly everywhere. In my closet I found a pair of sweats he called his "fat pants" for when we ate a big dinner at home. I even yanked the flannel shirt of his I'd stolen that still smelled like him. I wouldn't keep it around for any kind of "Brokeback Mountain" sniff.

All of Dave's stuff went back into the same brown bag he'd left me. I used a butter knife to maneuver the key to Dave's house off my key ring. He didn't have to worry about me holding onto this— he could have it back. I wanted to leave this stuff now so he wouldn't think I had a chance to get a copy made of the key. I banged out of the door and charged through the courtyard to my car.

I gunned the gas most of the way to Dave's. I thought of Dave and Chloe together, having dinner, watching a movie at home, and laughing about me.

Dave wasn't home. I'd been in such a full speed rush that I hadn't even thought what I would do if he was there. I left my car running and quickly took the steps up to his front door. I was nervous about being caught, although I hadn't done anything wrong.

I left the bag and scanned the street to see if anyone could see me. There was no one visible. I paused in front, waiting a minute. The inside of his place was dark. The windows were bare; he'd never gotten around to getting curtains. I moved a few steps toward the window, glancing over my shoulder toward the street.

Empty.

I leaned toward the glass, letting my eyes adjust to the interior dimness. I could just make out the dark shape of his couch and the big plasma TV that he'd splurged on last summer. He bought it after a big residual check from one of his "asses and ammo" shows.

I could also see his sneakers on the floor, pushed up against the sofa. That halted me. Dave had only two pairs of shoes, and if his sneakers were on his floor that meant he was out wearing his dress shoes, a pair of velvety dark Gucci loafers I'd given him last Christmas.

Thinking about his dress shoes, I trudged back to the car. I wasn't worried about getting caught now. Reversing direction, I eased my car down Rodgerton toward Beachwood. This was one of the few streets that led up to Dave's place; it was really the only direct way in, which meant Dave would take Rodgerton home.

I drove a safe enough distance down the street, then pulled over. It was a Friday night and close to eleven. Dave wasn't home and he was wearing his good shoes.

Date. Fucker.

I sat in my BMW waiting. I hadn't eaten dinner and my tummy growled. The best I could hope for out of this breakup drama was dropping a few pounds. I pulled out one of the "disaster Zone" bars that I kept stashed in the glove compartment in case of emergency. I devoured it in three bites; I was so hungry I sucked the waxy frosting off the cellophane wrapper. Catching sight of myself in the rearview mirror sucking on the wrapper, I thought of what a pig I was. No wonder Dave cheated on me with Chloe.

Glancing at the clock, I made a contract with myself about how long I would stay there. *I'll lurk until midnight,* I told myself; anything more than that is psycho. I didn't know what I hoped to gain by staying. Would I see Dave with Chloe coming home for the night? Maybe I'd see Amy from Atlanta? I turned on KCRW and stared out the window. Tinted windows gave me anonymity. I wouldn't even crack the windows, and it was getting warm quick. I was trying to be undercover.

I waited.

After twenty minutes, I gave up. I didn't want to wait till midnight, and by leaving early I felt like I was demonstrating a lot of control. Dave could come home from his date and find his stuff at the door. I didn't care.

The next morning I woke up groggy, feeling hung over but knowing I wasn't. I would have preferred the hangover. If I'd had somewhere to go out to the night before, someone to down tequila shots with, it wouldn't have been so bad to feel shitty in bed on a Saturday morning. Instead I was waking up in my bed with my cat as company. I felt like I was breathing lonely.

I decided I would approach my new singlehood like a pro athlete. After all, I was going to have to "get back out there." Put myself on the market. I was going to take yoga, I told myself, drive out to Malibu on the weekends and take long, soul-searching walks on the beach. I would eliminate all the "white stuff" that Oprah talked about—sugar, flour, and potatoes.

That afternoon I headed to Whole Foods on Santa Monica Boulevard and packed my cart with "Whole Woman" vitamins and scoured the packaged food labels for "all natural" and "whole grain" before I went to do some damage in the fresh produce section. I was trying to figure out the difference between "organic" and "heirloom" tomatoes when I bumped into my friend Bernie, who wrote for some lame CW sitcom.

"Dani! So how have you been doing? Married yet?" he asked.

I bit my lip for a second, realizing that this was the kind of moment when I would just have to face up to my single situation. Telling Steve was different from telling someone like Bernie. He wasn't in my first or second circle of friends—not that I'd told them either, or my mother. But Bernie was definitely on the C list.

"No, Dave and I broke up . . . a while back." I gestured over my shoulder, as if it were way far back.

"Wow," he said. "I'm shocked. I really thought you guys were doing the whole thing . . . all the way. He seemed so into you."

"Yeah. Unfortunately he was sticking it into a lot more than just me."

"Man, really? You know, I saw him once with this blond girl, at Starbucks . . . but I just let it go."

I took this in. "You didn't say hi or go up to him?"

"Er, no," he stammered. "You know, I just figured . . . it was, you know, none of my business."

Now he was not even looking me in the eye. He dug his hands into his pockets and started to draw something invisible on the linoleum floor of the produce aisle with the tip of his sneaker.

"You mean, you saw him and thought he was messing around on me and you didn't even say anything?"

"It's like I said," Bernie managed. "I thought maybe they were just friends hanging out."

"When do *you* ever go to Starbucks with a blond you're 'just friends' with?"

He smiled. "Yeah, you're right, but I just thought I should stay out of it."

Bernie could tell that none of this was going over well with me, and as I took a deep breath to fuel my telling him off, he brightened, as if he had hit on an idea. "You know, if you're back on the market, I know of this great guy to fix you up with. Are you up for it?"

I started to shake my head. "No way. No fix ups."

"Hey, what do you have to lose? He's a great guy. I've known him since college—we went to school at Columbia. He's been a writer on *The Simpsons* for years, and he just signed a new deal with Fox to develop a new show."

Now he'd piqued my interest a little. "A writer . . . really? So he's funny?"

"He's a frigging riot . . . and he's Jewish," he threw in.

I paused and thought about it for a half second. "Well . . . I don't think just getting together for some coffee or something could really be that bad. And you're saying he's not a freak. He's funny and Jewish and cool."

"Yes, yes, and yes." Now Bernie was feeling somewhat vindicated. "So I'll give him your number, okay?"

"Okay." He had talked me into it.

"Great, and no hard feelings about that other thing, right?" Bernie held his hands up in the air as a truce.

"Right." We said good-bye and I shook my head as I walked away. How many other women were there? And did everyone know? It was bad enough that I had to deal with his betrayal, but the fact that everyone knew he was cheating on me made me feel so much worse. When a man cheated on a woman and people knew, it was as if he were proclaiming to the world that you were lousy in bed. Because if he was getting laid with any decency, why would he stray and mess that up?

I took my sad, single-girl salad home and sat in front of the computer, trying to come up with a fresh way for our investigators to talk about a dead body lying on a metal autopsy table. Writing the dialogue wasn't really that hard, but coming up with creative new murder ideas was tough. The "Marilyn" story had been money, but there weren't too many of those. And with all the forensic shows on the air now, we were all tragedy whores looking for the next great scandal.

Online, I came across a story in Canada where police had suspected a well-respected doctor of being a serial rapist. The guy worked out of one of Toronto's biggest hospitals, and police tailed him for months, finally gathering enough circumstantial evidence to get a warrant for some DNA testing. The doctor passed the DNA testing, even though one of the victims had ID'd him from a police lineup. Canadian police were mystified over the negative test results. Over the next two years, they asked for more DNA samples, thinking maybe the negative result was the fault of shoddy lab work, but still they got no positive match.

It wasn't until the fourth time they extracted blood from him that the nurse practitioner noticed something strange about the sample. She thought it looked old; the blood was too dark in color. After a thorough examination, investigators found that he had surgically implanted a vial of someone else's blood under his skin near his own vein, so that when the sample was drawn from his arm it wasn't his blood, but blood from the vial. It was totally gross to imagine someone thinking that up, but it would make for great television.

The light grew dark in my little house, and I hadn't realized when the time passed from being late on a Saturday afternoon to the middle of Saturday night. I took my salad plate into the kitchen, rinsed off the remnants, and slid the lone dish into the dishwasher.

Saturday night and there was no date, not even a bad date. I padded back to my computer and went back to my Web surfing, looking for new stories of murder and revenge to inspire me. I smiled to myself: When artists talked about being "inspired" by someone else's work, it pretty much meant they were ripping it off.

Everything is inspiration.

ELEVEN

'd put off telling Ina and Lauren about the breakup, just because I didn't want to deal with their I-told-you-so's and are-you-OKs?!? I finally broke the news to them a month after Dave returned my shopping bag of stuff. Both girls ended up being cooler than I expected, and frankly sounded more relieved than anything. I confided in them about the drive-by, and trying to check his voice mail and e-mail, and they didn't seem to judge me too harshly. We'd all done it.

A few days later, Ina called with her first attempted fix up.

"This guy is great. I can't believe you don't already know Garrett—he's amazing. Do you know who his dad is? His dad is that director guy who does all those action movies. They have their own jet and—"

"No sons-of-the-successful. You know my rule. Remember Jack? That guy I dated in college?"

"He's not like Jack," Ina said. "This guy has a job, for one thing."

"What kind of job?"

"He produces with his dad, but not in a handout kind of way. He's the real thing. He's great looking and funny."

I was still suspicious. "How do you know him?"

"We just know him from being around in the scene—something you need to get out into, missy."

"We meaning you and Larry?"

"Yes, he knows Larry, but will you stop it already with your bitchy-pants, Dani? It's obvious from your crankiness that you need to get laid."

"Thanks for that, Ina. If I want this kind of affirmation, I'll call my mom."

I thought Garrett sounded pretty good, at least to meet for a beer or something. But then Ina hit me with the real story.

"There's just one thing . . ." she started.

"One thing?" I echoed back. "Is there something wrong with this guy that you should be telling me about?"

"Well, um . . . I wasn't going to say anything. I was just going to let you guys go out, but now that you're kind of into the idea, I feel a little guilty."

"What? How bad could it be?" I asked.

"Well, he kind of killed a guy?"

"He kind of killed a guy?" This was a first. I had to hold the phone a bit away from my face to actually give Ina my "Oh no, she didn't just say that" face through the receiver.

"Yeah, not intentionally or anything like that. He'd been dating this girl, Bridget, for years and she broke up with him and he was devastated. She started dating this new guy and, well, the story is kind of fuzzy, but there was this party up in Benedict Canyon and Bridget was there with her new guy and Garrett showed up. There was some sort of shooting . . ." She trailed off.

"Some sort of shooting?" I prompted.

"And a gun Garrett was carrying accidentally went off. It shot the guy and the guy died."

"Are you fucking saying you're trying to fix me up with a murderer?"

"No, it wasn't like that. He was never charged with murder. He actually pleaded out to second-degree manslaughter. His dad hired one of O.J.'s lawyers, and he got him the lesser charge."

"This guy buys O.J. justice and that's supposed to make it okay? Ina, excuse my language, but what the fuck?"

"Okay," she said. I could tell she was a little deflated. "But knowing how you're into murder and stuff, I thought you'd be intrigued, and it *was* years ago."

"I am *into* murder, as you put it, but I don't want to date murderers. Do you think I would ever try to fix you up with a murderer? Even if it would get you away from Larry?"

"*Enough.* I get it," she said. "I'm going now." I heard the phone click.

I loved how somehow in all of this I was the one out of line. I slammed the phone down.

Thankfully I had Lauren to see that night and complain to. My indignation actually helped me divert a bit of the hurt of Dave's cheating. Fixing me up with a murderer? It just wasn't something a friend would do. Trying to arrange a date for a good friend with a murderer was the work of a Frenemy.

I lead-footed it up Franklin to the new house Lauren had moved into a few weeks earlier. Her house was in an area just east of the Hollywood Hills in Los Feliz. Stopped at the red light at Beachwood Canyon, I tried to keep my eyes focused straight ahead. This was the light I used to take to go to Dave's. The three of us all lived within three miles of each other. I prayed I wouldn't have any run-ins with my ex for a long time.

Passing the Mayfair Market, I made a left and climbed into the hills. Lauren's street was technically in "The Oaks" of Los Feliz, which borders Griffith Park. The LA *Times* had dubbed this area "one of the hottest nesting grounds for young Hollywood," so now every couple with a baby seat in the back of their Volvo was driving around on weekends doing lookiloos at open houses.

Lauren never talked about how much money she made, but I knew that even though she worked on cable, she had to be earning pretty good money to buy a place in this neighborhood. I'd been a little offended that she never asked me to check the place out during her escrow. Didn't she understand that real estate was my cardio?

Obviously she wasn't interested in my input. Normally, I would have gone behind her back to find out the address and drive by, but I'd been so consumed with everything with Dave, I'd even slacked on that.

"Wow," I said from the driveway. The place really was amazing. Midcentury modern set on a bluff. The grounds were perfect. Lauren had bought it from a gay couple relocating to New York. That was striking the mother lode in real estate. The gays always redid everything with great taste and style.

Lauren was waiting at the front door.

"It's stunning. I'm overwhelmed," I gushed.

"I know—can you believe it's mine?"

"Show me!"

Lauren began giving me the professional tour, starting in the living room with its original, walnut floors and walls of glass that drew the eye to the breathtaking view of Hollywood below.

"Oh, man. I never even saw this place in the open houses," I told Lauren.

"I know. It wasn't even on the market. My Realtor had a heads-up and showed me the place before the listing went out, and I made an offer and got it."

"It's so special," I said, sincerely. With every room I envied her more: the bathrooms with their terrazzo floors, the master bedroom with its wood-burning fireplace. The flow was great. It was a house you wanted to come home to, a place you wanted to have friends over for a barbecue. It was a purely California house, something you'd find only in Hollywood. Lauren's tour ended in the kitchen, in front of the clear glass door on her Sub-Zero refrigerator.

"I saw this on one of those kitchen design shows," I exclaimed, peering inside. I winced slightly. "I guess you have to keep a neat fridge."

"You sound like your mother," Lauren remarked.

"Great."

"Dani, it means a lot that you love it. I know how you are about houses," Lauren said. "Now, about you. Are you okay?"

Rubbing my hands against the caramel countertops, I let my fingers follow the veined marble. I tried to distance myself from Lauren's all-seeing eyes. "Yeah, I am. I am sad. I don't want to see him, and I don't want him to be happy with Chloe or anything."

"Are you doing any stalking?"

"Yes," I confessed. "A little, just a few drive-bys, but nothing major. He changed most of his codes and passwords six months ago, way before the trouble, so I haven't been doing any snooping like *that,* if that's what you're getting at."

"Good," she answered. "Doing that is only a world of hurt. You know that, right?"

"Yes, I know." I hated it when she harped on me. I tried not to think of myself the way I was the night before, curled on my side in bed crying uncontrollably because I'd found a birthday candle that I'd saved from the red velvet cupcake Dave had given me last year for my birthday.

"Do you think he's dating Chloe?" Lauren asked.

"I don't know. I saw in the trades that she's been in Prague shooting a movie about vampires for the Sci-Fi Channel, so whoever he was out with that Friday night, it wasn't her."

"Maybe he's already cheating on Chloe, too," Lauren said, trying to make me feel good.

Looking for a distraction for my misting eyes, I spied a man's baseball hat on the kitchen counter. Lauren had been dating this indie filmmaker Michael for six months.

"Is Michael living here with you?"

Lauren followed my eyes to the baseball hat and her face flushed. I knew that look, the look of total infatuation and great sex. That was the look of always knowing there'll be a message light blinking on your cell phone, and that someone would be waiting at home when you drove in from the airport.

"No, he's got his own place, his 'bat cave' as I like to call it. We stay over a lot, but he likes to retreat to the 'cave' when he has his freak-outs."

"Are things okay with you?"

"Oh yeah. It's just the 'tortured artist' thing." She shook her head in exasperation and pulled out a bottle of white wine from the fridge. "He loves me, but he says he can't help but fuck it up."

"Does that mean he's fucking other people?"

Lauren pondered for a moment. "I don't think he's sleeping with anyone else, but it's just that he's just so impressed with artists, and he thinks that because I do what I do, I can't possibly understand him."

"But you're amazing. You're good at what you do, you're kind of famous and smart and beautiful . . ."

"Yes," she said, shrugging. "I know he loves me, but last weekend when we got the *New York Times* delivered on Sunday, I saw they had a feature in the magazine section about hot new up-and-coming female artists in Manhattan. There were a couple of really beautiful women in there. The article featured each one in a full page photo with a piece of their artwork—paintings and sculptures and stuff."

"So?"

"Well, when I saw the article, I waited until he was in the bathroom and then I tore out the pages of the more attractive women. I didn't want him to be leafing through that thing and all of a sudden become smitten with some beautiful artist he thought would understand him in a way that I don't."

"Lauren, I know I can be a bit crazy . . . but that's crazy!" I felt an embarrassing sense of triumph.

"I know." She laughed. "But why put that temptation in front of him when I know it's one of his 'things'?" she asked, emphasizing "things" with her fingers. "Want to know how I keep him?" she asked.

I smiled. "How do you keep him?"

"Well, you know he eats guacamole every night, and he loves to mash up the avocados very precisely. It's like some kind of therapy for him when he's home after a hard day being an independent film-maker."

I nodded.

"Well, every few days, I put a little crushed-up Viagra in there, and then we fuck like rabbits."

"Are you kidding? I can't believe you've been holding out on me with that one." That was one for the record book. I thought Lauren was my Sane Friend.

"I know." She grinned. "He thinks it's all me . . . and I let him." She finished pouring the wine.

"Cheers to that," I said, and we touched glasses, then burst out laughing.

It was a fun night, but when I drove home my heart started racing as I approached the turn for Beachwood Canyon. Unable to resist, I turned right, following Beachwood as it wound up through the hill to Dave's house. It was a moonless night, so I felt I wouldn't be conspicuous—I'd do one quick pass in front of his house and be out of there. From the stop sign on the corner, I could see that his VW wasn't in the covered driveway. Dave was out again, or maybe he was just shooting late that night. I allowed myself to drive past his house and make a U-turn a few houses down. Swinging back around, I slowed to just over five miles an hour as I cruised by the front of his place. The inside was dark, the way it had been before, but in the middle of the window I could make out a beautiful potted orchid, prominently set on a small table. Dave wasn't into orchids, so I thought that was odd. Maybe it was a corporate gift someone from the network had sent him, or maybe it was a gift from a girl and he felt obligated to display it.

Giving the orchid one last look, I gunned the gas to go home.

TWELVE

It took another two weeks for me to be rewarded for putting myself "out there," with a voice mail from Mr. Katz, the *Simpsons* writer.

"Hi, this is Grant Katz. I'm a friend of Bernie's. I think you've been warned that I'd call. Well, anyway, give me a call back and let's see if we can set up a time and place to meet."

Even though I'd checked the messages just a few minutes after he phoned, I did what any woman would do: I waited two days to call him back. Because it was summer, we had occasional weeklong breaks from shooting, to let the staff catch up on writing and posting shows. So I could be pretty flexible about getting together. After another round of returned calls and messages, I was in my car on a Wednesday night, heading toward Sushi on Sunset for my first meeting with Grant.

I went over in my head what I knew about him. I had Googled him and the whole thing was looking promising. He had written for the *Harvard Lampoon* and somehow had ended up on *The Simpsons* as one of the writers and producers. I also found out that he was thirty-three, which was okay. He wasn't so old that you'd think there'd be a problem with him (like, what was wrong with him that he never settled down), but he was over the initial I'm-successful-in-Hollywood-and-am-going-to-nail-everything-in-sight phase.

I checked my lipgloss in my rearview mirror as I waited for the valet to open the car door. I didn't want to look like I was trying too hard. I'd only thought about my outfit for an hour. I finally settled on a skirt, short but not too short, and a sleeveless mock turtleneck in baby blue that would bring out my eyes. I'd thrown a matching cardigan over my shoulders, hoping it looked effortless.

My car door opened and I carefully slid my legs to the left, with my knees firmly glued together. Then I stepped out. Valet guys never thought anyone was hip to them sneaking a snatch peek as women exited their cars. Usually women were so busy juggling their purse and cell phone and grabbing the valet ticket that they left themselves vulnerable for a few seconds, while the valet guy angled his head down for a prime view of her real estate. I could tell by his disappointed look that I'd foiled his plan. Smiling, I took the ticket and walked past him into the restaurant.

As I entered, my eyes took a minute to adjust to the dim lighting. It was really dark. I was never really a big fan of sushi. When my friends would pressure me about it, I would just say it was a "texture thing." Lauren loved going out for sushi on dates. She thought the whole hand to mouth chopsticks thing was autoerotic. But when Grant suggested we meet here, he asked, "You do like sushi, don't you?" to which I replied, "Oh yeah, of course I do. I love it."

I peered around the sushi bar counter and didn't see any men waiting alone. "Shit," I muttered to myself. I hated being early. I'd even driven up and down Sunset a few blocks each way to help kill time, and I was still early.

Looking over the dark railing into the dining room, I could make out some couples sitting in the black leather banquettes deep in conversation. I waited a bit and no hostess came up to seat me, so I decided to go sit on a stool at the sushi bar. I self-consciously crossed my legs, deciding not to put my purse on the sticky floor underneath me. I balanced my bag on the stool next to me and waited. A couple was seated a few stools away. She had multiple earrings, piercings, a lot of makeup, and a leather miniskirt. He sported dirty jeans and aspiring ZZ Top facial hair, and his short-sleeved shirt revealed beefy arms covered in tats. I could make out some of his armpit hair sticking out. Jesus, he shouldn't have that stuff out. It was like a woman's bush.

The waitress approached them and handed over a couple of hot paper towels wrapped in plastic. The woman tore through it and cleaned her hands furiously, while he wiped off his face with the towel and then threw it in the middle of his place setting. I could see the clock from where I was seated: 9:10 PM. Grant was officially ten minutes late. I didn't understand how people could be late. I was never late. I always allotted extra time whenever I had to meet up with someone or had an appointment. I just thought it was so rude to be late, especially for a meeting with someone new. Glancing back at the rock-and-roll couple near me and over by the booths, I realized that this restaurant was somewhere you would go when you didn't want to be seen by anyone you knew. The place was all shadows, and who would come here for sushi? If it was a real date, you'd go to Roku on Third Street or Matsuhisa if the guy really wanted to impress you.

I was starting to lose a bit of my confidence. It was 9:14 and fifteen minutes late was *really* late. I went over word by word our conversation about the plans. Maybe this was the wrong time or the wrong place?

I was thinking I should leave when the black door burst inward and I saw Grant enter. I knew him right away. He was wearing a dark blue sweater and a suede caramel-colored jacket and khakis. The pants were a dead giveaway; all male writers wore non-wrinkly pants, for all those hours spent sitting in front of a computer. We locked eyes in the dim room and he rushed directly to me, nearly colliding with a waitress en route.

"Dani, I'm so sorry I kept you waiting. I never do that." Grant extended his hand. His grip was firm, and he put an arm on my shoulder, not quite a hug, but physical contact in an assuring kind of way.

"It's okay," I lied. "I just got here."

Grant sat down and signaled for the waiter. "Dani, before we get started, I have a confession to make. This isn't exactly a blind date for me."

He was talking like a kid who's done something naughty.

"Really?" I asked, intrigued. "What do you mean?"

"I saw a picture of you in that TV Guide article about Maggie Black."

"Oh God!" I exclaimed, feeling embarrassed. "And you remembered me from that? That's surprising."

"Well, it stood out in my mind because I remember showing it to the guys in the writing room and saying, 'Why doesn't anyone who looks like this work with us?'"

"Oh," was all I could eke out. This all pleased me greatly. His tardiness was forgiven.

Grant insisted on ordering for both of us, which was cool with me. He was obviously really excited about the sashimi and said something about "pure protein." As if that should electrify me. He was what some people would describe as "folliclely challenged," but I liked that. A smooth head was sexy. If anyone was going to have crunchy, product-loaded hair on the pillow it should be me, not the guy lying next to me. I'd take someone who was a Nice Jewish Guy who looked like Grant any day over a hotheaded Irish guy with a full head of hair.

We went back and forth with the usual basics. We both had the

Kabuki of it down: He told me his funny, self-deprecating story, and I fired back with mine. Neither of us mentioned any former relationships. The first date was when you revealed your best self, not your real self.

"How did you become a writer?" I asked.

"Well, much to my parents' disappointment, I didn't become a lawyer."

"Really?" I asked, acting surprised. I already knew a lot of this from the Google search.

"I had every intention. I graduated from Columbia and was in my first year of law school at Harvard when I realized it just wasn't for me. I started writing for the *Lampoon* and one thing led to another, and I knew this is what made me happy."

"When you knew you weren't going to go through with law school, how did that phone call home go over?"

"It wasn't a phone call, it was a visit. I had to tell them in person." Grant sobered a little. Even though it had been years, the scene was still fresh and obviously a little painful.

It was time to change the subject. "How did you get out here to LA?"

"I landed my first job writing on the original *Roseanne* show. People had started recruiting from the *Lampoon* and I got lucky."

"Lucky? I've heard horror stories about their writers' room. Are any of the stories true?"

He smiled. "My first day there, Tom Arnold came in and handed out numbered T-shirts to all of us. He and Roseanne didn't want to have to learn any of our names. They just wanted to call out our number when they spoke to us."

"That's crazy! Do you remember your number?"

"I sure do, it was eighteen, and I still have the shirt."

"You should frame it."

"I know, but everyone has those kinds of stories about first coming to LA."

I told him about working for Les Moonves. I saved my escapades with "Norma Jean" the rock star. She wasn't for a first date. When our food arrived, Grant dug in and I hesitated. I was never sure if you were supposed to put the whole piece of sushi in your mouth or if you could bite part of it off the chopsticks. I always felt like whatever I did, it wouldn't be seemly. I carefully picked up a piece of California roll and raised the chopsticks to my mouth. I opened wide and closed around the entire piece and immediately regretted it, because my mouth was so full the rice was threatening to spill out.

Grant asked me about work, but I was careful to temper my answers about the morgue stuff; guys sometimes found all that blood and guts talk a little scary.

"So you're writing on *The Simpsons*, but working on a new show also?" I asked.

"Yeah. It's a busy time." Suddenly he seemed tired. "I had been playing around with a couple of ideas for pilots, and Fox picked one of them up, so I'm kind of doing double duty, writing on *The Simpsons*, and starting to cast the pilot. We're hoping to start shooting the pilot in six weeks."

"Wow, that's fast." I said, impressed.

"Very fast."

"What's the new show called?" I asked.

"The Grant Katz Untitled Project," he answered, in an official sounding voice.

"Oh." I laughed.

Grant told me he had just gone on a vacation alone to Mexico. "Alone?" I asked, teasingly. The effects of two Sapporo beers were kicking in. "How was that?"

"It was great. It was the best thing I've done for myself in a long time. I lay on the beach with a stack of books and just relaxed and read."

I nodded my head in understanding, but I didn't understand. I couldn't imagine anything worse than going away on vacation alone.

Sitting there, a half-eaten plate of sushi in front of me, I felt more relaxed than I could remember. When I finally checked my watch, I was surprised to see it was a little before midnight.

Grant paid the check and we agreed we'd better go; we both had to be in the office early the next day. Pushing open the black door, I was immediately hit by the rush of the traffic on Sunset. We made our way over to the valet. This was the first time we had actually stood side by side, and I realized I was about an inch and a half taller than him. My head towered above his. I started thinking that if I wasn't wearing heels we might be more eye to eye, but even in sneakers I would be taller.

Grant took my valet ticket and handed both of them to the valet, slipping him a twenty. Nice. I always took the guys who had "grabbed a meter" to be a sign.

We both stood there awkwardly waiting for our cars. I decided to be quiet and to let him dictate on what note this date would end. But then I burst out with, "Do you like what you do?"

He seemed surprised by my question. He looked down and shuffled his feet. "Of course I love writing. I just worry sometimes about the pace of it. It can really be draining. Sometimes when I'm working on something and having a tough time, it's like looking directly into the sun."

"I know. It makes your head hurt."

"Exactly. I just try to push through, and I remind myself that even the most talented and successful writers struggle. It's not easy for anyone."

"You think?" I asked. I never had anyone to talk to about this stuff. I was always too busy trying to convey that I was supremely confident when I was actually a mess of insecurity.

The valet whipped around the corner of the lot with my BMW, pumped a bit too heavily on the brakes, and jerked the car to a stop right in front of us.

"Well, here I am," I said, starting to make a step away from Grant and toward the black asphalt of the parking lot. I could just make out the headlights of another car being brought around by the valet, slowly pulling behind my BMW.

"And here I am," he said, mimicking my singsong line.

I turned to smile at him. He *was* funny. Then I noticed his car. It was a Nissan 300 Z, with a glass moon roof. I didn't know what to make out of that. I couldn't even remember seeing a Z in years, but obviously this car was fairly new and loaded, as they say in the classifieds.

I was taking all this in when he touched my arm and I turned my body slightly toward him. "I'm glad we did this. I had a great time."

"Me, too," I said, a bit breathlessly.

Then he turned his face slightly and kissed me.

He was warm and I could feel him through my clothes as he pressed himself against me. His hand behind my head guided me toward him. His lips touching mine were firm and I could just make out a bit of moistness behind them as he pressed even closer to me.

He slowly pulled back. "You take care." He smiled and then turned toward his Z.

I wanted to try to play it cool, so I just smiled and nodded. Turning, I dove into my car and pulled the door closed behind me.

My heart was starting to race a little bit. The kiss was nice. And it was more than a blow off kiss. Those kisses are bone dry.

I pulled out onto Sunset and made a right toward Hollywood. I left my window down and the wind blew my hair back and I felt so good. Free, kind of wild. I didn't know why, but I felt like a grown-up. I drove the entire way home with a smile splitting my face in half. The fact that another man could make me feel like this let me know I was over all that Dave stuff. I didn't have to do a Dave drive-by that night.

THIRTEEN

The next morning I jumped out of bed before the alarm rang. Brushing my teeth, finding something to wear, burning my English muffin and not caring—all the things I did every morning somehow seemed special and fun. I charged down the hall at work, saying "Good morning!" to everyone, even Evil Janet, and "Hey, you!" to the creepy intern whose name I didn't know.

The morning flew by as I went over the shooting schedule and fixes for the show that week. My office line rang and I picked the call up before Azita could get to it.

"Hi, Dani." My heart sank to the floor with such a thud that my feet shook.

"Hi, Mom."

"I just want you to know that I really loved the show this week."

"Oh really?" This was surprising. "Well, thanks so much. I'm glad," I answered cautiously. I closed my eyes and tried not to exhale too heavily into the phone. We were in reruns, so I knew the show that just aired was from earlier in the season.

"How's Dave doing?" she asked.

I hadn't mentioned the breakup during my phone calls with my mother these last few weeks, and she hadn't asked any direct questions. I just didn't feel like having the kind of conversation about it that we were about to have. But I had to tell her sometime, I reasoned. "We broke up a while ago," I said quietly.

"What? But you liked him so much. I thought he was going to be my son-in-law."

I didn't respond. Anything I said could and would be used against me in a court of law.

"You should really be more careful about the men you have me meet," Mom said. "There's no point in my forming an emotional attachment to them if the two of you are just going to break up."

I'd forgotten that this was all about her. "It really is a long story," I said. "It's complicated. I just think it didn't work out and that we're going to be better off apart than we were together."

"Did he break up with you?"

"It wasn't really like that," I replied, imagining what Mom would say if I told her what happened.

"Dani, were you a bitch to him? You know how you can be so bitchy sometimes. I've always told you to be careful about that."

"I guess you'll have to ask him." Any kind of relationship conversation with my mom ended up going nowhere. "You know, Mom, I really have to get back to work. I have to go write a show with someone."

"Well, hearing your news, I have the perfect gift for you. It's a new self-help book that I saw at the bookstore, called *Crazy Time*. It's for when you're trying to get over a divorce. You need to know that right now you're in your Crazy Time and that's probably why you're so miserable."

"Mom, *Crazy Time* just sounds like another name for having your period, and yes, I am in a *Crazy Time*. You're right. I have to go. Bye, Mom."

"All right then, love you. Proud of you."

"Thanks, Mom, me too."

I hung up the phone. That could have gone so much worse. I loved how *she* was sending *me* self-help books.

"Hello." Rich poked his head through the doorway. "You got a sec?"

"Uh, yeah, I've got time, what's up?" I asked.

"What are you reading?" Rich approached my desk, which was a disaster zone littered with books and Post-it notes. He picked up my copy of *Infamous Serial Killers* and then one of my forensic books, the three-inch-thick *Forensic Guidebook for Beginners*. "Whoa. Definitely not chick-lit material."

"I call them dick lit, because most of those books are just about a woman trying to score some guy." Then I reddened a bit because I'd just said "dick" to someone I didn't know that well.

"I would have thought you were beyond a guidebook for beginners," Rich said. "I would have pegged you for more of a pro."

"I'm not a doctor, that's for sure," I replied. "I like using the entry level books because the language is so complete. It spells everything out in pretty simple terms for someone to understand."

"You mean the average viewer?"

"Exactly."

This exchange felt kind of awkward. Rich wasn't really the type of guy to hang out and chitchat. He was much too serious for that. My eyes scanned the navy blazer he wore over his white button-down shirt. Suddenly I was relieved he was no longer on the police force. I was glad there was no chance he would get shot in the face while on duty.

He glanced down and I could tell he was getting ready to say something important to him. "I was thinking the other night about your stalking problem."

"My stalking problem?"

"Yeah, remember you called me a while back about that plate number, but it was a false alarm?"

"Oh, yeah." I shrugged. "I'd been followed home a few times and I would occasionally see this one guy hanging around in front of my house, but I haven't seen him in a while."

"A lot of people truly believe that women have a natural instinct for sniffing out trouble, that there really is something behind women's intuition," Rich said. "This guy Gavin de Becker is a noted expert who specializes in protection for people who are targeted."

"I've heard of Gavin."

"I've met him a few times over the years. He's a cool guy. He consulted with the government about how to improve security at the White House. Gavin's book is called *The Gift of Fear*. You should check it out." Rich looked at me seriously. "Don't ignore those feelings. Always go with your hunches."

"I definitely feel sometimes that I do have a secret sense," I told Rich. "Just a feeling, ya know? When I go with these hunches and let them drive me, I've found I'm usually right."

"Okay." He headed to the door, then turned toward me again. "Be sure to check out that book."

"Okay."

I let him leave, counted to twenty, and buzzed Azita.

"What is the deal with Rich? I think he may have just been in here hitting on me," I said.

"I think he's hot." Azita giggled and jumped up on my desk, so that she was sitting on the edge with her legs dangling. She was in one of her usual naughty girl outfits: a plaid Catholic girl skirt topped with a tight T-shirt. Two bouncing ponytails completed her look. All she was missing was a lollipop.

"That guy is definitely armed and dangerous. Do you think that bulge in his pants is a gun?"

"I'm ignoring you," I retorted, turning back to my computer. "I have work to do, Azita."

She wouldn't be deterred. "He doesn't give any of the girls here any notice—he just comes and goes. But the other day he was asking some questions about *you*."

Damn, I was so busted. Maybe he knew my whole story about being stalked and followed had been bullshit.

Azita was picking up steam. "Well, I try to put things together sometimes, ya know? I think Mr. Armed and Dangerous thinks you are still with your ex. Maybe he just assumed you were because you were always so crazy about Dave and you've never really given off that vibe of being available."

"Even I wouldn't date someone at work. Just tell Rich that I'm dating someone but that it's not Dave."

"Cool, mama, anything. You want something from Starbucks?"

"No, I'm good, thanks."

In our usual script meeting that afternoon, Steve wasn't there, so I took over, giving quick, minimal notes on the latest draft of an episode helmed by one of our staff writers.

"Okay, I think that's it," I said. "See everyone tomorrow." Evil Janet was out of the door in a flash, after staring daggers at me the entire meeting. The rest of the writers all exchanged confused glances about wrapping up early. They quickly grabbed their yellow legal pads and headed for the door, starting their usual late morning conversation about what they were eating for lunch.

I checked my voice mail at home every hour that day to see if Grant had called. I went over his timeline in my head, from the scraps of information I had garnered from our date. I knew he was going to wake up early and work out with his trainer. The schedule for a sitcom was pretty routine, which meant he would have to be at the office by nine at the latest. It was now 3:15. I was sure he'd had meetings. It was a

Thursday—was that a blocking day for them? His hours might not be as regular if they were blocking or if it was a tape day.

We'd met on a Wednesday, which meant there was plenty of time between then and the weekend for him to make a plan with me and not seem overanxious. But he didn't call that Thursday.

Or Friday.

By Friday night, I reasoned that maybe Grant was nervous about us; maybe he didn't know what the next move should be. Sometimes men really wanted a woman to make the first move, to give them the sign that you were into them and wanted to wave them in.

Boldly, I sent Grant an e-mail late Friday to see if he wanted to go hiking over the weekend. I phrased the invite casually: "Hey . . . I'm going to Griffith Park hiking and if you want to get some fresh air, maybe we could meet up." That was casual, no pressure. Now all I could do was wait.

I waited around all morning Saturday. I heard nothing. As part of my effort to get in touch with my inner Weight Watcher, I decided to hit a Pilates class to kill time until the hike, part of my new A.D. (After Dave) self-improvement regimen. Later that afternoon, I found myself pacing back and forth in my living room willing my phone to ring. I wondered if maybe an accident on Mulholland Drive might have knocked the phone system down and he'd been trying to call and couldn't get through. I checked my cell for the hundredth time to see if anyone had called and it hadn't registered. No luck.

To try and kill some more time, I got on the Internet and began Googling Grant again with some of the info he had mentioned. I read some of the articles he'd written at Harvard for the *Lampoon* and also found some writing he'd done for *The Onion;* I laughed in all the right places. Then I started assessing the e-mail I'd sent him. Should I have not been so eager? Should I have waited? Was the e-mail too bland and not funny? Was it e-nilla? I logged on to AOL to see if he'd sent me anything. Grant was a comedy writer; he probably had tons of funny lines at the ready that he could dash off to someone . . . a little sunshine and a smile in their e-mail box.

I'd gotten nothing from him. I did a quick buddy search and saw he wasn't online. I was getting ready to log off when suddenly I was gripped by an impulse I couldn't ignore.

I went ahead and logged off but remained on the sign-in screen. I typed in his e-mail: speedracer11@aol.com. He'd told me Speed Racer was a secondhand Halloween costume his parents had made him wear every year.

I stared at the password slot. Carefully I entered p-a-s-s-w-o-r-d. I promptly received an "invalid password" response. Next I tried s-e-c-r-e-t for the password. Again, I was dumped back to the main sign-in page.

My chest was tight. I was now committed to cracking this. I wouldn't be denied. I had read once in *Maxim* that most men used their first name, the name of their pet, or the pet name for their penis as their password. Since I didn't know the latter two, I entered g-r-a-n-t-k-a-t-z. This time, instead of the main screen coming back up, my screen went blue and then popped up with that aggressively cheery "Welcome to AOL" greeting.

My heart was beating hard. Speedracer11 had seven new messages. I clicked to enter the "New" messages box and scanned the subject lines. None of them seemed flirty or suggestive. I didn't know what I was looking for.

I started clicking and opening the messages.

A friend confirming plans to play basketball that weekend. Now I knew what Grant did Sunday mornings.

He had mail from one of the writers from *The Simpsons* sending him some new pages for the next episode. There was also an e-mail from a college friend asking him about some tech stock.

I couldn't make much out of any of these. There was nothing incriminating so far. I decided to click over to his "Sent" messages folder.

Blah, blah . . . e-mails to Mom, the writer guy, the college guy. A message to a friend whose e-mail was JoeinLA. My heart started thudding again as I scanned the e-mail Grant sent to JoeinLA. I made out the word *dating*. Backtracking, I started from the top.

```
Sorry I won't be able to make the alum dinner
this year. I've been finishing up my work on
The Simpsons and I been working on ideas
for a new show on Fox. LA really is good, and
Yes, I have been dating. I went out with a
girl I really liked this week and I'm being
fixed up with woman Saturday who's also a
lesbian.
```

I pushed back from the desk and said out loud, "A lesbian?" Grant was excited about his upcoming date with a lesbian?

I knew Grant had to have been referring to me as the girl he "really liked," so if he liked me why was he taking out the lesbian? And he was taking her out tonight, Saturday night—that was prime time! I was obviously a second-position date when he relegated me to the Wednesday night slot.

I could feel my armpits start to get damp. My heart was beating a thousand times a minute. I pulled my chair back to the desk and started checking the e-mails I had read back into the "New" box. When I was done, I shut off my PowerBook. I just couldn't stand the thought of being in second position, especially to a lesbian.

I needed immediate assistance with this one. I called Lauren to see if she could meet me at AOC for drinks before dinner. Michael was out of town, so luckily she was free to meet up.

I hated to rely so much on Ina and Lauren to decode my dating life, but I didn't have much choice. Not counting Rachel, my imaginary friend at work who came in handy whenever I *didn't* want to see Lauren and Ina, I had few other girlfriends. Most of the women I knew had tons of girlfriends they'd known since they were all cheerleaders at UCLA, all of them still best friends forever. Now these BFFs loaded their strollers into their SUVs and met up for Ice Blendeds at the Coffee Bean on Sunset to complain about their husbands. Or they dragged themselves in a posse all the way to the Valley to take that Cardio Barre class that was supposed to be the best class in LA, the one they thought would get them an ass like Jessica Biel's. But at UCLA I had been a loner girl determined to leave Arizona and my messy mom and dysfunctional dad behind to make it big as a writer, and I didn't have time to hang around tossing my hair with sorority sisters. No checks came from home to pay for school and all the partying. With the people I did know, I had one rule, then and now: no intermingling of the friends. There were no weirder people than your good friends' other friends.

Meeting Lauren at AOC was a smart call. Wine, cheese, and warm bread were exactly what I needed. The place was always packed, but Lauren knew Caroline, one of the owners, and she was always cool about getting us a table. The dark wood bar was polished under the crystal-stemmed wineglasses. I searched for my friend's strawberry blond head above the late-afternoon drinkers packing the bar area. Lauren was easy to find; she was almost six feet tall and always turned heads. People always thought they knew her. "Did you go to Beverly High?" someone would come up and ask.

"No, I didn't go to Beverly," Lauren would answer.

"I know you from someplace . . ." the person would push.

Lauren would just demur and shrug her shoulders. She didn't

want to blurt out that they knew her from TV. She thought that would make her seem like too much of an asshole. Lauren was the kind of ultimate success story I envied. She started at *MoreTV* as an intern the summer before she graduated from college and managed to get hired on as staff. After a year of learning the business, she was made a producer for the news. Someone in the news department, as she put it, "had a hard-on for her" and also gave her a shot on camera. She never felt bad talking about the guy in news because, as she put it, "Everyone had to blow someone to get a job in the business, and at least I didn't screw him."

Lauren was already at a table and waved to get my attention. I leaned in and she pecked me on the cheek.

"How's the Fonz?" was the first thing I asked her.

Lauren had been dealing with her overly attentive and slightly amorous new female boss, who bore a striking resemblance to the Fonz. Or as my mom would put it, "She sure wears a lot of pants." Lauren's new boss was Cheryl Fox, a ball-busting executive whom the corporate powers brought in to get the cable network running, as they put it, "firmly in the black."

"Cheryl is a freak, as usual." She rolled her eyes.

"What's going on now?"

Lauren took a deep breath. "Yesterday I had to go into wardrobe for a fitting for an evening gown to wear for a gala charity dinner I have to cover for work, and the girl who was doing my fitting told me Cheryl had called down to see when I would be in for my fitting." She sighed. "So there I am, half naked, and she walked in with a 'Hey, Lauren, I didn't know you'd be in here.'"

"Why don't you complain to Human Resources?"

"Because I don't want to be thought of as being uncool." She took a big gulp of her wine. "It's not like she's a *guy* who's also my boss trying to get me in the middle of changing."

"But that's just it. If it were a man walking in on you, you wouldn't think twice about reporting the guy."

"I know, but I don't want to come off as being homophobic. Maybe she just wanted to talk to me."

"What did she 'talk' to you about when you were standing there half naked?"

"She was all hot about some guy she had just met and was starting to see." Lauren made a face.

"I don't know what the big deal is and why she thinks she has to fake it," I said. "Everyone in Hollywood is gay. C'mon, there's Rosie and Ellen on TV every day . . . and nobody really cared when those girls used to make out on *The O.C.* every week."

Lauren agreed. "She's pretty powerful in Hollywood, so I think it's even stranger that she feels like she has to keep putting up this whole facade so no one finds out her not-so-secret secret."

Cheryl was universally reviled in the offices of *MoreTV*. Soon after she joined the company, she proclaimed that the parking in the building was costing the network too much and that everyone would have to park off-site and be shuttled in. Who ever heard of such a thing? The 2,000 employees had to comply—and they all passed her Porsche, which remained in its reserved spot in front of the elevators.

Ms. Fox also thought the company was spending too much money on paper cups and sent out an e-mail advising employees that if they wanted to drink beverages at work, they'd better bring in their own cup from home, and if they were expecting guests for a meeting, they'd have to bring in extras for them.

She'd be mortified if she had any idea her current assistant had scrawled an obscene message on the underside of her desk, smiling to herself every day knowing Cheryl's knees rested unknowing just a few inches below.

"She keeps e-mailing me to go out to sushi with her," Lauren said.

"Are you kidding me? What are you going to do?"

"Well, luckily, I'm out of town a lot in the next few weeks, so I can keep putting it off, but at some point we're going to have to have sushi together."

"Well, order the spicy tuna at your own risk."

"You are so gross." She giggled.

"I write about dead people all day. What do you expect?"

"So how are you doing after the whole photo thing?" she asked. I had already filled Lauren in on the picture of Chloe's breast.

"I'm okay," I assured her, swirling my wine. "Hey, it's not like I didn't know they were together, ya know? It just shows what a conniving wench she is."

"What did you do with the picture?"

"I ripped it into a million little pieces and tossed it." I smiled.

"Well, I'm glad. I wouldn't want you obsessing any more over it, and who knows, it could have been a mistake. Maybe it was from someone else, and meant for someone else who works at the show."

I gave Lauren the hand. "Lauren, stop. Can't we just accept that it was a photo Dave took of Chloe's breast? He obviously gave her the picture, and she sent it to me to mess with my head."

Lauren made a face. "You never let Dave take any nude pictures of you, right?"

"Of course not! Would you ever let Michael take nudie pictures of you?"

Lauren mysteriously smiled. "I'll never tell." We laughed.

Suddenly growing serious, she fingered her empty wineglass. "Things are just good for me right now—with the new house, with Michael, and with work. Everything I've been striving for is finally happening." She pulled out a small brown gift bag from her purse. "But enough about all this crazy stuff. I brought you a little present."

"Oh, really?" I was so thrilled that as I took the bag my eyes almost welled up with tears. No one had given me a present or done anything sweet like this for me for such a long time. Dave was always giving me presents, just a note or something funny, but when all those little things stopped I realized how much I missed the little stuff, too.

Carefully opening the inner tissue, I discovered two red candles. "Wow, thanks!" I exclaimed. Secretly, I thought they were an odd choice, because I didn't have any red in my house.

"They're for feng shui," Lauren explained. "Do you know where the southwest corner of your place is? You're supposed to light them in that corner and they will bring romance and passion into your life."

"Really?" I asked suspiciously. "Does this stuff work?"

"Absolutely. Paula Abdul attributes her success on *American Idol* to feng shui. She says she had someone come in and do her whole house, and right after that was when everything took off."

"But we agree Paula Abdul seems totally whacked, right?" I raised an eyebrow.

"She's totally crazy. But feng shui works, I swear."

"Okay. I'll go home and burn them tonight. Maybe Grant will pick up on the love vibe."

Now Lauren got animated. "Okay, tell me about what's going on with the guy."

I gave her a quick report, cutting out a few bits here and there to make me seem a little less desperate.

But Lauren was staring at me as if I were a total nut job. "You broke into his e-mail?"

"That's beside the point. He was two-timing me."

"Wouldn't you actually have to be together . . . you know . . . actually be boyfriend-slash-girlfriend to be two-timed?"

"You know what I'm talking about. He took me out on a Wednesday, kissed me at the valet, and told me he would phone, and then he called a lesbian."

"All guys are into the lesbian thing."

"But he finds that more interesting than me. I'm just someone who wore a twinset on our first date."

"A lesbian somehow has promise for guys. It's a fantasy for them, like having sex with twins. All guys want twins," Lauren said with authority.

The waitress brought us food, little plates with cheese and meat, big enough to share. We ordered white wine. I was slathering soft cheese on bread and getting ready to have a third slice when I looked up to see Lauren staring at my hands.

"What are you doing?" she demanded.

"I'm eating."

"I'm talking about the *way* you're eating. You're eating funny. You're right-handed, but you're doing everything with your left hand. What are you doing?"

"Oh, don't worry." I shrugged. "I read in a magazine that to eat less you should reverse the way you hold your silverware. So if you're right-handed, you hold your fork in your left hand. It's so awkward to eat that you naturally eat less. It's been proven in a study," I assured her, putting the piece of bread slathered with cheese into my mouth with my left hand.

"Dani, that is the craziest thing I've ever heard. Stop it."

"No way. I think it's working. Soon I'll have such a perfect ass that Grant will want me instead of *five* lesbians."

Lauren ran her hands over her face and was quiet for a moment, then asked, "How did you know what his password was?"

I rolled my eyes at her. "Guys are so easy to figure out. They keep it simple. Having his password be his name is practically inviting me to read his e-mail."

"You're going to have to stop. I bet he will still call you."

"I don't want him to call me now. I know what he's into, and it's not me."

I tried to focus on my food, spearing an olive with my fork. I didn't do anything wrong—every girl I knew had read her boyfriend's e-mail at least once.

"You're ruining this. You're ruining something that was fun by being psycho," Lauren said.

"I'm not a psycho. I'm just checking. I'm investigating. I had a hunch, I looked into it, and I was right—something *was* up. Guys are always fucking around. Having this info just levels the playing field."

"*Hello*, Dani. Would you like to have a private moment alone with your Crazy?" Lauren stared at me like I was a lunatic. "This isn't your TV show. He's not a criminal who needs to be apprehended in fifty-two minutes of a television drama."

I pouted. "I'm just disappointed, because I really thought we would be good together—he was such a 'good-on-paper' guy."

"You sound like you were already picking out your wedding dress." Lauren drained her wineglass. "I guess you really are over Dave."

"Grant's just the kind of guy that I would really go for. We would be really good together. He's my type." It felt good to obsess about someone other than Dave. I stewed some more, wondering what kind of woman would be a lesbian and would also somehow get fixed up with Grant. What matchmaker would say, "Hey, you like pussy, and so does my buddy Grant—you two would be great together!"

Lauren held her hands up to calm me down. "Maybe you should take a break from all this dating and just spend some time on your own."

"I'm not good on my own. With Dave, things were so much better than they are now."

"No, things weren't 'better with Dave.' We never heard from you, ever. You could never make a plan—you were always holding out to see what Dave would spring on you. You would never make your own plans unless you knew for sure the two of you weren't doing anything."

"Lauren, that's not—"

"Why do you wax poetic about this guy? What else did he have to do to show you what a dick he was? You never saw him clearly for who he was."

"I did in the end," I answered quietly.

Lauren pulled her wallet out of her purse. "What I'm trying to say is that I think you should maybe develop more of a relationship with yourself before you jump into another thing with some guy. Be on your own for a while."

I stared back at her. "No way," I shook my head. "That sounds like a horrible idea. How would being on my own ever make me feel better?"

"Well, I just think that you obviously have some *issues* you've never dealt with, you know, because of your parents being so crazy."

"Yeah, well, they're crazy, and they were shitty parents, but if you look at me now, a big success in Hollywood, they must have done something right. Right?" The wine and the conversation were beginning to make me a little agitated. A couple of people seated nearby turned and frowned at my loudness.

"You're a success despite all of it," Lauren said, "but you're not happy, and I'll say it again—you were never really happy with Dave, even when you were together."

"That's not true—and my parents didn't make Dave mess around on me."

"Then why did you sabotage it? Why did you go looking for something unless you were really prepared to find something?"

"I don't know why I went looking." I'd come to AOC to unload to Lauren about Grant. Bringing up Dave and my parents didn't seem fair. Maybe she wasn't as good a friend as I'd thought. I remembered how Lauren put Viagra in her boyfriend's guacamole . . . like *I'm* the crazy one. It was time to go home.

FOURTEEN

Nicole Brown Simpson wore bikini underwear from Victoria's Secret. That was classy. I squinted at a police photo from the 1994 crime scene. I'd requested the pictures because we were kind of ripping off the O. J./Nicole thing for a *Flesh and Bone* episode. Studying the actual crime scene photos was invaluable for giving me details for Maggie and her team on the show. I'd never seen these pictures before and was surprised by all the gore. Nicole lay on her stomach in a huge pool of her blood, wearing a black minidress. It had ridden up and you could see her bottom hanging out of her Victoria's Secret panties, one buttock cheek totally exposed. She'd had two kids, and her bottom in death was a little lumpy—not by normal American Ass standards, but by LA standards. As beautiful as she'd been in life, it wasn't a flattering shot, and I wished for her that someone had pulled her dress down to give her a little dignity. Sure, it would have meant tampering with a crime scene, but the murderer wasn't going to be apprehended on the basis of her panties showing.

My office phone rang. "Hi, it's Dani," I said absently, still looking at dead Nicole.

"*Buenos días, señora*, I'm calling from the Palmilla to confirm your reservation for the Labor Day holiday."

"Oh shit," I said out loud.

In my misery about Dave I had forgotten about other couples and their happiness. Jon and Catherine, two friends of Dave's, were getting married in Cabo over the Labor Day weekend. Destination weddings were all the rage in Hollywood circles and everyone in town was "running for the border" to get married. Because *Flesh and Bone* was going to be in production through most of the summer, I wasn't going to be getting an extended vacation the way writers did on most shows, which halt production during the summer months. Going to Mexico with Dave for a long wedding weekend was something I'd been so excited about planning. Shortly after receiving the "save the date" card in the mail, I'd bought my bathing suits from net-a-porter.com, so I'd have the chicest Missoni and Pucci bikinis at the pool. I'd also been clipping articles about anti-cellulite treatments in anticipation of getting a little rear end tune-up for our trip. In the last weeks, what with just trying not to have a nervous breakdown, I'd not thought about it at all. Now here was a woman not only confirming the reservation, but also calling me "*señora*." How the fuck did she know how old I was? I could *still* be a "*señorita*." Was there a cutoff age?

I should have canceled this reservation when Dave and I broke up. "Well . . . ," I began.

"And good news! We have it here in our records that you called a couple of weeks ago to see about upgrading your room, and we *were* able to free up a villa with private plunge pool for your stay. These are really hard to come by—the villas are our most exclusive accommodations."

"Oh, that's great news," I said, feigning excitement. Then I kicked into investigator mode, like one of the characters on my show, trying to solve the riddle of how I came to receive this phone call. I had made the original reservation back in March, and that must be why they had my office number in their records. Dave must have made this upgrade request, but they'd messed up the call-back number.

I closed my eyes and felt the tears start to well up. Dave was not only still going to the wedding, but he had also requested this special villa. It wasn't something that a low-key guy like him, who was happy to stay in a Holiday Inn Express most of the time, would usually do. He was trying to impress someone. I couldn't believe it. I couldn't believe he was taking someone on *our* trip.

I imagined him with a willowy date in a formfitting dress, mingling at one of the pre-wedding festivities with margaritas in their hands, both of them bronzed from the sun and sharing a postcoital glow.

Going to the Palmilla had been a dream for me ever since I saw a special segment on *Oprah* about John Travolta's birthday party there, where he'd rented the entire resort. This was supposed to be *my* trip. I'd never get to go there and afford to splurge on a villa with a plunge pool, especially now, when I would only imagine I was in a room that Dave had occupied with his wedding date.

I couldn't believe this, after all this stupid crap with Grant.

"So we can go ahead and confirm?" the reservationist prompted.

"Actually, we won't be needing that villa after all. The stock market is down, if you know what I mean. . . ." I laughed, trying to sound nonchalant about my fake imaginary financial setback. "Do you have something with a mountain view for those dates?"

"Let me check." She was all business. "We do have a mountain-view room available, but it's two double beds, not a king as you originally requested. Is that okay?"

"Two double beds is fine." I smiled into the receiver. This was starting to not feel so bad.

"And we can go ahead and confirm your couples massage in the room upon your arrival. It's obviously going to be a little tighter, space-wise. We have you confirmed with two female therapists."

"Oh that's great—but wait, would it be possible to get the massages with two male therapists?"

Dave hated getting a massage with a man; he thought it was something only a gay guy would do. I always thought he was just worried about having his penis "shift" like George's did in that episode of *Seinfeld*.

I listened to the woman from the hotel type away on her end. "Okay, perfect! We're all set," she chirped. "*Vaya con Dios, señora.*"

"*Vaya con Dios* yourself."

I clicked off and stared into space for a moment. Dave had someone serious enough in his life to take to Jon and Catherine's wedding. Those wedding photos would circulate for a long time—you didn't just take some bimbo one-night stand. I knew he wasn't with Chloe; she was still in Europe playing a vampire princess in that cable movie. I had Grant, who was juggling me with a lesbian. Life didn't seem fair. I buried my head in my hands on my desk and tried to do some yoga breathing exercises. I was feeling a little unglued and panicked.

"Dani, are you okay?"

I jerked myself upright guiltily, to see Rich standing in my doorway.

"Is this not a good time?" he asked. For once he seemed almost tentative.

"No, it's okay. Just a little bit of a migraine, that's all."

"You're sure it's okay?"

"Yes." Now this was getting old. "Come in, sit." I gestured toward the chair.

I watched Rich move to take the chair. He looked good. His dark hair was clipped shorter than usual and he had a bit of a tan, as if he'd spent a lot of time outside over the weekend. He was wearing a crisp black jacket over a simple gray cotton T-shirt. It was not a ratty T-shirt or something picked up at the Gap; I could tell from across the desk that it would feel plush beneath my fingers.

"So?" I asked, trying to be professional.

Rich leveled a look at me. "You asked me to meet with you, Dani, about some questions you had about an interrogation scene . . ."

He was trying to lead me into why he was here. I'd been so distracted by the Mexico phone call that I felt a little blank upstairs.

"Oh, yeah, of course. I'm getting stuff ready for the O.J. Show and I wanted to go over some basic things about interrogations." I looked up from my notebook. "You do know about that stuff, right?"

He smiled slightly. "What do you need to know?"

"Well, I've heard so many things about this left side/right side thing when it comes to interrogating someone. Is it true that people look to the left when they're lying and to the right when they're telling the truth while being questioned by police?"

"There's no way to tell if people are lying by their behavior, but you can come close," Rich said. "There *are* different theories about which way someone is looking while being interviewed, but I think there are broader signals you can look at during an interrogation that will clearly give you an idea that someone is trying to mislead you."

"Like what?" I asked, my pen poised above my pad of paper.

"The guilty tend to touch their hair and face. They'll pick off things like lint from their clothing when they talk."

"That's pretty obvious."

"Innocent people act very differently from guilty suspects. Innocent people sit up straighter. They answer questions eagerly and look at the interrogation as something they can do to clear their name. Guilty people look at an interview situation as something they just need to get through. Innocent people would like to sit and talk and be helpful, to prove they're innocent."

"All this you glean from observation, and it doesn't matter what they're saying while being questioned?" I asked.

"An experienced investigator can watch a tape of people being interrogated with the sound off and be able to tell seventy-five percent of the time if the person is being honest or not."

"That's a crazy number," I said.

"It's a high percentage," he agreed, calm as ever. It was funny, because even while talking to Rich now, I felt closely observed. I wondered if he could see through me and have an idea of what I just orchestrated on the phone for Dave's Mexico trip, and that with his help, I'd ferreted out the identity of the woman who had ruined my relationship. I was suddenly, self-consciously aware that I was kind of a mess. My hair was piled on top of my head in a sprawling ponytail, and my morning lipgloss had long been transferred to the recycled paper rim of my latte. Panicked, I wondered if I'd remembered to put on deodorant that morning. Did I smell? I definitely felt like I was perspiring after the excitement of the hotel call and now under Rich's intent gaze. He was watching me so intently, I knew I'd never be able to sneak a furtive sniff of my armpit.

"So how are you?" he asked.

"I'm doing good, good." Now I felt compelled to follow up. "And you?"

"I'm fine," he replied.

"So is fine good? Because when I say I'm fine, it doesn't mean fine," I heard myself rambling.

Rich's eyes were steady on my face. "How's that thing working out for you?" he asked. "No more follow-homes, I hope."

At first I thought he knew about my Dave drive-bys, but he wasn't being snarky. I realized he was asking about the cherry-red Mercedes lie I'd fed him when I'd gotten him to look up the plate number.

"Oh no, no problems." We looked at each other for a few seconds. This was starting to get uncomfortable. It was those cop eyes. It was like I shouldn't even *think* of a lie or he would totally see it all over my face. Fucking cop—or ex-cop, I corrected myself.

Rich sensed my change in attitude and stood to leave. "Well, if you have any more questions about the interrogation, you know how to reach me."

"Sure. Thanks a lot, Rich." I tried to sound breezy.

"Oh, and did you get the pictures?" he asked as he stood to leave.

"What pictures?"

"The Nicole Brown Simpson photos. I heard around the office that you'd been trying to locate some crime scene pictures, and I happened to have a few at home."

I had no idea the pictures were from Rich.

My eyebrows shot up. "You just happened to have some grisly crime scene pictures lying around your house?"

Rich turned in the doorway and gave me an odd look. "You're not the only one who's into this stuff." Thunderstruck, I was, for once, speechless.

My eyes stayed on the door after he was gone. Fucking cop.

There were no calls from anyone to make plans for the rest of the week. Heading home at the start of the weekend, I thought how Fridays were the night that Dave and I always spent together. We went to Blair's in Silver Lake on one of our last dates. Their specialty was short ribs, and I'd have to diet all day in order to indulge. Since the breakup, I'd head straight home at the end of the workweek and collapse. I missed those short ribs and I missed having a date for dinner.

I surveyed my house and realized the place was a disaster area. I started putting things away in drawers, threw a load of laundry in, and picked up stale drinking cups in the living room. The house was such a wreck it would be embarrassing if someone stopped by unannounced. Granted, there wasn't much chance of that happening, but you never knew.

Per Lauren's instructions, I'd figured out where the southwest corner of my house was. It wasn't hard; I knew the 405 freeway was west of me, and that LAX was to the south. Since having dinner with Lauren, every night I would carefully light the two candles, hoping I was activating some positive feng shui. I didn't know what I expected, like some gorgeous guy to come bursting in the door as soon as I put down the matches, but nothing had happened yet.

I clicked on the news to see if anyone famous had died or gotten married since I'd last read the paper. The news in LA was always the same: a freeway chase followed by a celebrity being arrested, getting divorced, or becoming pregnant. Then the weather report of partly sunny and with a low of seventy degrees.

Paul Moyer's voice boomed out at me from the television, telling viewers about a missing woman, Veronica Davis, who had left the Universal Studios lot and hadn't been seen in two days. She lived only a couple of miles from the studio and police said she never made it home.

I looked around at my surroundings. There was the cat, the cat box, my desk. The computer I should be writing on and wasn't. My message light was dark. I could be dead and no one would notice. How long before someone would notice me missing and come over and break down my door, only to be assaulted by the stench of my decaying body?

I felt gross after all the cleaning and hopped in the shower. As soon as the hot water hit my body I could hear the phone ring. Normally I would just let it go, but I was feeling somewhat desperate for human contact. I lunged for the receiver and hoped it was not a telemarketer.

I checked the caller ID. "Private Caller"—never a good idea to pick up. I knew that when Grant called from the studio it said, "Fox Television" or when he had called me from his house it said his number.

"Hello?"

"Hey . . . it's Grant."

I couldn't believe it. . . . What if he sensed what I was just thinking of doing? What if he knew that I broke into his e-mail? I tried to fight down my panic and sound nonchalant. "Hey, how are you?"

"Sorry I haven't called. The last week has been crazy trying to lock down this episode."

"No problem. I've been swamped too," I replied, trying to sound like I hadn't ever looked at the clock or calendar to calculate the seconds since I last saw him.

"So how have you been? How's this week's show coming along? Who dies?"

"I'm still working on it. I'm always looking for new ideas." I brightened up a bit. "Did you see this thing about the woman who works for Universal Studios in accounting? Police believe she was followed home and now she's missing—she's been gone two days."

"No, I've been buried."

"Oh . . ." I was a little deflated. I always forgot that I got a little more excited than most people about murdered wives and missing female accountants. "She left work at her usual time, but she never made it home to her apartment in Studio City. That's less than a ten-minute car ride home. You really wouldn't think you could get in trouble driving such a short way home." I tucked the towel tighter around my chest. "I'm always looking to the news for ideas, and this may come in handy this week. We could change this up a little bit and make it part of the B story of an upcoming show."

"Wow . . . you really are into that stuff. Well, I'm glad that you're focused and that it seems to be going so great." He seemed impressed.

"Yeah, thanks." Ouch, that came off a little more abruptly than I thought it would. I didn't mean to cut him off.

"Well, besides checking in on your writing, I wanted to know if you were busy later this weekend. It would be great to get dinner again."

"Yeah . . . it would," I gulped out. I wondered if the lesbian had canceled and that was why he was calling me, second-position girl.

"So how 'bout tomorrow night? We won't go to sushi this time, I promise."

So she *did* cancel. "You noticed I didn't eat much?" I teased.

"You hardly touched a thing, and you looked a little sick when you had some of my sashimi. I didn't want to give you a hard time because I was trying to impress you . . . and it left more food for me."

There he was, being so cute again. I could hear the smile in my voice when we arranged when and where to meet. I would never give away to him that I was free on a Saturday night that was less than twenty-four hours away, so we made the date for the following Wednesday night at Musso's. I told him I would meet him there. I didn't ever let guys come to my place until after a few dates. I knew they could really tell a lot about you from your place and there was plenty I was still trying to hide.

Hanging up, I threw myself naked across my bed and bounced up and down a few times, as if someone had just asked me to the prom. I thought about inventing some sort of sexual disease that was plaguing the lesbian community. I could say I had read about it for the show. Maybe I could bring this up casually over dinner.

Later that night, I was online checking my e-mail and I felt the pull . . . I clicked onto Amazon.com.

Amazon was a huge discovery. No one liked to have a bunch of different passwords. So I always knew if I could get the one password for someone's e-mail, it was probably the same password for all the other accounts. The great thing about Amazon was that your screen name was your home e-mail, so if you were investigating someone you immediately got that right.

I punched in Grant's e-mail address on AOL and then waited for the prompt for the password. Again, I logged in Grant's first and last name. The three seconds crawled by as the computer thought about my answer and then the "Grant's Amazon.com" screen popped up. I clicked over to "Your Account" and then to "Recent Orders." I knew that someone as busy as Grant didn't have a lot of time to go to the store; he probably bought a ton of stuff online. First I checked to see where he was shipping everything. I could see that his address was on Kings above Sunset. Very nice. Real estate up there was pricey and it was hard to find anything to rent, which meant he probably owned, which was great.

He'd bought box sets of DVDs: Hitchcock and Scorsese. I made a mental note to bring up a couple of their movies during dinner. Grant had also bought a bunch of diet books, including *The South Beach Diet* and *The Abs Diet*. There were a few workout tapes also. He looked fine to me, but maybe he'd secretly been a chub when he was younger, so he had a complex about it.

He'd gifted *The Three Tenors* CD to an M. Katz at an address on Park Avenue, which I figured was his mom. Park Avenue was another good sign, but I knew he came from money because he went to Harvard. The strange thing was that he had purchased a half-dozen DVD box sets of Monty Python for different people. Why so many copies of the same set? I read through the addresses. One went to a Tiffany, others to a Sabine, a Monica, a Margo, and a Summer who lived in Santa Monica. "This is part of his foreplay," I said out loud. He was a comedy writer and I bet he wanted to "enlighten" the chicks he dated. Maybe it was a test to see if his dates had a good sense of humor. I loved John Cleese and thought he was hysterical, so I knew I'd pass. At least he wasn't sending box sets of the Three Stooges to women. I'd yet to meet a girl who was a Stooges fan.

I logged out of my AOL account and wondered when I'd get my set of DVDs. Pushing back from my desk, I stared down the hallway to the bedroom. I knew I should call it a night and get some sleep.

But the computer was batting its eyelashes at me. I grabbed the wooden desk edge and pulled myself back to the keyboard.

I couldn't help myself. I logged on to AOL under his screen name.

I clicked through his sent messages. Nothing more about the lesbian. In his new mail there was something about a stock to buy. Just before I logged off, one more new e-mail clicked into his box, with an attachment. In the body of the e-mail, the sender had written: "Thought you would dig these. They're right up your alley."

That begged me to open it up. Maybe it was something that would tip me to the perfect gift to buy him, something that would elicit the reaction, "How did you have any idea I was *such* a Beatles fanatic? You're the best." He'd lean over and kiss me and I'd feel the magic warmth of being half of a two again. My knowing "the perfect thing" would definitely make him like me more.

I moved the mouse and clicked twice, waiting for my tip to open up. But what I saw was not what I had been expecting.

There were two photos. Both taken on the beach, both featuring naked women. But they were not women. They were girls. From the size of the pubescent breasts, I judged the girls to be thirteen or fourteen. They were wearing absolutely nothing, and lay across a striped beach towel with their legs spread wide open.

"Holy shit." I'd discovered his penchant for child porn. Now he was guilty of not only being a lesbian lover; he was into these kinky photos. These photos were against the law—just how far did this fascination with young girls go? I thought of that guy on *Dateline* who did those specials, "To Catch a Predator."

Online kiddie porn could be a stepping stone to creepier stuff. What if he instant messaged young girls in chat rooms? I swiftly moved my cursor to sign off and hoped my computer wouldn't sound an alarm at a national child porn watch group and send police to my door to arrest me. When the screen went blank, I stared at it anyway, imagining the images that had just infected my computer. Thankfully, the pictures were in the body of an e-mail, not downloaded to my desktop. But still I knew they would always be on my hard drive somehow. What kind of guy would find that kind of filth sexy? Or even amusing? I might love watching real autopsies and examining blood spatter at crime scenes, but this was really sick.

He was a loser, pathetic really. He could go to jail for this stuff. Let him marry some other desperate woman who would think he was a great catch and then discover his stash of kiddie porn while pregnant with their second child. I was way beyond that.

Now it was time for bed. I powered down my computer and headed down the hallway. My head hurt and I felt defeated. I didn't bother brushing my teeth and I let my clothes fall to the floor as I peeled them off. Sinking into bed, I pulled the duvet up close to my neck. I dreamed of kiddie porn and me running down Sunset Boulevard in a wedding dress.

The show was crazy the next week; we had to replace an actress who had broken her leg. Auditions were going on just down the hall from my office to recast the role of "Bridgett." For days I had leggy blonds hanging outside my office waiting to get called into a session with the casting director. I was so busy, and the leggy blonds sent me into such a tailspin, that on Wednesday night I fell into a wine-induced coma on my green marshmallow couch while watching an episode of *American Justice* on A&E. The ringing phone woke me up.

"This is Dani." I was so exhausted I used the greeting I employed at work instead of just plain "hello."

"Uh, hi, Dani, it's Grant."

Holy shit. I had totally blocked out our plans.

"Hmm, hey."

"I was at Musso's waiting for you. I mean, if you couldn't make it you just had to call me—it would have been cool. But just to not show. . . ." He trailed off.

"Oh, God, I'm *so* sorry . . . I . . . well . . . I just forgot. I've been really swamped at the office and when I got home I just passed out."

"You're asleep?" he asked tightly.

"Yeah." It wasn't exactly a lie, and I had the just-woken-up-by-the-phone voice. "I'm sorry . . . maybe we could do it another time?" I ventured. "I'll call you next week."

"Sure. Call me next week when things calm down."

"Okay, Grant . . . good night."

"Good night."

We both knew there wouldn't be a next week. I wouldn't call him and he wouldn't call me because I was the one that stood him up.

Grant Katz was history. He had been so cute and funny. Too bad he was such a perv.

So now that I didn't have any guilt left from the violation of breaking into Grant's e-mail, I started checking it every couple of days, just to check in and see how he was doing. Even though he was a "Chester the Molester" as my mom would have said, I was still interested in monitoring his life and times.

I read about his new show getting picked up by the network. I learned about his golfing vacation plans with his buddies, and other dates he had. I never came across any more nudie pictures of underage girls. But maybe he was just being careful; maybe he had his own private stash of photos at home.

A couple of weeks later I got home late after another bad fix-up date, some guy who worked in business affairs at Paramount. He spent the first twenty minutes of our date explaining why he hated his mother. I smiled and nodded at what seemed like the appropriate times. I tried to read the time upside down on his Cartier watch. Two glasses of wine and I was out of there. There was no TiVo love waiting for me, so I got ready for bed, and then made my way to the computer to log on to Grant's e-mail. After a few weeks, it had become a habit, something I did at the beginning and the end of my day.

Tonight I came across a message from a Harvard college buddy who was working at some tech firm in Silicon Valley and was e-mailing him about a "sure thing" stock tip. I wrote down the name and did a little googling of my own to find out more on his company. Anagen was a biotech start-up with several big drug patents pending. I reminded myself that the rich were a very exclusive group and helped each other get richer in these kinds of ways. And his buddy after all did go to Harvard. The rich only got richer, and everybody had inside information; that was the way this world worked. Martha got busted for something that was only standard practice.

I had recently received the big check for writing the Marilyn show solo, so I called Alec, my business manager, and told him to buy, buy, buy. He was, of course, a little dubious. "You know, Dani," he began, "you should just concentrate on the business of being Danielle Hale and let us concentrate on the *business* of Danielle Hale."

That one made me shake my head, and I told him again to put in the buy order. Hearing the insistent tone in my voice, he relented.

A week later the stock split. Then soared and split again.

I made a lot of money. Now when I logged on as speedracer11@ aol.com, instead of checking his e-mail in and out boxes, I first checked on how his stock portfolio was performing. Thank goodness AOL made it easy to monitor those things from your personalized home page. Grant was becoming a savvier investor, and now when his friends e-mailed him about a "new great stock lead," he would write back and tell them to call him at his office. No need to have an e-mail trail. But there was a trail for me to follow; it was there in what he was buying and selling in his online portfolio. In only a month, starting with that first stock split, I continued to make money.

During one of these visits, an instant message suddenly popped up from someone named Cooterfiend.

"Hey man . . . where are you?"

I froze at the keyboard, thinking that if I made any noise at 7870 Camrose Avenue that this guy would sense it, and send the Internet police to my house.

"Dude, I thought you were in a meeting with the writers?"

Panicking, I unfroze long enough to log off.

Fuck, I was busted. Maybe it wouldn't amount to anything.

But it did.

Trying to go cold turkey, I abstained from logging on to Grant's account, but after waiting a full week, I couldn't resist. Punching in his screen name and his regular password of "grantkatz" I received this response back: "Invalid password, please re-enter."

Maybe I'd entered a typo. I punched in the password again.

No luck. My window into the fabulous and perverted life of Grant Katz was closed. Going cold turkey from Grant's e-mail was a million times harder than just not getting a call for another date with that guy who worked at Paramount and hated his mother.

I had come to rely on Grant's e-mails for some excitement; the voyeuristic charge I got would keep me going for days. And now, nothing. It was like a breakup.

I started driving by Dave's every night after work. I had it down to a very well thought-out route. I would stop at the corner stop sign and see if his car was in his parking slot. Because I usually finished up late from work, the cover of darkness helped me blend in. I'd let my car pause at the stop sign and suss out whether he was home.

Seeing his car there was a reward. It made me feel good to know he was not out at some club or bar. I didn't see the cherry red Mercedes again. Whoever he was dating didn't seem to drive. I never spotted a new car in the driveway. I preferred to think of the mystery girl-friend as not driving; I didn't want to dwell on the notion of Dave's always picking her up and bringing her back to his place just to be nice.

A couple of times I pulled past his driveway and saw the re-flection of the TV through the top of his window. I knew if I stayed long enough I'd be able to make out what he was watching, but I wasn't that interested, and lurking like that seemed a little des-perate. If Dave's car wasn't there, I'd punch the gas all the way back to my place.

I resumed googling Dave to see what he was working on. I knew he wanted to work in features, but he was just doing episode after episode of TV. At least he was busy. I also monitored Chloe's career on IMDB.com. She was still in Europe on that movie shoot, which meant she hadn't been about to fly off to Mexico for Jon and Cather-ine's destination wedding. I guess that was why I never saw the cherry red Mercedes. Dave had another Mystery Woman, and I couldn't fer-ret out who it was.

I slogged through some more dates, all setups from Azita, Lauren, and a couple of distant friends. One was with an actor who flat out told me on our first date that he thought dating me "would be really good for me during pilot season." There was a stockbroker who used the N-word casually during dinner. Like Grant the porn perv, he was another good-on-paper guy, with a three-million-dollar house in Hermosa Beach. He ordered martinis with extra olives and had his initials stitched into the cuffs of his shirt. The racist also had a man-icure. Touching up my lipgloss in the ladies' room, I realized his nails looked better than mine.

Saying good night at the end of one of these hopeless dates, I'd pull around the corner from the restaurant and park. I'd sit in the dark with my hands on the steering wheel and think about Dave, Dave and me, Dave and Chloe, and Chloe's breast.

I started doing all my busy errands on the weekend in Studio City. I liked the anonymity of the Valley, all the happy couples pushing their strollers. Most of the new moms still carried around the extra baby weight, and it made me feel better about myself to sit at the local Peet's Coffee and read the paper.

In late August, about four months after Dave and I broke up, my anonymity at Peet's was blown. "Dani, is that you?" It was Janey, my college boyfriend Jack's sister.

"Hey, Janey. How are you? You look great." I meant it; she did. No baby weight on her—she looked like she'd dropped at least ten pounds.

"I'm good, you know, still acting. I'm in a showcase at my acting school for the next couple of weeks, if you want to come check it out."

"Oh, wow, that would be great." Nothing put a chill up my spine more than the idea of checking out someone's play, or a "showcase" for acting talent.

Jack was my first big relationship when I came to LA. He was cute, and his dad had been a somewhat well known television star back in the '70s. His father's star had since fallen, but he was still well known enough to command respect at any of the large delis in the Valley.

Jack was a singer, and I couldn't remember how we met, but I'd been crazy about him. His mom wasn't around and he'd needed someone to take care of him, so I had.

He loved coffee, so I taught myself to make the perfect cup of joe. I did his laundry and ran him a bath every morning as a treat. Taking care of Jack replaced everything else in my life, and he became my hobby. Night after night, I could be found sitting in the back of a dark club smelling of stale beer, singing along to his songs. He was a little like Robert Smith of the Cure (but without the makeup, thank God). Jack had a serious David Bowie complex and during songs he'd start dancing and twirling all over the stage. That worked for Bowie, but it didn't really work for Jack.

When Jack's mom came back from an extended European stay, she decided to sell her house, where Jack had been living with friends. Suddenly, at the age of twenty-seven, Jack was faced with having to pay something called rent. It was a new word to him.

A senior in college, I couldn't stand the couple I was living with, a husband and wife in Culver City who grew six-foot pot plants in the backyard and screamed at each other constantly. Renting a room for $200 a month had certainly been a winning deal, but when the husband starting getting paranoid that I'd steal his stash, I knew it was time to move on. So moving in with Jack had been kind of the natural thing to do. We hadn't been dating that long, but. . . .

Jack and I found a place together way out in Burbank in the North Valley. His best friend had previously lived in our unit, so we'd inherited his black lacquer bed frame and dresser. Very *Miami Vice*. For a while things were great. Jack still bought me a nice dinner once a week, thanks to an AmEx card of his dad's that he still had in his possession. In addition to his music, Jack was also an actor and spent a lot of time in acting class. He'd regale me with stories of all the famous people who had also studied in his class, stars like Meg Ryan, Sean Penn, and Belinda Carlisle before the Go-Go's. After class, he would head over to the Golden Apple on Melrose and peruse the new comic books. He thought of his extensive comic book collection as an investment and what he called a "nest egg for the future." I nodded my head and agreed, not minding the boxes of musty comics stacked around our apartment. Our drinking glasses were monogrammed with the brand Coca-Cola in swirly letters; we got a free glass with every three tanks of gas from the corner gas station.

At night we'd rent movies, or "films" as Jack called them. Whenever we'd go to a theater to see a movie, Jack always made us stay until the very end so we could read all the film credits. He'd always exclaim, "Kirk Balaban! He's a good friend of mine," or "Joe Damon! I've known him since we ditched classes at Crossroads." I wasn't even sure then what a grip or a gaffer was.

Besides getting good tables at delis, Jack's dad also commanded star treatment at Temple Beth Israel, the huge synagogue up near Mulholland. Jack had never seemed that religious to me, but for the Jewish holidays that year, we went to services with his dad. We were in the overflow venue, the Bel Air Church on the other side of the 405 from the temple. I figured this was the "B" service; maybe you had to donate more to make it into the real place. I'd always thought it was weird that we were in a church, with all these depictions of JC on the cross.

My own religious affiliation was a little more ambiguous. My dad was an atheist and my mom Southern Baptist. Growing up, I'd usually gone to church or Sunday school with whoever lived near us and could give me a ride. So I learned some of the Book of Mormon with the Mormon kids, and the Bible with my Catholic friends. There were no Jewish people in Arizona. I knew Steven Spielberg was from Scottsdale, but he was honestly the only Jewish person I had ever heard of from AZ. But now I felt comfortable with Judaism; the emphasis seemed to be on the family, and Judaism didn't punish you as much as the other religions I was familiar with. So I tried to have an open mind and bend with the breeze. I never converted, but I always referred to myself as an "honorary Jew."

Things started getting bumpy with Jack when I started interning on different shows, mostly because Jack didn't get my work ethic. He was an "artist," something that he'd throw in my face from time to time, letting me know that I could never understand him, never feel something as deeply he did. Jack would tell me to quit my job and stay home (and do what, I didn't know). Then he started talking about our having a baby and getting married. I looked around our Van Nuys apartment and felt the roof falling in. The power lines strung at eye level outside our front window seemed menacing.

From then on, any little thing Jack did made me crazy. I once heard someone say that the things that make you fall in love with someone are what make you hate them later in the relationship. For instance, I'd always thought it was cute when he left his underwear on the bathroom floor—I'd move it to the hamper and smile warmly to myself. That got really old after a while. Another initially endearing trait was that Jack never had any cash. Whenever we'd get in the car, he would grasp the steering wheel, exhale loudly, then announce, "I've got no money and no gas." I didn't know why he was so shocked, because he took out only twenty dollars at a time from the ATM. So, before we went anywhere, we'd have to go to the bank, then to the 7-Eleven to buy two packs of smokes for him, and finally over to the gas station to put four bucks' worth of gas in the car. This left him with six dollars, and I'd cover whatever expenses we'd have for the rest of the day. Whenever I suggested he withdraw forty bucks on the weekend or think about filling his tank all the way up, he'd just glare at me.

I knew things were winding down when we spent New Year's Eve going to the Union 76 station by our apartment and filling up the tank completely. Jack had found an old Union 76 card that his dad had given him years earlier. It was due to expire on New Year's Day, so we had one last chance to use it. After that, I kind of checked out of the relationship and, after a couple of months, I moved out.

"So, how's Jack?" I felt compelled to ask, even though I couldn't have cared less.

Janey hesitated. "He's good. You know, he and Melissa have two kids now."

I'd known he'd gotten married and had a little boy. He was kind of like a kid himself, so I bet he was a good dad. "Does he have a job?" I asked.

"Kind of . . . ," she said. "He's writing too, and they just bought a house in Tarzana."

I didn't ask what he was writing or what the kids' names were. I didn't care.

I'd always liked Jack's sister Janey, but she was the really fucked-up one in the family; lots of daddy issues. As we talked at Peet's that afternoon, she acted sweet and glad to hear I was writing on *Flesh and Bone*. She had started her own dog walking business, which she described as "very lucrative." It paid for her acting classes and I guess walking dogs paid for the coffee, too.

Janey gave me a flyer about her showcase and we hugged good-bye. She had to make a workout class at Barry's Boot Camp in Sherman Oaks. I guess that explained her newly svelte figure. I tossed the flyer in the trash with my stale coffee cup on the way out.

When I got home, I did a search of Jack's name online. I wanted to see what he was "writing." I still found the idea of him holding down a steady job hard to grasp. I finally came across some documentary where he was listed as a "creative consultant." I took that title to mean that he'd helped out on the project but had not been paid.

Googling Jack's name brought me to a photo diary he kept on Flickr. I'd never checked out Flickr before. Millions of registered users used the online photo site to show and share photos. Jack had been keeping a photo diary since the birth of his first little boy. With just a few clicks of the mouse I could view pictures Jack had taken in the past ten years. Baby pictures of his kids, a nude shot of his eight-months pregnant wife artfully done in silhouette. (C'mon, does *anyone* really want to see that?) There were Christmas pictures from last year with a large fake tree in their living room. I could just make out the couch next to the tree in one of the photos. It was the couch Jack's mom had given us when we moved in together. How was that even possible? How could he even have the same couch after all these years?

Besides the pictures of his kids and home life, Jack had devoted a large folder of pictures to his old band. I guess they'd never gotten signed. He'd scanned ticket stubs from big shows at the Roxy and the Palladium, displaying them next to grainy photos of the band performing onstage. I remembered the shirt he *had* to wear for every show. Jack had bought it at a store on Melrose back when shopping on Melrose was cool.

I was still bothered by the fact that he still had the couch eight years and one wife later when I saw another familiar face from the past: my face. Or as my mother would say, my old nose featured on my old face. Along with the concert pictures, Jack had scanned photos of a party backstage. Did that guy ever lose a roll of film? I didn't even remember this shot, but there I was, with my big hair, big nose, and very little skirt. That part of the '90s wasn't good for fashion.

Written in the margin of the picture was the caption, "Miss 1998, talk about a Miss-Take!" with a bold arrow pointing directly at my old nose.

Miss-Take? Miss 1998? If this was an example of his writing talents, I was worried about him feeding his wife and children. I couldn't believe that fucker had sneaked in that shot of me. Did he laugh about it with his wife?

I was sure I was the only girl in the picture who didn't now have two different children with two different fathers. Jack must have known that things were going so well for me now, and he wanted to shit on me by putting the old photo with the nasty caption on there. I quit out of Flickr and turned off my computer. What a jerk. I should just be glad that life in Tarzana hadn't ended up being my life.

FIFTEEN

The Idea sprouted at work, where all my ideas usually start.

The Idea came while I was writing a scene where Maggie would have to peel away the skin from a corpse's finger and slide the skin over her own latex-gloved finger in order to take a fingerprint. As a body decomposes, the fine ridges that make every finger unique sometimes become impossible to print correctly. This technique would be very visual, and in the latest memo from the network we'd been told, "the science should be more sexy." I decided that the memos were just another way for people to make you crazy. The really smart and successful people just didn't read the memos, but I wasn't successful enough, so I couldn't escape.

In this scene, Maggie would show the novice investigator how to lift the fingerprint. The sight of Maggie slicing the skin from the finger of the corpse would make the newbie nauseated. Postproduction would add a little sound effect to emphasize the cutting. Sliding the skin on her own finger, Maggie would look seriously at the newbie:

MAGGIE

The body tells its own story. The body is trying to tell
us what happened the night she was killed. If we
can lift a fingerprint, we can identify the victim. That's
our first step in finding out who murdered her.
The fingerprint is the key.

The key.
So that's when the Idea first came to me.

My desk calendar was flipped to September and I'd marked a little red heart on the first Sunday, Jon and Catherine's wedding in Mexico. I'd drawn the red heart months ago, when I'd first found out their date and thought things like colored-in hearts were cute. I knew Dave would arrive in Cabo for the wedding and not get his requested Ocean View Villa, but be stuck with a small Mountain View double room. My stomach tightened thinking of the date he was taking on the trip. Who was she? No one wanted to take me anywhere. I was sure she was someone who could pull off a one-of-a-kind vintage dress with incredible style. All the other women would be drawn to her, asking her where she found such a great dress, and she'd shrug delicate shoulders and reply, "Oh, this? I found this at a thrift shop for twenty dollars." As for me, I wouldn't feel good about myself unless I had the new "it dress" mentioned in the pages of some magazine.

So who was Dave dating? If it wasn't Chloe, maybe it was an actress from one of his shows; maybe it was that blond from Starbucks that Bernie had spotted him with. I knew the clues to discovering her identity were accessible. I knew I could figure it all out if I was just given a little something to work with. This was the shit I did at work on a daily basis. One thing I knew, as the heart on the calendar approached, was that the identity of Dave's date would be detectable in his house, and even though I'd given him back his key, I knew where he kept the emergency lockout key in his carport.

They were in Mexico now; they'd arrived this afternoon. Everyone in LA kicked out early on a Friday before a holiday weekend. Plus I knew Jon and Catherine had planned a cocktail reception to welcome everyone on Friday night. I smiled, thinking of the male masseur. That would be a turnoff for Dave. They wouldn't have sex right after a massage from a guy—he'd be too nervous that being able to have an orgasm so soon after a man's hands had been on him would make him gay.

So that was how I found myself parked on Dave's street at nine at night on a Friday. If I'd been normal, or at least not crazy, I would have been on a date with someone great right now, on my second glass of Pinot. But here I was, dressed in black, sneaking up to my ex-boyfriend's house under cover of night.

The moist crunch of the grass and leaves under my Pumas made me feel a little 007 as I crossed the street. I reminded myself that James Bond was a little cheesy; I should imagine myself to be Jason Bourne. Even though there was no one around, I faked a spy move and tried to be invisible behind a tree, pressing my stomach into the scratchy bark.

I'd be Mrs. Bourne . . . but didn't Mrs. Bourne die in the second movie? Whatever. I slipped toward the carport. Dave had changed his pass codes on his phone a long time ago, but I was pretty confident that he wouldn't have found a new place for the key.

Dave's VW was resting in the covered driveway, but I wasn't worried he was home; he'd never leave his car at LAX, even for a brief weekend trip. He'd once explained that his car was "catnip" to the various nefarious types that prowled LAX looking to steal. He usually threw in a few racial slurs in his description of the prospective thieves. Classy guy.

I crept my way up to peer into the window of the VW. The car was glossy from the lone streetlight illuminating the carport. Peeking in, I saw a script thrown across the backseat. I also spied a half empty bottle of Evian. Instantly I corrected myself: a half full bottle. Listening to all those Tony Robbins tapes was really paying off.

Moving past the car, I saw my objective: the pile of wood slats resting against the far wall. Shortly after Dave first moved in, he'd had a leak in the bathroom and the plumbers had ripped out the flooring to get to the pipes that needed to be repaired. Following the work, Dave's landlord had to replace a good-sized chunk of the flooring, and these golden slats of walnut had been left over.

Dave would never move the emergency key—this was too great a hiding spot. All you had to do was to move a few slats and you'd find the key secreted between a couple of the wood pieces. Reaching for the wood, I really did feel like Jason Bourne.

It was dark and I hadn't thought to bring a flashlight for my covert mission. I'd retrieved the key a few times with Dave, so I thought I remembered where to look. My heart raced as I slid the slats apart, and I realized I was holding my breath. Nothing. With both hands I started to disassemble the small woodpile, throwing planks to the side as I made my way down. I was making a lot of noise and sounded like a coyote going through someone's garbage can, and I got scared that someone might come looking. Dumbstruck and feeling defeated, I turned to leave.

Suddenly I realized I could be caught, and for what? What if one of his neighbors had seen me rooting around in the carport and called the police? I'd been so focused on the mission I didn't really consider what would happen if someone saw me. I could be humiliated, and lose my job, and my job was all I had right now.

Quickly crossing the street, I tried to act nonchalant as I hastened my way to my car a few houses away. I wouldn't have really gone in Dave's house anyway—this was just something for fun, I told myself.

Safely in my car, I pulled away from the curb and told myself again that I wouldn't have really have gone in. This was just a fun research trip; I'd go home and write about this. I could use this for one of my upcoming shows. Of course, the woman looking for the key outside wouldn't be the "bad guy"—she'd be the one on the right side of the law. Leaving Dave's house behind in the rearview mirror, I vowed to myself never to drive by again.

"Dani, there's a call for you."

"Did they say who was calling?"

"Troy Zarcoff."

My heart leaped. I had been waiting for this call. I counted to ten before picking up the phone. "Hi, this is Dani."

"Hi, it's Troy Zarcoff. I'm Mark's friend."

Mark was a friend of mine who made huge money producing cheesy teen skin flicks. He had married "the Wicked Witch of the West Side," as my girlfriends and I liked to call her, but he was still a nice guy. Whenever I saw him, though, he would linger just a little too long when he'd kiss me hello or good-bye. His lips would rest uncomfortably on mine, and I could feel his breath on my cheeks, rustling my eyelashes. I knew that all I had to do was make a slight movement and he'd have his tongue down my throat. And the last thing I needed was trouble with a married guy. Mark always regaled me with his past exploits. He'd had "ass sex," as he liked to put it, with half the actresses in Hollywood. Despite the ass sex and the mild attempts at hitting on me, there was something really charming about Mark. I remembered him telling a story of being at the famous Hotel du Cap, one of the most exclusive and expensive hotels in the world and a playground for Hollywood, two weeks every May during the Cannes Film Festival. And they took only cash. No credit cards allowed. Mark stayed there as an executive at Paramount. The du Cap was famous for its bellinis. One flute of the champagne and peach juice cocktail set you back fifty bucks.

Mark told me of holding up his empty glass and asking the French waiter if he could get a pitcher of them. I didn't think you ordered "pitchers" of anything in France. That night his bar bill was twelve thousand dollars. Because the hotel didn't take cards, the studio had to wire money to settle the bill.

I had met Mark through Dave; they had been friends at UCLA film school. Mark had graduated and Dave hadn't, although he told everyone he had. We had double-dated a couple of times with Mark and the Wicked Witch of the West Side, although the dates always seemed a little tense.

Mark had reacted well to the news that Dave and I had broken up. The first thing he said was that he never thought it was healthy for a guy to be as into me as Dave was. If only he knew that while Dave might have seemed like he was into me, he was actually into everyone else at the same time. I had tried very subtly to pump him for information on what Dave was up to and who Mystery Woman was, but he was too cagey to spill the news I wanted.

Still, I was surprised when Mark called to say hi and brought up that he had the perfect guy he thought I should meet. Troy Zarcoff used to run Zephyr Studios, as in being the president of Zephyr Studios. The trades reported a few weeks ago that Troy was leaving the studio and becoming an "independent producer" with a production deal. I remembered his quote saying he was "thrilled to be embarking on this incredibly creative new venture." Which meant, you've been canned and they're paying you a fraction of your original deal so you won't sue them, but good luck producing on your own.

Troy had a reputation for being a bit of a player, but according to Mark, that was all in the past and he was really looking to settle down. I hadn't had a date in a while and I figured I didn't have much to lose.

"Yes, Mark told me you might phone," I said, smiling. These things were always so awkward.

"Yeah. Mark tells me you're not an actress."

"No, not an actress, and no aspirations in that direction."

"Good, because I'm kind of off actresses for the moment."

I took this as a good sign, but didn't want to overanalyze the implication of "for the moment." It either alluded to a recent nasty breakup or a self-promoting actress trying to weasel her way through him for a big break, but it also suggested I might be a rest stop on the freeway leading to a starlet trophy bride.

There was an uncomfortable pause for a few seconds. I wasn't sure what else I was supposed to say to Troy. He was the one calling me to make plans.

"Well, I don't know if Mark told you, but I have season tickets to the Lakers and I was wondering if you'd be interested in checking it out with me. The game's on Thursday."

"Sure," I replied quickly, trying not to seem as desperate as I felt. "I love the Lakers."

We decided he'd pick me up. "Great," I said, though it didn't make me happy—but he wouldn't have to come far inside. I told him how to get to my house. He said he lived "way out in Malibu," which put him in the GU category (geographically undesirable), but it wasn't as if he lived in San Bernardino. And everyone knew that Malibu spelled m-o-n-e-y.

My buzzer rang exactly at six thirty. I had known he'd be on time, because we were trying to make the tip-off.

I let him in. "Hi, I'm Dani," I said. I started to put out my hand for a handshake, but he came in for a kiss, which was a little surprising, but I hadn't had sex since May, so it was fine.

Troy was a little odd-looking, definitely Jewish, not that there was anything wrong with that. His face was a little pale and he had a *nose*, but allowances had to be made for the man who had earned billions for a studio. A successful bachelor in Hollywood had his pick of any-one. See a model on the cover of a magazine? Have your assistant call her in for a meeting to see if she wants to act. Just tell her she has "that star quality" and deserves to be in movies.

"So you want to get going?" Troy asked me.

"Sure."

It felt a little funny for the two of us just to be standing there in my living room staring at each other. I followed him out and saw that he had parked his brand-new mega Range Rover in front of my place. Up here in the hills, the streets were pretty narrow, so this kind of thing isn't that great of an idea. Cars were already bottle-necked behind him, and I caught a nasty look from someone in a Prius a quarter way down the hill.

"Sorry, sorry," I called to the cars, before hopping in and slamming the door behind me.

At the Staples Center, Troy had the best-of-the-best VIP park-ing. We arrived just in time for the national anthem, performed by Seal, complete with light show. This *was* Hollywood.

Our seats were great, seven or eight rows behind the Lakers bench. Troy and I made a little small talk as the game began, but he didn't seem that into it, as if he regretted making plans with me. Fi-nally, after an uncomfortable silence that lasted for minutes (who ac-tually comes for the game?), he looked down glumly and said, "When I was at Zephyr I had their seats whenever I wanted, right on the floor."

"I think these seats are great," I chirped, trying to be easygoing.

He made some sort of sound of acknowledgement, but I got the feeling he wasn't impressed that I was impressed. "I share these with a buddy. They're fine, I guess."

He really seemed sad about the seats. I was working on my light beer and he had a Coke. When I went for a second drink I asked him if he wanted an Amstel. "I don't really care for beer," he said, sipping his Coke. "I'm just really into wine right now. I've been working on filling my cellar over the last couple of years."

Okay, but no beer at a basketball game? I asked myself. This guy was really down.

In the second quarter, I tried to cheer him up. "You know, I hear that Vivid, the company that makes all those porno movies, has its own box."

Now I had his attention. "Really? Where?"

"I'm not sure what box it is, but it can't be that tough to find, if it's filled with porn stars."

His eyes started scanning the boxes that lined the rim of the Staples Center. Now that I'd given him something to be excited about, he couldn't have been less interested in our date.

During halftime he bolted from his seat and headed for the mezzanine. I was practically running to keep up with him. Halftime at a Lakers game was prime time for the scene, crawling with people you'd expect to find loitering around a VIP bar at a professional sporting event: The men, the "Masters of the Universe," were getting payback for all those years growing up as the nerdy smart kid. A lot of the guys were as well groomed as the women, with waxed eyebrows, lots of product in their hair, and just a touch of Botox around the eyes to give them that little lift. The women were plastic blonds in too-tight jeans and tummy-baring tops with spray-on tans. Any guy who got lucky tonight would wake up in the morning with his sheets looking like he'd wrestled a bag of Cheetos all night. The guys downed manly drinks, and the girls sipped Cosmos out of plastic cups.

"Yo, dog, how are you?"

Troy and a supergroomed studio exec type, who had better highlights and whiter teeth than me, shared some sort of soul handshake, which looked really stupid between these two very white guys. "I'm good, I'm good."

"How's the new gig treating you?"

"It's going good. We're just getting started, so things are just beginning to get off the ground. Building a new company takes time."

The handshake guy's eyes drifted toward me, and suddenly Troy remembered I was there. "Oh, sorry, let me introduce you to Dani Hale. Do you know Dani? Dani, meet Jay Ravich."

Everyone usually assumed that everyone knew each other in Hollywood.

I shook hands normally. "Nice to meet you."

He kept shaking and didn't let go of my hand. "Hey, didn't I meet you at Scott Rosenberg's house? At that big barbecue he has every summer?"

I wasn't sure. I would have thought I'd have remembered Jay; he was kind of cute, but I knew he was an agent, which was a turnoff. I'd gone to Scott's barbecues for years and maybe we had met when I was in the Dave bubble and I didn't give any guys any kind of once-over.

"Yeah, of course." My lightbulb went off a little, as I finally got my hand free. Jay had been at the barbecue with John Parkinson. JP, as he was called, worked in the TV department at William Morris and managed to be friends with the entire working population of Hollywood. JP always knew who was getting fired and who was screwing whom. When I was offered my contract from Steve for *Flesh and Bone*, I went right to JP. He helped negotiate more money and signed me to the agency.

The crowd's cheering broke up our group, so we said our goodbyes and headed back to our seats. Troy seemed in a little better spirits after seeing his friends, but he still had one eye on the game and the other looking for that porno skybox.

We bailed at the top of the fourth quarter because the Lakers were ahead by twenty points. Back in the Range Rover, I wondered what we'd do now. I had a vision of Troy driving up my street and opening the door to make me jump out of the moving car so he wouldn't have to stop.

"I was thinking we'd get dinner at Dan Tana's. You cool with that?"

I was a little surprised. It was a school night and it was almost ten. I was having a pretty good time, even with Troy's bouts of distraction. I reasoned with myself that he had a lot on his mind with starting the new company and maybe he was thinking about work more than women, or at least women who weren't in a porn skybox. I told him that was great and didn't mention that I had to be in the office early for a meeting.

Dan Tana's was completely dark inside; my eyes had to adjust before I could take in the room. I had heard how great the restaurant was but had never eaten there before. The maître d' greeted Troy as if he were a visiting dignitary, and we were swiftly escorted to a prime back booth. As I sank into the rich leather, I glanced around. "Being here makes me think of that Phil Spector shooting."

Troy regarded me blankly. "Why?"

"You know, this is where he had dinner that night . . . the night he allegedly shot that woman. He had dinner here and left a $500 tip on his credit card. Then Spector headed over to the House of Blues, where he picked up this waitress Lana and took her back home to his house in Alhambra or someplace. Hours passed, and he called the police to say she'd shot herself, that it was a suicide."

I was really into telling the story now. "Investigators carefully examined all the forensic evidence and found through the gunshot residue and various skull fragments around the room that she didn't pull the trigger. That she was murdered."

He stared at me. "Wow, that's a lot to take in."

His dry response made me laugh. "I am *very* into this stuff."

I ran to the ladies' room, and when I returned he was furiously texting someone on his BlackBerry. "It's just a buddy of mine . . . this thing is a lifesaver. I don't know what I'd do without it. Do you have a BlackBerry?"

"Yeah, but I'm kind of technically challenged. I don't use it much," I replied. Truthfully, except for the occasional e-mail from Lauren and Ina, I really didn't have anyone to correspond with now that Dave was out of the picture. No little messages signed "xo D" during the day.

"Well, I'll give you my instant-message account and you can e-mail me whenever you want."

"Okay." I beamed. Troy didn't catch my glow. I watched him cast his eyes down to text his friend. This was a first. His fingers flew across the keys, tapping out something that must have been pretty hysterical, judging by his pleased expression.

Troy broke away from his Crackberry when our food finally arrived. As our plates landed on the table, I realized my shrimp scampi was swimming in garlic. There would definitely be no make-out sessions tonight. But maybe that would be a good thing with Troy; maybe we should take it slow.

When Troy pulled up in front of my house, I had no idea what to think. I began my "It was really fun, got to go, see ya soon" good-bye. But he jumped out of the car and came around to open my door. "There's no way I'm not walking you in, like a proper gentleman."

I was a little surprised by his sudden interest. I hoped he didn't think anything was going to happen. He was just walking me in.

Once we were in my place, I turned around to thank him and give him my "great time, good night" thing when he moved toward me and pushed me against the wall and started madly kissing me.

It wasn't unpleasant; it was pretty nice. His lips were very soft and I could feel him through his pants as he pressed himself harder against me. After a bit of this, he pulled back to get a breath. His lips were pink and swollen and I was sure mine looked the same.

"Good night, Dani."

"Good night, Troy. Drive carefully."

"Okay, bye."

After he left, I brushed and flossed, then went back to the bathroom to use the Listerine. Padding into bed, I pulled the duvet up to my chin. I felt the bed jiggle with the familiar weight of Lucy jumping up and settling into her spot. I hoped Troy liked garlic.

The next day at lunch, I ran to the mall and bought a new Black-Berry. My old one worked fine, but it was a few models out of date and using it was like holding a loaf of bread against my face. The new BlackBerry was sexy and svelte. I smiled, thinking that the next time Troy went out with his friends, he wouldn't be able to stop texting me.

Back in the office I pored over the new manual. The buttons were awfully small, but it was a cool new toy to have. For once, it was an asset to have bitten-down fingernails; they maneuvered quickly over the keys.

After a couple of hours of fiddling with the BlackBerry and not writing a scene featuring double cadavers, I managed to figure out how to send and receive e-mail. I was smooth with normal-sized computers, but this was going to take some getting used to.

I IM'd Troy. "I just traded in my old BlackBerry for one like yours!" After an hour he responded, "Cool . . . I hope you like it."

And then nothing the rest of the day.

I waited a couple of days, thinking maybe his battery had been dead and he couldn't text anyone.

"What are you doing?" I texted.

I waited and waited. After three hours, I got a message back: "Just working, boring. Take care, T."

I tossed, or more exactly threw, the BlackBerry off my desk. I wasn't having a fit. I was aiming for it to land in my bag on the floor, but it missed by a few feet. Being so accessible to everyone made me ultra-aware that no one really needed to reach me or wanted to reach me that badly. But thank God my mother didn't use e-mail. Feeling bad, I walked over to retrieve my BlackBerry from the floor. The moment I picked it up, the shiny bullet came to life in my hands, vibrating. For a second I thought I'd damaged the phone and that it was starting to explode in my grasp.

But when I looked down at it, I saw I had a text message—from Troy: "Capo for dinner, Sat 8. OK?"

My heart fluttered like a freshman girl's. "OK," I texted back.

Azita interrupted me as I hit "send." "Time for the weekly pitch meeting. Everyone's already in the Room."

I grabbed my notebook and folder with news clippings I'd cut out from the paper—you never knew where the next great idea would come from—and dashed to the meeting. We were in the thick of the fall season, and we'd pretty much plotted out half the shows for the year, but that still left us with a dozen show ideas to come up with.

"Okay, anybody got anything new?" Steve said to the assembled group.

"How 'bout Internet child porn?" I offered up. "It's edgy and controversial—it would be great for sweeps."

Steve relaxed into his chair and jotted something in his notebook. "Go on, Dani."

"Well, we have a successful woman, owns her own business, that kind of thing. She's getting married to a great guy and thinks she has it made. He starts acting a bit distracted, not just the normal work-distracted stuff. So she goes digging a little, checking up on him. She looks in his computer e-mail and finds kiddie porn. She confronts him with it and he explodes, killing her." I looked around the conference table. "Sounds great, right?"

Blank stares.

Sam, one of the staff writers, piped up, "That sounds a lot like that writer guy who was convicted of killing his wife. They found her at the bottom of the staircase, remember? I think she found his kiddie porn."

"Michael Peterson," I cut him off. "That story is so *old*. It's been done *everywhere*. And it wasn't kiddie porn—she found gay porn on his computer. Who cares about gay porn?" I said this last part to the rest of the table. The guys all squirmed. "Gay porn is boring," I added.

Sam was picking a fight now. "Okay, this guy has child porn in his e-mail account. He could just have received it from a pervert friend or something. You can't help it if someone sends you something sick."

"Yes, you can," I interrupted. "If a friend sent you filth like that, you just e-mail him back that it's not okay. 'Don't send me any more kiddie porn' is what you write him." I looked around the conference table for support. "You guys know what I mean, right?"

People shifted a little bit in their seats before nodding. Steve was writing down a few notes. "Dani, you know how it is in the Room here, we're just bouncing ideas back and forth—that's what the Room is for."

"I'm not pitching a tired idea about gay porn and the Staircase Murder," I retorted. "This is about Internet snooping, and a relationship in a sensitive stage. The fiancée has a gut feeling and looks to see if there's something to her feelings, and she ends up being right. But we make her our victim. When she confronts him with the e-mail, he flies into a rage and she ends up dead. That's our story."

"But doesn't she deserve it?"

We all turned to the far left of the room to find the voice. It was Evil Janet, with a chair pulled into the crowded room against the far wall. From where I was sitting, I could still see Janet's nails. She'd drawn a single black stripe down the center of each nail to the tip. It looked like she'd used a Sharpie instead of polish.

"She went looking for something where she shouldn't have been looking. That's a bad thing to do," Evil Janet said. "The core belief system of someone who would do something like that is totally out of whack."

Steve interjected excitedly, "Yes, this is the moral dilemma for the show. We all know that she didn't have it coming, because no one deserves to be murdered, but she wasn't an angel." He turned to me, his face alight. "Dani, this is great, this is fantastic! You should really run with it."

"Okay, as long as we all recognize that possessing child porn is an illegal offense," I said, sounding dour. I was glad Steve was jazzed about the idea, but getting a green light felt like a consolation prize. They were all ganging up on the *she* in the story.

"It's also an illegal offense to break into someone's e-mail," added Evil Janet.

"Enough, we get it!" Steve looked around the room. "I just want to remind you all that a lot of eyes are on the show. Les is looking for ideas to bolster the network's drama portfolio, so feel challenged." He gave a mock thumbs up to all of us.

After the meeting I was still annoyed at the other staffers and especially at Evil Janet. As I settled in behind my desk, my phone rang. "It's Dani," I said, sounding more irritated than I meant to.

"Hey beautiful, it's JP. How's my writing angel today?"

Even though he was full of shit, no one could be too annoyed with JP. He was too good an ass kisser. After generic chat about things, he got to the point. "I got a call from a buddy of mine—you remember Jay Ravich, the lawyer?"

"Yeah, I remember him. He's the guy who says I met him at Scott Rosenberg's barbecue."

"He called me first thing Friday morning after the game. He was asking a lot of questions about you and wanted to know what the deal was with you and Troy. I told him you were a good friend and a rising client and I didn't do this sort of thing. I'm no pimp."

I let him get away with that one, for now.

"So Jay plays hockey out at the Icoplex with a guy who is a good friend of Troy's. Jay thought he could find out from that guy if Troy was really that into you, or not into you. He felt that if he got the green light from Troy, then I would feel cooler about fixing you both up."

This whole thing was unbelievable. "I'm so glad you two worked all of this out so I didn't have to be involved at all. Why would Jay even think I would be interested in going out with him?"

"He just—"

"Let Jay know that Troy is taking me to dinner at Capo on Saturday night."

This news elicited a low whistle from JP. "Fancy."

"Very fancy," I agreed.

"This is definitely going to be a date with a capital *D*."

"You bet," I said, trying not to sound as happy as I was to have trumped Jay Ravich.

"Have a great time on your 'Capital D' date, and I'll let Jay know things are good between you two."

"You do that."

I spent Saturday morning getting my hair highlighted by Jennifer J at Juan Juan. (Ashley Judd was there at the same time!) I went shopping and decided against jeans and went with a skirt that wasn't too short and some great sandals. I wore jeans on our first date to the Lakers game and I'd been told that I had nice legs, so why not show them off? And even though I was meeting him at the restaurant in Santa Monica, I hid my library of self-help books in the closet. Who knew if the night would end up back at my place?

SIXTEEN

I arrived twenty minutes early for dinner. I couldn't help myself. Spying a meter across the street from the restaurant, I eased into the spot and got comfortable. Keeping one eye on the digital clock, I watched the traffic blow by, studying the passing cars. I knew Troy would be driving in from Malibu, so he would be coming from the north down Ocean Drive to Capo. Even though the sun had just gone down over the ocean horizon, the tourists were out in force, driving their neon-colored convertibles distractedly as they still tried to take in the view.

There was just something not that cool about Santa Monica. Having not grown up in California, I had always expected Santa Monica to be glamorous, but it really wasn't that impressive a place. Most movies set in California were shot in Miami Beach. Anybody wanting to make Santa Monica glamorous should really look to the redevelopment of South Beach as a guide.

Finally, after sitting in my car for twenty-eight minutes, I decided that eight after eight was the time to go in. I'd order a drink at the bar and try not to look like a high-end prostitute.

I had never been to Capo, but I knew of it by reputation as one of the most expensive places to eat in LA. The owner was some rich guy who wouldn't advertise or go after coverage in magazines. He wanted the word of mouth about the food and exclusivity to be restricted to a choice clientele.

I stepped inside and waited for my eyes to adjust to the dim lighting. I was surprised to see Troy there, seated at the bar. He must have beaten me by quite a while. I couldn't believe it. Maybe he was really looking forward to the date, too.

He made a slight move to get up and I met him halfway for a hello kiss. "I hope you haven't been waiting long," I said. "I'm never late."

Troy smiled. "I just got here. Don't worry. You look beautiful."

"Thank you." He was regarding me so intently that I got a little uncomfortable. "So, what are you drinking?" I asked.

"I've really gotten into drinking this heavy, dramatic wine. Have you ever had a Barolo?"

"No. I usually drink white wine," I answered.

The bartender offered to pour me a glass and I nodded for him to go ahead. I cast my eyes over Troy's shoulder and around the room. The restaurant was beautiful, with linen tablecloths and candles everywhere and soft lighting. Even on a Saturday night, the place seemed empty, with only a few couples scattered among the tables. Maybe I should call it more *intimate* than empty. There were no windows. I had expected there to be a great ocean view. I reminded myself that the actual ocean was blocks away from this location, even if it was on Ocean Drive. Go figure! I saw that all the tables featured very cute salt and pepper shakers. I was glad my purse was big enough to accommodate them when I left.

"Hey," Troy began. "I didn't want to call and cancel on you, so I thought I'd show up early. I was hoping maybe we could skip dinner . . . because I have to go take care of this work problem."

"Oh," I said.

"We're just having this issue with the new pages for a script, and one of the actors isn't happy. There's this fund-raiser over at Brian Robinson's house, and I was thinking if we swung by there and made an appearance I could take care of it. Then we can bail and the night is ours."

"Oh, okay, sure. I understand." I was so disappointed. I wanted those salt and pepper shakers, but I took his not canceling the entire date as a sign that he wanted to see me.

"I'll drive, and we'll only go for a little bit, I promise," he said.

"It's no problem. I bet it will be great," I added, trying to be cheery. Maybe it was for the best that this was going to be a spur-of-the-moment kind of plan; I'd already worked myself up about the dinner date. Knowing I was going to a party would have sent me over the edge.

It wasn't far from Santa Monica to the huge Palisades home of the Robinsons. Brian Robinson had made his mark producing commercial holiday movies and summer blockbusters as well as an Oscar-winning film the previous year. I'd seen him having lunch at the Ivy, at the number one table inside, the week after he won the Oscar. Well-wishers were lined up out the door to kiss the ring, Hollywood style.

In the Robinsons' brightly lighted driveway Troy pulled up to the valet parking, which I saw was being handled by Valet of the Dolls, babes in shorts running up and down the hill parking cars. We got out and headed to the massive stacked-stone entranceway. Party talk buzzed from inside. Troy didn't bother ringing the bell; he comfortably opened the front door.

Inside, the place was even more stunning than the outside. With an über-rich producer type like Brian Robinson, I had been expecting his home to be some sort of McMansion, with a Tuscan-inspired stucco exterior, a screening room, and a five-car garage. But this house was a showplace, an original Neutra, impeccably restored, with walls of glass that opened onto the backyard. The party was already at full throb. The first person we saw was Drew Barrymore, walking around with no shoes, kissing everyone hello on the lips.

"Troy . . . my boy!" I heard a female voice exclaim. This was Mrs. Robinson. I recognized her from pics in *In Style* magazine, taken at fabulous parties a lot like this one. As she approached, I thought she was so anorexic and so tan she looked like a walking X-ray. She threw her stick arms around Troy and kissed him hard.

Troy pulled back a little. "Miranda, looking as beautiful as ever. Brian is a lucky fuck."

"You flirt. I'm telling." She kept her arms wrapped around his neck and she wasn't letting go.

Troy suddenly remembered I was there. "Let me introduce Dani. Miranda, this is Dani Hale."

"Oh, hello!" She limply took my hand. "Welcome, welcome. I don't know where Brian is but I'm sure you'll be able to find him. Everybody is here." She winked over Troy's shoulder at me. "Don't worry, Dani, you'll be fine."

I guess I didn't look fine. I tightly smiled back at the missus and we endured an awkward silence. Then something behind me caught her attention. We turned to see a girl who was around eight, dressed from head to toe in Missoni. She was straining to carry a tray loaded with canapés.

"Isn't she darling? We always like to get the children involved any way we can, and she begged to be able to pass out the hors d'oeuvres. Lily, hold the tray flat—you don't want to spill any on Mommy's new floors."

With a scared look in our direction, Lily snapped to attention and steadied herself and the plate.

Miranda's hands were constantly in motion fluttering around as she talked. It could have been the edge from diet pills, but I suspected she was trying to draw attention to her fabulous jewelry. Her ring finger glimmered with a six-carat canary diamond, and stacks and stacks of microdiamond bangles adorned her wrists. I recognized them from the window of Martin Katz on Burton Way.

Miranda noticed me admiring her ring. "You like my droolery? Don't you love the ring? When we got married, Brian gave me a tiny, tiny ring. It only would have been worse if it had been a marquis cut." The thought of this was so ridiculous it made her throw her head back and cackle. "This was a present after *Green Eggs and Ham* made four hundred million. And believe me, after what having three kids did to my body, I deserve every carat."

She turned to Troy. "Do you like the house, honey? You with the architectural eye?" Mrs. turned to include me in their conversation. "We've *finally* gotten through the work here. You should have seen it when we moved in. I refused to stay here with all that dust, so we rented up at Tigertail for over a year. It's great to finally be home."

Suddenly she was distracted, or maybe she was faking it. With another squeeze of Troy's hand, she moved on to greet some bigger names. Troy and I got our drinks. I felt silly sticking so close to him; I felt like one of those "helicopter girls," always hovering over her date.

"Are you going to be okay if I break away for a sec?" Troy asked. "I see my actress I have to deal with."

"Sure, no problem, I'm fine." Troy was turning away into the crowd of incredibly sleek physiques before I even got the sentence out.

I was hoping I didn't look as awkward as I felt. I knew people went to parties on their own all the time. It was just that these were movie people and it was different. You couldn't have a normal conversation with them, like "Where will you go on vacation?" or "What part of town do you live in?" If you asked direct questions, they thought you were working for the tabloids and digging for dirt. Celebs never wanted to be specific about their neighborhoods, because that would let the paparazzi know what Starbucks to stake out in the morning for a no-makeup and sweatpants photo. All conversation had to be about superficial stuff like the weather and how incredible the party was. I drifted out through the open glass doors onto the lawn and saw Brian Robinson surrounded by a handful of admirers near a faux fire pit that was electrically burning.

"I mean, if you haven't been to China, you've got to get yourself there. The Ecstasy you can get there is amazing, and the women are incredible," Brian was saying. "I'm telling you, there's nothing the women in China won't do for a Westerner. It's like how it was here in the States in the '60s and '70s—they're going through their own sexual revolution right now."

Like frat boys, the group of forty- and fiftysomething men nudged each other and laughed at the thought of a wild Chinese sex partner.

"Just don't look at their teeth," Brian added. "Communist dentists obviously aren't well versed in cosmetic dentistry. I like them best when their mouths are full of something; namely, me!" Again a big laugh. He was grinning so broadly I could see his entire mouth of capped teeth. They were Chiclet teeth, and his smile looked like an even row of tombstones.

I saw Troy leaning against the guesthouse wall with his arm above the head of Jennifer Aniston. He was bending in close and they were having an intense conversation. Their body language was a little intimate, but I was sure they were talking about the problem on the film. I was thinking about moving in for a closer vantage point to maybe catch what they were talking about when a voice startled me.

"So have you donated to her fund-raiser yet?"

I jerked around, feeling a little busted for staring at Troy and Jennifer, but happy that someone was finally talking to me. The voice belonged to a man I guessed was in his late forties or early fifties; it was hard to tell in Hollywood. He was weaving back and forth a little, waving an amber-colored drink on ice.

"Not yet. It's for an environmental thing?" I squeaked.

"Yeah, Miranda Robinson is this big anti-fossil-fuel proponent.

She drives her hybrid SUV all over Brentwood crying about air and the damage we're doing to our planet." He was a little slurry at this point and his drink was sloshing precariously in his hand.

I recognized this man now: He was a director who did something good a long time ago and now only directed movies for the studio his wife ran. I didn't see the wife anywhere. He inched closer to me.

"So she drives the hybrid like she's making a difference, but she insists on flying privately on the studio's G4 whenever they go to their house on Cape Cod. She's probably using a hundred times the fuel for that trip than she would have if she had been driving a Jeep Cherokee for a decade."

"Wow," I said.

"Fucking cunt," he said under his breath. His eyes focused on me probably for the first time and he took a step closer. I could smell his Boozy Breath. Hearing BB using the C-word was my cue to leave.

"Oh my God! Rachel! There you are!" I exclaimed, waving to someone over his shoulder. "Rachel, I've been looking for you everywhere!" I scolded. "Excuse me," I said to BB. Instantly I was moving past his shoulder toward my imaginary friend. This conversation would not have ended well. I headed inside to find the ladies' room.

About half a dozen people were waiting for the bathroom. No famous faces, though. If I was going to wait in line to escape that guy, I should probably try to really go, I reasoned, so I stood there, wondering what Troy was saying to Jennifer.

I could hear the two guys behind me in conversation. "Let me tell you—first class sucks. It's gotten to the point where I really can only stand to fly privately. So I called up Bob and said, 'Fuck you, if you won't let me have the plane.' Ratner goes all over town bragging about how he has it at his disposal? I mean, *Rush Hour* was a long time ago."

"You should definitely have priority over him," said the other guy.

"No shit." His eyes swept the room, flickering over all the beautiful women, and he changed the subject to something important. "Dude, this party is total lace."

"I know, man, but I didn't realize that Drew has turned the big uh-oh three-oh."

"Yeah, she's about to expire like spoiled milk. I remember jerking off to her in that *ET* movie when I was a kid."

"Dude, me too! Give me some high . . . now give me some low." They slapped hands and I surmised that they were both gay.

Troy interrupted. "Hey, there you are. I've been looking all over for you. Are you ready to go?"

"I'm so ready."

"What, were you not having a good time?" he asked, steering me toward the front door and our freedom. "I know Miranda is a little eccentric."

"Oh, it's not her. Just weird guys hitting on me."

"I bet that happens all the time. I'd think you'd be used to it."

He was being really charming. If only he were like this all the time. Fortunately, I was getting used to his bouts of distraction.

The Valet of the Dolls driver pulled up in Troy's Range Rover. I checked my watch and saw it was after eleven. There wasn't a lot we could do.

"Okay, now I have to make all this up to you." He was smiling as he grabbed the wheel. "Well, we've certainly done the high thing already tonight—how 'bout going for a little bit of the low?"

"The low?"

"Yeah. I'll take you to one of my favorite bars. We'll have a drink and relax—it's not Hollywood at all, no one will bother us. That is, if you don't mind divey places?"

"No, I love divey places. I'm in."

"Great."

He drove back toward Capo, where my car was still parked, and made a turn into a driveway a few blocks down.

"Have you ever been to Chez Jay?"

"No, I don't really come down here to the beach that often."

"You'll love it. It's great."

He was right that it was a dive. The place looked like a strong gust of wind would knock it over. Hawaiian knickknacks on the walls, straw on the floor. Troy found us the last two barstools and ordered us double margaritas.

"Margaritas to celebrate!" He clinked glasses with me.

He was in a great mood . . . so it must have gone well with Jennifer at the party. "I almost bought this place last year," he told me. "They had been having a tough time, but they got it together."

"This place is great." I said in a hollow voice. It might have been great if I were a freshman in college and this was the only place that would take my fake ID. Chez Jay was, literally, a shack. I took another sip of my margarita and tried to ignore the fact that we were within walking distance of Shutters, with their extensive selection of wines and their tranquil lobby bar overlooking the sands of Santa Monica. Troy insisted on another round, complete with a tequila shooter. With the wine at Capo, drinks at the party, and now all these Chez Jay margaritas, I was more than a little shitfaced. Somewhere after the second margarita and the tequila shot, we started kissing, more like sucking faces, as if we were a couple of high schoolers. I didn't care that people were looking. It wasn't like there was anyone here that I knew. Now I felt great. I was proud of myself for getting through the evening's change in plans and the party. Troy was obviously really into me, and I felt all warm.

Troy paid the check. It was getting really late and Chez Jay was getting ready to close. Back in his Range Rover, he was on top of me before I could get my seat belt on. More furious kissing. He helped me move into the backseat and flopped on top of me, putting one hand up my shirt and the other up my skirt. I started pulling his shirt out and sliding my hands up his furry chest. My head was spinning and I was glad I was lying flat because I might have been weaving at this point if I had been upright.

I knew we shouldn't be doing this in a car—I knew he wouldn't have any respect for me if we actually had sex like this—but I hadn't been with anyone since Dave last May, and that was almost six months ago. Troy had my panties down now and I kicked a leg free to flick them all the way off. Now his hands were really everywhere. We had plenty of room in the Range Rover; this was probably a selling point. I had rolled on top now and his shirt was off. His eyes were closed and his head was thrown back as I came in again to start kissing his neck.

Smack!

"Ouch!" I yelled out. What the fuck?

Smack! And then *smack!* again.

He was spanking me, or to be more precise, he was smacking me *hard* on my bare bottom. I felt like I'd just sat in ice cubes. I rolled off him, sat bolt upright, and pushed him to the side as I tried to find my panties.

"Hey, what's the matter?" he said, a little fuzzy.

"I'm not feeling well," I mumbled. "I've got to go."

"Are you okay? I thought you were into it." He watched me straighten my top and wriggle into my panties.

"Yeah, I'm fine. It's just been a long night."

Troy tried to focus on me and what I was doing. He moved back into the driver's seat and fixed his clothes. He looked totally composed as I continued my wrestling with my panties. Watching me with disinterest in the rearview mirror, he waited patiently for me to fix my clothes. Troy made no offer of apology; he had dead eyes.

"Are you okay to drive?" he asked.

I knew I wasn't, but I couldn't deal with him trying to take me home.

I don't know what I said, but soon I found myself in my car and heading up San Vicente back toward Hollywood. I rolled the window down and hoped the air whipping my face and hair would keep me alert. Driving was definitely not a good idea. I gripped the steering wheel tightly with both hands and tried to drive the speed limit and stay in my lane.

I made it home without killing anyone. I took two Tylenol and drank a big glass of water and hoped I wouldn't feel as bad in the morning as I knew I was going to feel.

The water and Tylenol didn't help. I woke up Sunday morning feeling horrible. When I did a scene-by-scene breakdown of the night before, my stomach became even more sour.

I was immobilized on the green marshmallow, surfing through 500 channels of nothing, when the phone rang. I would just have let it go to voice mail, but each ring seared right through my temples and into my throbbing head. After five rings, I feebly picked up the cordless.

"Hello?"

"Hey . . ."

I froze. It was Dave, his voice low and familiar. It had been four and a half months, but there wasn't any need to say who it was.

"How are you, Dani?"

"I'm great, Dave," I said, sitting straight up, trying not to sound half dead. "And how are you?"

"I'm good, I'm good."

Ha, he was just good and I said I was great. We exchanged incredibly civil banter about what was going on at work. I had seen an episode of *Law and Order SVU* he had directed and he had seen an episode of *Flesh and Bone* recently and noticed I'd gotten sole writing credit again. I was not sure why this conversation was going on so civilly. I didn't feel like being civil. What was behind all this?

"I was wondering if you could meet me for coffee?" he asked.

Coffee? "You don't drink coffee."

"I do now."

I processed that. I felt like there was an ambush coming.

Rolling over to lie on the couch, I held the phone tight to my ear. I hope my voice didn't give away that I was horizontal. "Why do you want to have coffee?"

"I just felt like there was some stuff we should talk about."

What could we talk about? We were over, although I still thought about him every hour on the hour. We'd given back each other's stuff. He'd changed his passwords and hidden his house key in a new place.

I felt like a cross-examining defense attorney when I fired back, "What do you feel like you have to tell me in person, face-to-face? Do you have some sort of terminal illness, or are you going to break it to me that you're getting married or something?"

Silence . . . and then more silence. My heart started beating faster with each passing second.

"Well," Dave said, "I didn't want you to find out this way, but yeah, I am getting married."

The hair on the back of my neck stood straight up and I felt my arms flush with goose bumps. Suddenly I was freezing and felt like I was going to throw up. This was more than the aftereffects of Chez Jay.

"Anyone I know?" It took a heroic effort to keep my voice steady. I couldn't believe he was doing this over the phone.

"I'm marrying Madison. You know, Madison Jasper."

I definitely knew Madison Jasper.

In an instant I flashed through everything I remembered about her. Madison was the youngest daughter of the famous Hollywood producer Morgan Jasper. He was that guy who made a fortune in the '80s and '90s making all those TV shows with shoulder pads and bad hair. I remember an *In Style* magazine at home pictorial of the family estate high above Sunset in Beverly Hills. The three Jasper daughters wore matching white dresses and Madison was glued tightly to her father's side, his arm protectively around her.

Just last month, I'd read an article in *Glamour* magazine about Madison that said she was now focusing on being an "independent film producer" and was turning several of her father's old TV series into feature films. The title of the article was "Hollywood Princess."

Dave had directed an episode of *Magnum Force* last season for Morgan, and was hoping to be asked back this year to do more. I'd seen the family sometimes in the VIP first row pew at St. Monica's for morning services.

One Sunday, Dave lingered in the lobby after morning church services, hoping to catch Morgan's eye and casually reintroduce himself. I remember Dave introducing me and the great producer's eyes locking on my breasts, hidden behind my fitted navy blazer, while he mumbled, "Nice to meet you." Dave never noticed.

The only time I'd ever met Madison, she was lingering in the church lobby after midnight mass services on Christmas Eve. One of her older sisters leaned in and whispered something in her ear as Dave and I made our way toward them. I grasped his hand in an unconscious territorial move. I saw her dramatically exhale and roll her eyes to her sister before another sibling pushed her in the small of her back to step forward and say hi. My first impression of Madison was that she wore a lot of makeup. I'm talking a full face of matte MAC. I could tell she was still using the same base that she had purchased the previous summer. Her face didn't quite match her neck.

"That was one of the cutest Christmas cards I've ever gotten," Madison said. Dave and I had sent out a card with old pictures of the two of us as kids on Santa's lap; inside the card we had a new picture of us both with Santa. It was cute, then; now it made me wince. It was the kind of card where the girl who got it would always say to her boyfriend, "Why don't you ever want to do something like this?"

I remember being surprised that Madison Jasper would have been on Dave's Christmas card list, but I shrugged it off back then, just figuring they'd met on the set sometime. Now they were getting married.

"Well, congratulations," I said, my voice artificially strong. Suddenly I pictured them together at Jon and Catherine's wedding in Mexico. He had tried to rent the Ocean View Villa for Madison. "I am a little surprised, but I guess I shouldn't be." I closed my eyes and definitely had "tears in my ears."

"I'm glad you're happy for us."

Was I that good of an actress? Did he really think I was sincere?

"I just had a really tough time rebounding from what happened with us," Dave went on. "When we broke up, I really felt like you had dragged me behind a truck. I never thought I'd be able to trust anyone again."

I could not believe he was putting the whole trust thing on me. "Umm, Earth to Dave. *You* were the one who cheated on me, so if anyone has any trust issues, I think I'd be the one."

I could hear Dave take a deep breath. "You know, I'm trying not to get all negative with this. I thought that because of what we had at one time, that we could have a conversation like adults." He was on a roll now. "I was hoping that we could be happy for each other."

"I always should have figured there was something up between you two," I said.

"Would you stop? You're not even listening to me!" Dave sounded really exasperated. "I entered therapy after we broke up. Even when I was away shooting *One Tree Hill* in South Carolina, I made the time to have a phone session once a week. Being in therapy really helped me give myself back to me."

I gripped the phone. My head was pounding relentlessly, and my right ass cheek still vibrated from my paddling last night. I was not in the best condition to be trying to grasp all this.

Dave's voice went all soft. "When I finally managed to work

through everything that had happened with us, I realized there was this amazing woman right next to me."

"Madison?" I paused. "Isn't she really young? Isn't she twenty-five or something like that?"

"Yeah, she's young, but coming from her kind of background, she seems really mature, so I don't feel like there's much of a gap."

"Yeah, I guess you would probably grow up fast with all that kind of money around you."

"It's more than just being rich . . . She's classy."

Smirking, I resisted telling Dave that the word *classy* just wasn't classy.

"So, when are you guys getting married?" I asked brightly.

"We're getting married on Valentine's Day."

"This Valentine's Day? That seems awful quick," I squawked into the phone.

"It's not quick when you're sure," he replied quietly.

I closed my eyes against the receiver. Of everything said during this conversation, this hurt the most.

"I'm sorry you're not happy for me," Dave said. "I'd be happy for you. You know I wanted a life with you." His voice started getting angrier, almost vicious. "I wanted to make a future with you, but you had to ruin everything. You always ruined every good thing. Any holiday or special occasion you always had to pick a fight." He was spitting his words into the phone. "You should really think about going into therapy."

I was too stunned to interrupt.

He was gaining momentum. "You don't have any idea what being normal is like because you're from such a fucked-up family. That's why you're so fucked-up and that's why *you* fucked *us* up."

"I am not fucked up." I wasn't angry. This conversation was draining everything out of me.

"Yeah, right. Your mom is a manic-depressive. You're the one with the dad who orders Chinese mail-order brides from a magazine. You have no idea what family is about. You have no idea of the importance of having that center."

"Dave, I'm aware that the way I grew up wasn't typical, but just because you're from a 'good Catholic family,' and you went to church on Sundays and said your prayers at night doesn't make up for the fact that you have been a world-class shit and been totally dishonest with me."

I realized I had vaulted myself off the couch and was pacing the length of my living room.

"You think you're a better person because of your religious beliefs, that you have a strong faith. But how do you explain the cheating? How do you explain your extensive porn collection hidden in your closet behind your rain boots?"

I was almost out of breath from getting all this out.

"Shut up, shut the fuck up, you are a psycho. You are a total psycho bitch!" Never in all the highs and lows of our years together had he spoken to me like this. His vehemence pushed me to cut him off.

"And you know what you are?" I shot back. "You are so not the person I ever gave you credit for being. I would probably have missed you these past months if I hadn't realized it was all fake." I was sputtering now. "There's nothing to miss when I'd been wrong the entire time. I was so, so wrong about you!"

Now he was silent. I knew that I'd wounded him, if only a little bit.

I flashed forward to the scene tonight in his bungalow, when he would kick back on his living room sofa while the fiancée brought him an ice-cold beer. He would just recount this conversation to Madison, saying how right he was about my being a psycho and no wonder he had been pushed to cheat, and how glad he was that *we* were over. Knowing what the postscript to this conversation would be only fueled me further. "I never should have given you my number that night at the airport."

Dave started to respond, but I cut him off. "I never should have believed you when you said that Chloe was 'just a friend.'" Then I went in for the kill. "And I never should have given you those seven chances before you were ever good in bed."

I placed the phone down in the receiver. I didn't slam it. I just hung up. I felt totally wiped out. He was marrying someone else and I'd said everything I needed to say.

SEVENTEEN

On Monday morning I couldn't face work. This was a first. Choosing to ignore the guilty voice in my head telling me that I was only hungover from the Chez Jay experience, I convinced myself that I must have some sort of food poisoning. I called Azita to tell her I wasn't coming in.

"I'm really sick," I told her. "Can you let Steve know? And tell him that I'm really, really sick."

"Ohmygod . . . are you okay?" she asked.

"I'm just going to stay in bed all day. Tell Steve if he needs me at all to call me at home."

"Sure thing, sweetie, and let me know if I can do anything."

Hanging up, I stared at the ceiling of my bedroom. A vein of patched drywall ran the length of my bedroom ceiling, a souvenir from the last big earthquake. If "the big one" were to happen now, I would be crushed under the falling roof and no one would come to find me.

I'd gotten no sleep the night before and now it felt good not to move. I pulled the covers over my head and stayed in bed. No one called.

The next morning, I sheepishly made my way to Steve's office. People who work on TV shows just don't call in sick, and I knew he was going to give me major shit.

"There you are!" he exclaimed brightly when he saw me lingering in his doorway. "Are you feeling better? Are you sure you're okay to come to work today?"

"Yeah, I'm feeling a little better, thanks." This wasn't the greeting I'd been expecting.

"Well, I'm glad you're here and that you're feeling better, because there's a lot going on."

"What's up?"

Steve kicked his feet up on his desk. "The network wants to bring back Assistant Number Two."

At first I thought the hangover was still clouding my ability to understand. "My Assistant Number Two? How can that be possible? We found her guilty of murder and put her away in prison."

"I know, but you know it was our highest rated show ever. They want us to figure out a way to bring her back. But there is one big problem."

"What, is the network chickening out again and having doubts about the necrophilia thing?"

"No, it's a casting problem. We can't get Jennifer Love Hewitt to do it this time."

"Really?" I asked. This was disappointing. "Was it a money thing? She was so perfect the first time around."

"I know, but she's back shooting on *Ghost Whisperer* and unavailable. But don't worry—we've got a great replacement."

I stared at him, waiting for the name.

"Chloe Johnson."

"Chloe Johnson?" A tsunami started in my head and rushed through my pores. Perspiration broke out on my upper lip. I blinked as my eyes started to well up and I grabbed the chair arm for support. "What do you mean? You're hiring Chloe Johnson?"

"She's someone the network really wants in the role, and this is coming from them."

"Well I think that's a terrible idea. She's not right at all."

"The suits are thinking of her as a Nicole Kidman type," Steve said patiently.

"She's more like a Pottery Barn Nicole Kidman. Very generic."

Steve looked surprised at my vehemence. "You know Chloe worked with Scorsese?"

"Oh that's right—I remember her playing the role of 'woman in crowd' in his last film." Normally Steve listened to me when I argued a point, but for whatever reason he was not budging on this one. "Is there some sort of history here?" he asked. "Because I don't get the huge problem with Chloe."

Looking down at my notepad, I saw I'd scribbled the word *bitch* in serial-killer handwriting several times. "The character is just very close to me and I think it's understandable that I would take a big interest."

"Listen, I don't know what to say. The first time around it was such a beautifully written role, and I think you should be glad someone of Chloe's caliber would want to play Assistant Number Two."

"Her caliber? She's twenty-eight. She's too young to have caliber. I'd say she's just a step behind Lindsay Lohan." None of this was making sense. "Forgive me, Steve, but could you please 'play it blond' for me and explain again why we're bringing back Assistant Number Two?" I was speaking very carefully, enunciating every word. "We found her guilty of murder and put her behind bars. What are we supposed to do, have some of the cast from *Prison Break* switch networks and help her escape her cell?"

"Dani, I get it," Steve said, "but the Assistant Number Two character keeps coming up on the testing cards with focus groups. We're thinking of doing a new two-part episode. We'll reveal that she was wrongly convicted, that someone planted evidence to implicate her in the murder, and now she's going to get her justice and be freed from prison."

"I'm still not sure it makes sense," I said slowly.

"It makes sense in TV Land. Enough said. Remember when JR got shot on *Dallas*? It ended up being Pam's bad dream, and the audience still watched—they love going along for the ride."

I was speechless. I could tell Steve hated my sour expression.

"Listen, Dani, it's been decided. I've already got postproduction working on this whole thing. We just have to edit out Jennifer Love Hewitt in a few of the scenes from the previous show, and then we drop in the same material re-shot with Chloe. It's all going to edit together smoothly. The Room is working on an outline and some new pages for tomorrow."

"You're having the Room work on Assistant Number Two?" I asked, feeling territorial. After all, Assistant Number Two was based on me, and the show was the first I'd earned sole credit for. "I call in sick for one day, and all this shit hits the fan?"

"Dani, I suggest you get over this, because Chloe is over in wardrobe having a fitting at this very moment."

Chloe was on the actual premises. Grinning tightly, I stood to leave. "I guess I have a lot of work to do and should get on it."

I was almost through the door when Steve called my name. I turned around. "Oh, and because she's going to be featured on the show in such a big way, we have to give her a name. No more Assistant Number Two."

I waited.

"Her name is Doheny. Kind of an exotic version of Dani, don't you think? If you want, we can call her Doheny Hale as a tribute to you." Steve came around the desk to give my shoulder a squeeze. "After all, Assistant Number Two is all Dani Hale." He squeezed my shoulder again for emphasis, pleased with himself for smoothing his writer's ruffled fur.

"Great." I smiled brightly with dead eyes.

After spending hours trying to scheme a way for Assistant Number Two to get out of jail free, I left work as soon as I could. My head hurt, and the episode in Troy's Range Rover, the hangover, Dave's Hollywood Princess, and the return of Chloe were all too much to have to handle in a seventy-two-hour period. I started to drive around aimlessly, and wound up in front of Pinkberry Yogurt. Mercifully, they were opening in ten minutes, and I ordered the biggest size and inhaled the giant cup alone at one of their plastic tables. I ordered a second cup on the way out.

I thought of calling Lauren or Ina to go through all this and see what they thought my next move should be. I decided not to call anyone. I went home to sleep.

The next day at work, I tried to be invisible, a white dot on a white wall. Ina called to see if I could meet up for a girl talk later.

"It's not really a good time," I told her. Thank God we didn't have videophones. If she could have seen the mess that I was, unshowered, with hopelessly unruly hair, slightly smeared mascara, and a half-eaten PayDay bar on my desk, there would be no way she would let me get out of a girl talk.

"Is something wrong?" she asked.

"Everything. To start, Dave is getting married," I quietly wailed into the receiver.

"Yeah, I heard," she answered

"You *heard*? How could you not have told me?" I practically yelled into the phone. "When did you find out? When did this happen exactly?"

"I just heard. It's not like I've been carrying it around for weeks. I thought we could talk about it tonight."

"Well, I can't. Things are too crazy at work right now. I can't believe you knew this and didn't call immediately to tell me."

"I'm trying not to be such a Frenemy, as you've called me in the past," she said, with a real resentful edge in her voice. "They're already registered on that wedding site TheKnot.com."

"They're registered?" The idea that Dave and Madison were registered made their getting married seem glaringly real.

"You can check it out if you want." I could hear the shoulder shrug in her voice. Ina *was* a Frenemy most of the time.

I was listening to Ina tell me it wasn't so bad, that it was good riddance, and that Larry had gotten a real, temporary job, but my fingers were flying across the keyboard, navigating to the wedding registry site. I had no idea about this concept of registering online. Sure, I'd gone into a Macy's to buy a gift for somebody's wedding, but I would never dare stalk someone by doing that. The thought of navigating parking at the Beverly Center, taking the escalator up to the store, and then seeking out a sales clerk to look up the registry with no intention of buying a gift—that seemed desperate and pathetic.

Knowing that I could just access a couple's registry from my desk computer was sheer opportunity, however. I saw you could register at several different places and have them all managed by TheKnot.com main server. They had everything from Williams-Sonoma to Pottery Barn. The automated site prompted me for the groom's name, and after entering "David Gallagher" and clicking the return key, I saw everything. Dave Gallagher and Madison Jasper, February 14th of next year.

They'd registered for terrible bedding from Calvin Klein. I thought I had seen the comforter set on an episode of *The Hills* last season on MTV. One of those bimbette girls on the show had these same linens in her bedroom. This was obviously the young bride's choice. Scrolling down to the appliance choices, I saw they'd also asked for a Delonghi Magnifica cappuccino maker.

"You shithead," I said to the computer screen. Dave hated coffee and had bought me the small coffee press for the nights I stayed over; he'd never entertain the idea of a cappuccino machine when I'd mentioned it, and now the loser was registering for an expensive Delonghi cappuccino maker. The slights never stopped.

I felt my adrenaline surge through me, and my heart started pounding furiously—I looked down and swore I could see my T-shirt on my left side pump up and down. Could the stress of everything going on in my life trigger a heart attack? Choosing to ignore it, I continued to click through the future inventory for the couple's happy life.

"Ina, I'm being called into a meeting. I've got to go." I hung up on her before she could even sputter a good-bye.

Asparagus steamer, ironing board, and Jenga board game from Bed Bath & Beyond. Twelve glass beer mugs. Had Dave started some sort of weekly poker night? Towels and more towels. They'd registered for complete sets in four different colors. Why would two people need so many towels? Remembering Dave's minuscule three-quarters bath at his place, I wondered where they'd even store so many towels.

Just as a goof I maneuvered through the pages and chose a simple crystal bud vase. Under "quantity" they'd asked for two of them. Checking off a single bud vase, I dragged the cursor to the "complete sale" button and clicked. It took a second for the "complete sale" page to launch, where I could enter in my credit card information and select a shipping option. There was no way I was going to buy Dave and Madison a bud vase, but suddenly I noticed the shipping information.

The new couple wanted their gifts shipped to an address on Bonnie Hill Drive. This wasn't Dave's address. I had no idea where she lived, but I was guessing she was an apartment dweller, not a home-owner, and Bonnie Hill Drive was all houses in the hills.

I grabbed a Post-it and scrawled the exact address. I mentally Mapquested the route and figured I could get there in about eleven minutes from work. I checked the clock. It was close enough to lunch to sneak out of the office. Hell, I didn't even have to bother sneaking; I'd eaten enough takeout at my desk to not get any grief for leaving for once. I headed for my car.

Taking the freeway up and over the hill to Hollywood would be best, I decided. The heat from the BMW's black leather seats sealed my cotton skirt to my thighs and reminded me of how that creep Troy Zarcoff had left my ass stinging Saturday night. My hands tightly gripped the wheel; I ignored the perspiration on my forehead and chin I saw in my rearview mirror reflection. I was on a mission.

It was midday, so there wasn't a lot of traffic on the freeway. Exiting Gower, I made the first left and then a quick right. The Scientology Center whizzed by. I knew Bonnie Hill was off Bronson, which meant the house probably had a killer view. Shit. I could feel my stomach turning acidic with the remnants of my late morning latte.

I almost missed the turn; the street sign was partially hidden by some overgrown foliage. Taking the turn, my car had to shift into a lower gear to accommodate the steep street. The painted curb numbers guided me higher, with some of the turns so sharp that I thought that this wasn't a street you'd want to navigate after having a couple of glasses of wine.

I felt I had almost reached the Hollywood sign when I finally spotted the address. I stopped the car and rolled down my window to get a look.

It was so much worse than I'd imagined.

A Sotheby's Realty SOLD sign was mounted to the front wooden door. The property wasn't gated, thank God, but a cream stucco wall ran the length of the property, shielding the home from view. The heavy Moorish door let me know this was a Spanish house, and my guesstimate on the dimensions of the property let me know the house was big, four bedrooms at least, and that, yes, they had a killer view.

Motherfucker.

This was my dream house.

It had been my dream home before they had found this place and bought it. I had talked constantly about this kind of house to Dave. He would never have thought to buy a place like this. Staring at the potted flowers on the walkway, I imagined the conversation the two of them would have had about buying a house, how they'd agreed on it, hired a Realtor, toured homes. Knowing as I did Dave's thirst for always scoring "a deal," they wouldn't have simply put an offer on the first home they saw. No, this took time. I went through the calendar in my head and marveled at how quickly this relationship had developed. They'd gone from first date to escrow in five months. I couldn't fucking believe this!

My knuckles were white as they gripped the wheel. I jerked the car around, banged a big green garbage can, and headed down the hill. Furious, I wondered how this was possible. I'd never seen this property listed in the normal Sunday open house guide.

I decided to skip the freeway and take Cahuenga back over the hill to the office. Taking the potholes hard somehow felt good as I seethed.

I slung my bag on my desk, reached for the computer, and punched in Zillow.com. I should have done this before heading over there—at least I would have been a little prepared for the shock of their house. Zillow was one of my great finds for peeking over the neighbor's fence. You could punch in any address in the US and through a database of public records pull up the purchase price of the house from over the years. I loved seeing what the nouveau riche overpaid for their trophy pads. I'd had no guilt when I came back from

Lauren's and looked to see what she'd paid for her new house ($1.8 million!).

Punching in Dave's new address, I only had to wait a few seconds to see that the house was currently in escrow for $3.3 million. All the air and energy went out of me. I leaned back from the computer. After all the open homes I'd gone to with Dave, after all the combined-income calculations I'd come up with, Dave and the Hollywood Princess had paid a price higher than I'd ever even hoped for. I'm sure they were buying the place with a little help from her dad.

Dave was getting married. He and I had circled the topic a few times and I'd had my seventh-inning-at-the-Dodgers hopes; I always counted on it happening. A year ago, I'd secretly purchased two bridal magazines, leafing through them covertly behind a closed bathroom door like an eleven-year-old with his first *Penthouse*. My greedy eyes soaked up the Vera Wang gowns and Ascher cut diamond rings. I'd imagined what the weight of the ring would feel like on my finger, and, knowing the bathroom door was locked, I'd delicately hold my hand against the page.

I was so lost in my misery I didn't realize my phone had been ringing.

"It's Dani," I answered.

"It's Azita," Azita mimicked back to me. She was always so up and lively. If only she could bottle and sell all that happiness, I'd buy a case. "Hey, boss lady, Steve wants to know if you can come into the Room to work with the guys on some of the new stuff for Assistant Number Two, I mean 'Doheny.' Production is hoping to come up with some sort of a shooting schedule."

Cradling the phone between by shoulder and ear, I closed out Zillow on my computer screen. Opening my work file for the episode, I scanned through to the new scenes. "Tell Steve I'm on my way."

"Sure thing, boss lady." Azita hung up.

Closing my eyes, I took in a few deep breaths, trying to calm my anxiety. I needed to clear my mind of Dave so that I could focus on writing for Chloe. I grabbed my notebook and headed for the Room.

Shooting continued on the episode with Chloe, and I tried to disappear.

Up until now, I hadn't usually worn any makeup to work. After all, my day consisted mostly of sitting in my office alone, and I didn't have to impress anyone. But now, I found myself spending some extra time in front of the mirror, carefully lining and concealing myself.

Troy hadn't called, and I didn't really want to hear from him, even if he did have an apology or an explanation for his behavior in the Range Rover. I sat behind closed doors in my office, polishing the pages for Assistant Number Two, a.k.a. Doheny Hale—grrrrr—and working on story lines for the following episode. I avoided going to set. But when I got up on Thursday, I knew what I had to do. I was going to have to confront this for myself. I couldn't go on like this.

I was bent over my laptop when Azita knocked and then opened the door. "Hey, Steve just called and he was wondering if you could come down to set? There's something going on with the pages . . . I think there's a problem."

This was my chance. With more bravado than I felt, I walked onto set, but hung in the back. They had built the crime scene set entirely onstage. Midcentury furniture, gray suede couches with throws—it epitomized what a rock star's home might look like. The only thing different here was the bloodstain on the rug, from where "Norma Jean's" body had been found. The scene was supposed to match what we shot the first time around, but now with Chloe playing the role instead of Love. We'd feature this flashback while Chloe explained her side of the story to the investigators.

OFFICER
So can you tell us exactly how the body was
when you found it?

DOHENY
She was on her side, her head was up here (she ges-
tures off camera) and her knees were a little bent.

OFFICER
Then those aren't your bloody footprints around the
body? You said earlier that you saw she was dead
from a distance. If that's so, where did all the
bloody footprints come from?

For her big moment Chloe bit her lip nervously, employing an Angelina Jolie bit of business in her acting.

DOHENY
Well, maybe I did go in close when I was checking
on her. I was really in shock so I'm not really sure
what I did.

Our director, Mick Gage, was a veteran of these kinds of shows.
He knew how to move along quickly on these heavy shoot days. Most
days we shot ten pages of script, whereas a movie shoots two or three.
Mick watched a monitor intently as the steadicam operator swung
around and was now tight on Chloe's face. I moved up to see the
monitor more closely myself.

There she was. I had actually dreamed about her face. I saw her
face wherever I went. In the doctor's waiting room, I saw her reading an old issue of *Redbook*. I saw her sitting in front of the Coffee
Bean on Sunset, and strolling down Larchmont. But when I'd look

again or double back to see if it was really her, it was just some pale and freckled chick. But there was no mistake today. Here she was in the flesh, all freckle-faced with "amazing eyes." Mick must have thought they were amazing, too, because he was shooting her tight, just as Dave had done.

"Cut!" Mick yelled. "That's great, everybody. We're going to break for lunch now, and we'll all be back here in an hour for scene thirty-three."

Chloe had been crouching with the two detectives, but after Mick's cue she stood and started doing some sort of yoga asana to loosen up the tight muscles. I stood observing her. I thought maybe I would see her do "the thing," whatever special thing that made Dave decide that blowing it with me was incidental.

Steve roused me from my staring. "Hey, Dani, come here." He was gesturing for me to come over for an introduction to Chloe. This should be good, I thought. I wasn't nervous anymore. I felt like I was in that scene in *Gladiator* where Russell Crowe turns around and surprises Joaquin Phoenix, who thought he was dead.

"And here's the person who you have to thank for the lovely words . . . Dani Hale." Steve patted me on the back.

Chloe reached her hand toward me and broke into a smile.

I had never seen her smile, and it lit up her face. We were shaking hands and she was actually talking to me. "Dani, it's so nice to meet you," she was saying. "I love the material."

We were shaking hands and her little hand was cool in mine. She was pretending she had never seen me before, never sent me Dave's photo of her freckled breast. *So we're going to play it that way*, I thought. I could be cool, too. "It's so nice to meet you, *finally*."

We stopped shaking and she asked me something else, but I couldn't concentrate on her.

"You're joining us for lunch, aren't you?" she asked as she turned with Steve and headed toward the craft service table. "I'm famished, as usual," she said, holding her stomach and smiling up at Steve. I noticed he was smiling back. "I'm just one of those people who eats and eats and fortunately doesn't gain any weight," she said.

I knew I was totally invisible as they started to move away.

"Sorry I can't join you," I called after them. "I'm doing only raw food this week and I brought my lunch in with me. Plus, I have a lot of work to do on the show." I quickly turned and headed off the set, banging open the exit door as I booked out of there.

I knew the two of them had never looked back. I was invisible.

She was playing it like she didn't know me, and I couldn't force the issue because she was working on my show, and her success ensured my success. I felt like the bat had been totally taken out of my hands.

I had been all ready for a fight; I had done the play-by-play in my head.

DANI
Don't you have anything you'd like to say to me?

CHLOE
Listen, I'm really sorry, Dani, I was really out of line.
I threw myself at Dave—I practically put his hand
down my pants myself. We'd been drinking,
and one thing led to another . . .

DANI
Well, I hope you used a condom. Dave sleeps around
more than a rabid coyote, and you never know what
he may have crawling around down there.

For months I'd thought of the attack and comeback I would have for both Dave and Chloe, and now that she was here in front of me,

I was dismissed like a mosquito that had already been swatted out of sight.

Not trusting my emotions, instead of going back to the office I headed for the sanctuary of wardrobe. I could gossip with Nicole, who handled all the costumes for the show. She usually had a fresh-baked batch of cookies or brownies wrapped in tinfoil on her desk, perfect medicine for my dark mood.

"Hey," I greeted her, ducking into the double-wide trailer and settling myself on one of the beaded sari cushions that littered the floor next to the racks of clothes.

"Hey, Dani, how are you?" Nicole acted as if it were totally normal for me to drop by wardrobe in the middle of the afternoon. I had interrupted her in the process of steaming costumes on a long metal wardrobe rack. Nicole was waving the steamer with authority over cranky linen and cotton. The steam was making curls spring up around her face, something that would drive most women nuts, but not Nicole. She was working that whole bohemian-chic thing with her look. No professional blow out in a salon for this girl.

"Any brownies?" I asked. There was no need to bullshit with Nicole.

"That good?" she asked, pointing to the lumpy tinfoil package on her desk.

I carefully peeled open the corner, and the aroma of double chocolate brownies instantly soothed me. "How do you bake every night and yet people on the show all still fit into their clothes?"

"I don't give any to the actors. I just bake for people I like." She smiled.

"Lucky me," I said passionately, shoving a second microbrownie into my mouth. "What's up?" I asked. I hadn't been to visit in a couple of weeks. Nicole always knew everyone's bad news. I loved it.

Nicole distractedly moved hangers between racks for the show's different talent. "*She's* with Steve."

"*She* is?" I didn't need to play the who-are-we-talking-about game. Life had a way of fucking with you. I was definitely going to need that third microbrownie.

"You didn't know?"

"No," I answered, stunned. "I hadn't heard that. I thought *she* was a favorite of Les Moonves."

"No, *she's* been Miss-Exclusive-with-Steve for a while now, at least a couple of months, which is obviously a big deal for him."

Danger alarms were going off in my head, but I knew better than to give Nicole an idea that any of this news mattered to me. I tried changing the subject. "What are you working on?"

"This is the dress for the party scene for Doheny that they're shooting tomorrow," Nicole said.

I eyed the black sheath and reached out to touch the material, although I didn't have to touch it to know it was expensive.

"Narciso." Nicole exhaled the name with reverence over my shoulder.

"That's not our usual budget," I remarked.

"No, but Chloe brought in a picture from a magazine. She thought this was the dress that she should wear for the party, and it's not like the boss is going to say no."

"That's for sure." I said. I couldn't take my eyes off the black sheath on the black velvet hanger.

Nicole had an official-looking pincushion thing on her wrist and was actually starting to apply a needle and thread to the magical black sheath.

"You do the alterations by hand?"

"Yeah," she said, folding the side seam with her two fingers. Nicole carefully punctured the black material with the needle. "Just a couple of well placed stitches will pull in the bust to make the bodice really snug."

"The dress looks tiny, but *she* has boobs." I was stating the obvious, and I couldn't help think of Chloe's freckled breast from the photo.

"Of course *she* does," Nicole answered.

"I guess they all *have* boobs. God doesn't really make size-zero women with size 36C bustlines, right? Well, except for Angelina Jolie."

Nicole bit off the thread to tie off the stitches. She smiled at me sympathetically. "Oh, darling, *especially* Angelina Jolie."

"Hey, what does that mean?" I begged, intrigued.

"Just think about it, my dear." Nicole quickly finished with her stitches, and started to leave with the dress.

"Where are you going?" I asked, still wanting to get to the bottom of her Angelina comment.

"They need this right after lunch. They're shooting the party scene next, and then they're finishing the rest of the party shoot in the morning."

"You're just going to leave me here? Alone? Do I need to lock up?"

"No, we keep it unlocked. Security comes by after we're all through and closes up everything for the night, but that's not till ten or eleven. Bye." She winked at me.

"Okay, bye."

I finally trudged back to my office. Azita had left me a note on my desk that my mom had called. I crumpled it into a ball and threw it in the trash.

Glaring at my computer screen, I tried to focus; there was still a lot of work to get done. The episode I was working on was entitled "Smells like Murder." A man is found dead and all leads point to a disgruntled business partner, but during the autopsy Maggie discovers his entire body is covered in a milky residue. After evaluation and testing, she discovers that it's antiperspirant. The victim had a problem with sweating through his clothes, and he knew he was going to a very volatile meeting with the business partner. He decided to cover his entire body with a thick coating of an antiperspirant and when he started to sweat, the toxins couldn't escape and he literally poisoned himself to death. The episode had a hook, but the network usually liked a little more action. A memo had come down from upstairs asking for "a little more blood" in the show.

"Bad time?"

I looked up and saw Rich waiting in my doorway.

"No, just figuring out how to write about a guy's BO," I replied.

"What?" He looked confused.

"Oh, it's nothing. I'm just a little slappy from too much caffeine. What's up?"

Rich seemed nonplussed; we'd been here before.

"You wanted to talk to me, remember? About the interrogation scene you're working on."

"Oh yeah," I had forgotten. All the Chloe drama had made me space about everything. "Sorry, Rich, can we talk tomorrow? I'm just kind of slammed now."

Rich held still in my doorway. He hadn't actually stepped into my office, but I hadn't invited him in either. "Sure, no problem, Dani."

But he remained at the threshold, watching me. "Bye, Rich." I said dismissively, turning back to my computer.

"Have a good night, Dani," Rich said, not moving.

I didn't know how long he stood there; I never glanced back to the doorway.

The light faded in my office, and the staff peeled away to go home to their families. I was fine staying late.

Tired and depressed, I headed out of the office into the deserted soundstages. When shooting wrapped, everyone cleared out of the soundstage and headed home pronto. The crew worked hard enough with their long hours; there was no extra credit for staying late. I passed the dark row of dressing rooms and trailers, stopping short when I realized I was in front of Nicole's wardrobe trailer. She had told me the doors remained unlocked until security came around late and sealed everything up. I hesitated at the door and checked to see if anyone was watching. The street was deserted. I cautiously reached for the door, and the handle turned in my hand and the door swung outward. I checked again to see if the coast was clear before stepping inside. Nicole wasn't the only one who knew how to use a needle and thread.

The next morning, I weaved my way between the desks toward my office, keeping on my shades to shield my bloodshot eyes from the staff. This was one of those mornings where I woke up and got out of bed, and my face would wake up a couple of hours later.

Azita waved to me from the far side of the office when I got close. "Hey, *mama, perfect timing.* I got a call for you."

"Okay, put it in my office." I felt a little overstimulated; I wasn't even at my desk and I was being hit with someone who wanted something from me.

"Hello, it's Dani."

"Hey, beautiful." It was JP, so I exhaled, relieved. He'd make me laugh and get the day off on the right foot. "How you doing?"

"I'm great, JP. What's up?"

"Well, I'm calling on behalf of my buddy Jay."

"Yeah?" I had no idea where he was going with this.

"Jay called to say that Troy called him and that Troy gave him the green light."

"What green light?" I asked.

"Yeah, I guess things weren't working out with you guys, and so Troy gave him the green light that he could make his move."

I was speechless. Jay got the news that Troy and I weren't working out. I wished I had gotten that message. I was still processing the spanking. Troy had finally sent me a text message last night explaining that he had been busy at work.

"So Jay is cool having Troy's sloppy seconds?" I felt the fight rising in me.

"No, it's not like that. C'mon Dani, you know how it is. Jay thinks you're hot and wants to call you up."

Cradling the phone between my shoulder and ear I stared a hole into the wall, furious.

"Just tell him I'm giving him the red light, okay?" I slammed the phone down. Fuck Jay, fuck JP, and fuck Troy. The whole thing was so very high school.

Defeated, I laid my head down on my desk and closed my eyes. It all seemed very RFK/JFK to me. Didn't the brothers pass Marilyn between them? John tired of Marilyn and handed her off to Bobby. Jackie was not pleased about all the attention Marilyn attracted after singing her breathy "Happy Birthday" to the president. Marilyn's phone records from the night she died were "lost" by the phone company, so there was no record of whom Marilyn spoke to on her last day. Depending on whom you talk to, they say Marilyn spoke with either Bobby or John on the phone that afternoon; one of them may even have come to the house that night.

Things weren't supposed to be like this.

I was still slumped over my pile of papers when Steve buzzed me in my office. This was strange. He never called me; he'd just yell for me or stick his head in my office door.

"Hi, Dani, can you come in here for a second?"

"Sure," I replied. What now? This was shaping up to be a tough day.

I closed his office door behind me and sat ramrod straight in the chair across from his desk. He looked a bit cockier and smugger than I'd ever seen him. Something was definitely brewing with him.

"Okay," I prompted.

"Well, I've got news and it's actually something I'm really excited about and I hope you will be as well."

I gazed at him, waiting for him to go on.

"The network wants to make Chloe a series regular."

"What?" I practically choked it out, trying to make it sound like a laugh. "That's impossible. Steve, I told you I had reservations about this whole idea of her being exonerated for murdering Norma Jean. I already think we're asking for a lot from the audience. To totally exonerate and make her a series regular is just too unbelievable."

Steve cut me off. "Dani, this is what we're *going* to do. Assistant Number Two is going to be grateful to Maggie and everyone in the lab for 'doing the right thing' and letting justice prevail to get her out. The character is a Hollywood insider, so it will make sense that she'll help the team out occasionally. Now do you understand?"

"And she comes to work at the lab?"

"Dani, what can I say? This is coming directly from Les." He shrugged, but as he talked I remembered he was discussing an actress who was also his latest girlfriend. "The thinking is that she's going to be a big star, and they want to try to latch on to her now, and you never know, the way they've been pushing this thing, they could be thinking spin-off." He grinned at me. "You've been such a big part in the success of *Flesh and Bone* that I wouldn't be surprised if they did spin-off this character into her own new series, and that you could be the show runner. Chloe's show could be *your* show."

How could I even start? "Wow, that's big" was the only reply I had for him.

Steve got up, came around his desk, and sat right next to me. "It's bigger than big—this is amazing news. You should be thrilled. I'm very proud of you." He trailed off and noticed that I was a little dazed. "Are you okay?"

"I'm okay," I said softly. I looked down and realized I was clenching my hands very tightly. "I guess I'm just a little shocked about all this. You're right, it is big news."

"If this works out right, you and Chloe could be working together for a very long time."

Azita interrupted us. "Steve, they need you on set right away . . . some kind of emergency with Chloe."

"Oh, really?" He looked instantly alert and worried. I was observing him *very* closely. "Did they say what's up?"

Azita obviously didn't know that Chloe and Steve were together, because she rolled her eyes. "Some actress drama. Her dress that fit yesterday is all of a sudden too tight this morning. I guess she thinks she gained ten pounds overnight, and she needs the big Executive Producer to come hold her hand."

Steve looked a little less concerned, but he grabbed his Black-Berry, ready to trot over to the stage to console Chloe. He turned to me absentmindedly. "You know, I think you should plan on getting out of here early today." He squeezed my shoulders, signaling we were done and that I should be happy. "You deserve it . . . smile!" He headed off to Chloe's aid.

I smiled huge, and with my Stepford grin frozen on my face, I turned to leave. Exiting Steve's office, I practically ran into Evil Janet hovering outside his door. She'd positioned herself in such a way that I had to brush against her to get by. What a freak.

EIGHTEEN

I didn't leave early; I worked until the light faded in my office and it got quiet outside my door, letting me know that people had headed home to start their weekend.

My phone rang and it was Ina, inviting me to come over for a last-minute barbecue.

"Hey, thanks, but I'm just not up to it tonight. There's a lot going on at work, and I'm just going to eat here tonight."

"Give me a break, Dani. You've got to get out of there and mingle. We've invited a bunch of guys from Larry's acting class over. These guys are *hot*."

"No murderers?" I asked.

"Are you ever going to let that go? Garrett's a great guy. Everyone is allowed to make mistakes. You should be a little kinder with your heart."

Ina truly was unbelievable. "I have a kind heart. Look, thanks for the invite, and the concern, but I'm doing okay. You don't have to worry about me."

"Well, I do worry. What are you going to do with yourself again this weekend? I mean, think about it—even Marilyn Monroe killed herself on a Saturday night."

"What?" I asked.

"You know—even the most beautiful, successful actress in the world killed herself over a lonely Saturday night. We're just worried about you, with the news about Dave getting married and everything."

"Marilyn didn't kill herself. It may have been ruled a suicide by Thomas Noguchi, the coroner, but there's enough evidence today that raises questions about whether it was a suicide or not."

"That's not true, Dani," Ina said. "I just watched this documentary on the Discovery Channel where they say Marilyn had tried to commit suicide four times before. It was just that she was finally able to pull it off that time."

I grimaced into the phone. I was glad Ina could set me straight about Marilyn, *finally*. "Why are you bringing Marilyn into this?"

"Being this alone isn't good for anyone, and breakups can be devastating. We worry about you not moving on after Dave."

"Who's 'we'?"

"You know, me, Lauren . . . Larry."

I closed my eyes and tried to do my anxiety breathing. This was almost as bad as talking to my mom. I ran my free hand across my face, and something flicked off my chin, landing lightly on my desk. It was just a tiny piece of something, but there was enough to get my attention. Distracted from Ina's rambling, I inched my face closer to the desktop, curious.

"That's weird," I said.

"What's weird?" Ina asked.

Ina's voice drew my attention back to the phone I was still holding, and I saw it . . . goo.

More specifically, it wasn't goo; it was someone's snot.

Someone had blown their nose and wiped the mucus all over my phone. I was beyond repulsed. I could see that the yellowish smear was firmly lodged in the tiny holes of the phone mouthpiece. I'd been on and off the phone all afternoon, tightly cradling the receiver against my face.

Flinging the phone onto my desk, I furiously slapped and pawed my face, panicked that more of it was on me, infecting me with germs.

Grabbing a handful of tissue from the Kleenex box on my desk, I grimaced as I thoroughly wiped the phone receiver down. Holding the tissue between my thumb and forefinger, I threw it into the trash as if it were a live grenade. I was going to have to go home and take one of those long, hot showers to try and wash all this away. Kind of like the shower the characters take in one of those Lifetime movies after something really bad has happened to them.

Who would have done such a gross thing? Chloe came to mind first, but I knew there was no way she would sneak in here and get her fingers dirty doing something like this. Sending me the anonymous picture of her breast in the mail was more her style. The only person evil enough to mess with me like this was Evil Janet.

I needed some sort of antiseptic. I frantically rummaged through my desk drawers looking for some kind of Handi Wipe, but there was nothing.

Totally grossed out, I looked helplessly around the office. I didn't want to have to call in Azita to rescue me. Moving to the bookshelf, I spotted the "Junior Detective Kit" Steve had given all the writers as a gag gift at the beginning of the season. The packaging proclaimed it to be safe for "twelve years and up" and said it was "packed with everything you need to gather clues and nab the suspect!"

Opening up the box I removed the rubbing alcohol, tweezers,

and plastic Baggies for evidence. Moving around to the trash can, I removed the balled-up dirty tissues and placed them in the plastic Baggie. I bet Bobby Kucerak down at the coroner's office could get someone in the lab to run some sort of DNA test for me. If I could prove Evil Janet did this, I bet I could get her fired—I mean, this had to be some sort of harassment or something.

Dousing more Kleenex in alcohol, I scoured my phone and desk, grinding the bits of wet Kleenex into the small holes in the phone receiver. The phone was wet, but it wasn't good enough. I had a better idea.

Removing the entire spiral phone cord, I sneaked into the hall and switched it out for Azita's. I had cleaned it up fine and she'd never know, and I would just feel better moving forward. I'd be sure to bring her a Starbucks on Monday.

Back in my office, I was going over the keypad with the rubbing alcohol once again, just in case.

The red phone light lit up with an incoming call. I pressed the speakerphone button and yelled into the receiver, "It's Dani."

"What happened? It sounded like you threw the phone down or something, and then we got disconnected," Ina asked.

"Sorry, I just dropped the phone . . . everything's cool."

"Whatever. But I still want you to come over."

I mopped down my desk again with the damp tissue. Now my office smelled like a hospital. "Ina, you're very sweet, but I'm okay. Actually I'm going to get a drink with Rachel from work in a bit, so you don't have to worry."

"You could bring Rachel to the barbecue," Ina offered. The speakerphone made her sound like she was calling from an airplane.

"She doesn't eat meat," I told her distractedly, "and anyway, she's got some stuff she says she needs a little one-on-one time with me to unload. But thanks—have a great night."

Ina wouldn't let me off until I promised to meet her for a late lunch the next day. I didn't particularly want to, but I had a feeling I'd feel better on Saturday.

Even Marilyn Monroe killed herself on a Saturday night.

It was almost nine; I gathered my things from around my desk, moving to go home. The night breeze on my face felt good as I made my way out to the parking lot. My hand firmly gripped the rich buttery leather of my Balenciaga purse. All the stores in Beverly Hills had been sold out of this bag, but I'd purchased it on eBay last week. It had been a gift to myself. With the holidays on the horizon, I knew there would be more "gifts to myself"—no one else would be buying me presents. I had a vision of myself struggling to bring the Christmas tree in the house alone.

In my purse were the plastic Baggies and a copy of the confidential crew list. Once in my car, I scanned the list for Chloe's name and address.

I saw she lived on Hollyridge, up in Beachwood Canyon, pretty close to Dave's house. I thought of her cherry red Mercedes parked in his driveway that night—she easily could have walked there instead. I wondered what would have happened that night if I had driven by and there'd been no red Mercedes. Would Dave have come over to my place with flowers and Christmas lights? Would we have bought the combined-income house? If her car hadn't been there, I wouldn't have had to have all the awkward dates and fix ups over these last few months.

Driving back into Hollywood, I took Franklin the short distance to Beachwood. The guidance system in my car told me when to turn left and when I would reach the address.

I followed Hollyridge Drive all the way up, winding my way carefully through the small streets and parked cars. I stopped in front of 2430 Hollyridge Drive and then decided to pull up a bit so I was a couple of houses up from her place.

I could see she had a high wood fence around her property. It was probably a security thing; I guessed her business managers and agents told her it would be dangerous for someone of her star-on-the-rise stature to be left exposed to the street.

I walked past the garage that housed the cherry red Mercedes and pressed the intercom buzzer. I waited.

"Hallo?" It was her.

"Hallo," I mimicked back. "Um, delivery from *Flesh and Bone*."

"Oh, okay . . ." She buzzed the door open and I quickly pushed through it, letting it close softly behind me.

A small courtyard led up to her front door. I could see the lights were on throughout her place. She must be tired, I thought; it had been a long week and she had worked really hard on the show.

Chloe opened the front door, expecting me to be the usual delivery person with new pages and script changes for the next week. But I knew there were no pages coming tonight. Steve was meeting with our director, Mick, right now, going over the rest of the schedule and seeing if anything additional needed to be written. Any new pages weren't going to be delivered until Sunday afternoon.

"Hi, Chloe." My greeting was friendly, nonthreatening.

"Who is it there?" she called out. She seemed a little taken aback that I was not a messenger.

"It's Dani, Dani Hale from the show."

"Ohhh, Dani . . ." she trailed off. I could tell she was confused and racking her brain as to why I was standing in her courtyard, inside her security fence. "Do you want to come in?" she asked, trying to be polite. She was wearing just her robe and slippers.

"Sure."

She opened the door wide for me to enter. I stepped into her house and surveyed the living room. An antiquey-looking umbrella stand (memories of Merry Old England). Overstuffed slipcovered sofas in some sort of floral fabric. The tabletops were filled with framed photos. I could make out one of Chloe in a bikini with a good-looking guy and older-looking photos of a smiling redheaded girl dressed in her Sunday best.

Behind the far sofa sat a baby grand piano. It figured that she would play. I'm sure she'd had a private tutor come to the house when she was a kid. I bet Chloe had had a piano recital that her loving parents attended, clapping proudly from the back of the room. My family couldn't afford a piano. I'd played the clarinet, and it had gone back to the instrument rental place after three months.

"I think I know why you're here," Chloe began. "Oh, how rude of me—sit down, I'll be right back."

She left me in the living room, and I heard the sound of a refrigerator opening and closing, so I figured she was in the kitchen. "Here . . . let's open some wine before we get into all this."

"Sure," I said. I watched as she poured us both healthy glasses of pink rosé.

"I love rosé wine, don't you?" she said, handing me my glass. "I was first introduced to it a few years ago in Cannes, and now I buy it by the case." Chloe took her glass and folded her legs up under her on the couch across from me. She waited for me to start.

"I'm curious, Chloe. Why do you think I came over here?"

"Well, I figure it has to do with expanding my role. The network wants to make me a series regular, with the possibility of the new show."

"I hadn't realized the news would have made its way to you yet."

"Steve told me. I'm sure you know we're friends." She smiled.

"I know about you and Steve," I replied.

There was an awkward pause as we looked at each other and sipped our wine. Even though I had scripted this entire exchange in my head on the drive over, I was faltering when it actually came to getting the words out.

I decided to push ahead. "I'm not here because of your expanded role on the show or anything having to do with work. I'm here because of Dave, Dave Gallagher."

"Ahhh, Dave, what a sweetie," Chloe said, sitting up straighter. She shook a well-manicured finger at me. "Please tell me you're not still pining for Dave?"

"I'm over Dave," I said.

"Well, it would be a shame if you were still hung up on him, because I hear he's getting married."

Chloe sipped her wine and smiled across the rim at me. She was actually enjoying this.

"I know he's getting married," I said.

She was infuriating, so relaxed on her couch, content to tease me and let me drink her wine. I was just a big joke to her.

"Chloe, don't you think you owe me something? An explanation? An apology?"

Chloe blinked her eyes twice. "Dave was a great guy, but he was just a little too possessive. I'm sure you know what I mean."

I didn't know what she meant. Besides his remarks about Steve, Dave had always told me that he didn't have a jealous bone in his body.

I pushed forward. "I know how you lied to Dave and told him I was cheating on him. That's how you got him to notice you in the first place."

This riled her a bit. "Look, Dani, I never lied to Dave. He was the one who wouldn't leave me alone."

"Well, that's not what he told me," I retorted.

Chloe's face darkened. "Look, you two were all but over. He told me he'd just been going through the motions with you for months."

I kept my voice as even and reasonable as I could, even though my nerve endings felt electrified. "That's not true," I said quietly. "We were together and happy. We were even talking about buying a house."

"He told me that you didn't understand his work," Chloe continued. "You didn't have the passion of a true artist. He thought you were—now, these are his words—a 'hack TV writer' and you would always wallow in television, but that he was meant for bigger things."

I just stared at her.

"He also . . ." Now she hesitated, as if what she'd already said wasn't hurtful, but what was coming was. "He also said that you two weren't really compatible physically. And that that problem was one of the big reasons that it would have never worked out."

"Shut up!" I was on my feet. "I don't want to hear any more of this crap from you, Chloe! All of this is just bullshit!"

Chloe gave me her Angelina Jolie lip bite again. "Listen, I know it hurts, but it's the truth." She smiled, just a little, but I realized she was hugely amused by all this. She found the fact that I was hurt then, and was still hurting now, amusing. She looked up at me. "And Steve has been honest with me about his 'thing' for you."

"What do you mean, 'thing'?" I demanded.

"You know," she said, raising her eyebrows. "Steve has always had it for you—that's why he wanted to hire you for the show. He told me that he's always had this fantasy of you two having sex on the desk. I'm fine with it. Steve and I . . ." She smiled. "We're both getting what we want from each other." She shrugged her delicate shoulders. "Big deal if he has an office crush."

"So you admit you're using him and he's fine with that?"

"Oh, Dani, guys don't care *why*." She grinned. "They don't care *why* you're sleeping with them. As long as they're getting it, they're fine."

"Guys don't care *why*?" I echoed. I'd never thought of it like that.

"No." Chloe smiled. "C'mon, the way you've played the whole Steve thing, you're obviously aware of the way things work in this town." She tipped back her wineglass, then smiled at me again and stood up. "And I'm fine with it, as long as Steve is around to clean up your mess if you screw up *our* show."

I watched her start to make her way around the coffee table. Seeing my face, she let out a little laugh. "And Dani, stop harboring all this animosity about Dave Gallagher. It wasn't like the two of you were going to end up 'old and crazy' together."

I lunged for her and my hands found their way around her neck. I started squeezing. I didn't want to hear any more of this. I just wanted her to shut up. My hands tightened around her thin throat, and I could feel her go from trying to be defensive to struggling to wriggle out of my grasp. I felt her tense into full panic mode. I held her neck in my hands and stared at her freckled face. She was gurgling now; she was trying to say something but my viselike grasp wouldn't let her.

At some point I had lifted her five-foot-three-inch frame off the ground. I was moving in slow motion, walking slowly one step forward and then another. My fury kept surging in fresh waves and I felt like the strongest woman alive.

I was so intent on staring at her freckles that I didn't realize that I had backed her into the wall. I could feel her shaking; I could feel her feet claw at the air like a bug on its back. Every couple of tries she'd feebly graze one of my shins, but it didn't really hurt. I loved being so much taller than her. I didn't see the freckles now; I saw her and Dave here on the slipcovered couches hanging out. Making out.

"Just shut up, I want you to shut up." I was hitting her against the wall now. She was bouncing off the wall . . . her head was snapping back and forth with each word as I said, "Shut up, shut up."

She didn't feel heavy, I thought. Maybe I had been getting stronger. Maybe taking all those classes at Barry's Boot Camp was actually working. I banged her against the wall again and thought of Dave and Chloe, Dave and Madison, and Troy spanking me.

My hands released her.

Chloe slid down the wall and crumpled onto her side near my feet. She lay there motionless, and the eyes that everyone thought were so amazing stared back at me unblinkingly. I crouched down close to her to get a better look.

Chloe was dead.

I was breathing heavily. I hadn't felt as if I had really exerted myself, but I must have. I wasn't tired, though. I was tingling all the way down the length of my body, ending at my toes, and I had never felt so high. I gazed down at her and thought of Marilyn, how in her house in Beverly Hills she had been found in the soldier's position. Chloe wasn't in the soldier's position. I thought she looked like she was in "child's pose" in yoga, but resting on her side with her arms extended above her head. I gave her a kick, sending her face-first into the floor. Now she looked good. Now when the coroner came he would write, "the body was found in 'child's pose.'" That one line would remain, long after Chloe was in the ground. Just like Marilyn's soldier's position.

I took a couple of minutes to compose myself. My eyes kept drifting back to Chloe to make sure she was dead.

My attack on her had been so sudden and so forceful that she really didn't have time to defend herself. The entire thing had been so one-sided that I knew she hadn't had the opportunity to pull any of my hair out during the struggle. Kneeling again by her side, I wiped her neck with the sleeve of my jacket. Lifting fingerprints off a dead body can be extremely difficult, but it can be done. I retraced my steps from when I entered the house. I hadn't touched the doorknob when I walked in. I realized I'd had a few sips of the rosé wine, so there would be DNA left on the rim of the glass. I picked up the bottle of rosé and the two wine glasses and moved into the kitchen. Pouring the remaining wine down the sink, I then flipped on the hot water with the side of my hand. I let the water heat up until it steamed and then I let it run over the glasses. My hand was turning red from the hot water, but it felt good, it didn't hurt, and the steam was rising into my face.

I carefully soaped each wineglass, paying particular attention to the rims. Grabbing a dishtowel, I dried both glasses and found the cupboard where they belonged. I replaced the two next to the six other glasses to complete the set of eight, in two rows, four glasses in each row.

With the dishtowel, I rubbed the cabinet door and then the bottle of Joy I had used. Then I had an inspiration. Moving over to my purse, I removed the plastic Baggie and dropped the dirty Kleenex onto the ground next to Chloe.

Picking up the empty wine bottle, I walked through the living room, giving the place one last look. At the table scattered with photos, I gave the picture of Chloe in a bikini a close look. Freckles everywhere. I knew it.

I stepped into the courtyard outside and closed the door behind me with the dishtowel. Everything was so quiet. These hills afforded a lot of privacy to those who lived up here. I thought that was a good thing. I left through the outer gate, which didn't creak, walked two houses up, and started my car, easing away from the curb. I decided to take the opposite way down from Hollyridge. I knew that if I just kept heading down I would eventually run into Beachwood Canyon Drive.

When I hit Beachwood I saw that it was garbage night and that the residents had all put their cans out on the curb. There were the regular cans and the recycling cans. I thought how I never recycled and that I probably should.

I pulled up close to a trash can without a lid and tossed the bottle and the dishtowel inside. The garbage truck would come early the next morning, well before someone would discover Chloe's body.

I rolled all the windows down and let the air blow in and lift my hair in all crazy directions. A few blocks down Beachwood I threw the plastic Baggie out the window. I hoped no one saw me litter.

I had always wondered, with all the research I'd done into murder, how much of a leap it was for someone when he or she committed a violent act. At what point did hating your husband or someone you work with provoke you into doing something? We'd all been taught right and wrong, but how close were most people to making that small step over the line?

Now I knew there was not much difference. For me, anyway, I was perfectly fine one second, and a minute later someone was dead and I felt exactly the same.

I drove past the Hollywood kids hanging out on the boulevard and up Highland to my place. There was a parking spot right in front. Usually I had to drive around to find a place to park, but tonight was my lucky night.

NINETEEN

Inside my apartment, nothing had changed. Lucy jumped up on the kitchen counter to say hello, reaching her head up toward my hand. I petted her gently and said, "I love you, kitty, Mommy's home."

I shed my clothes as I made my way down the hall, leaving each piece in a trail behind me. I turned the tub on hot and drizzled in some of my special lavender and rosemary essential oils, for a treat.

Naked, I opened a bottle of white wine that had been languishing in the back of the fridge. I used that new wine opener called the Rabbit. I loved the Rabbit. Funny that the vibrator all my girlfriends and I owned was also called the Rabbit. Should all women have two Rabbits?

I eased myself into the steaming water, leaned my head back to rest against the cool ceramic tiles, and closed my eyes. The glass of wine was precariously balanced on the edge of the tub. Everything felt so good. I was glad it was Friday.

I slept a deep, Ambien sleep that night, although I hadn't taken anything. The sun pouring in the window finally awoke me after ten. I'd never managed to keep my head on the pillow that long before, so I never knew how harsh the sunlight was midmorning.

I was bounding with energy, and went right to yoga over in Larchmont Village. My mat was right behind Renée Zellweger's. She looked amazing; there was no sign of that *Bridget Jones* weight she had gained. I concentrated on her cut arms and legs and reasoned that if she looked this good from yoga, maybe I could look like her, too.

Our instructor, Sparrow, did her usual handstand at the end of the class as a grand finale, her forehead dripping sweat in little rivulets that pooled on her mat. She was upside down, balancing herself perfectly, with her long legs reaching above her toward the ceiling. The rest of the class tried to follow her move. Renée got up okay, and so did the WeHo boys far in the back. The rest of us just managed to drill our heads into the padded mat and get halfway up with our legs bent, which was so not a handstand. Handstands were too much of a challenge, even though I was feeling superhuman today.

"Try and think of nothing," Sparrow said, holding her position.

I thought of nothing.

As Ina had demanded, I met her for lunch at the Newsroom on Robertson. I was on time, as usual, and downed two lattes in twenty minutes while waiting for her.

"I know, I know, I'm so sorry. Larry drove me here and we got stuck in some Bowl traffic coming over the hill." Ina threw her arms around me and I was engulfed in the cloud of her perfume, then felt a sticky lipgloss stamp on my cheek.

"It's okay." I let her off easy this time. "I've had so much caffeine I'm totally wired. Still no driver's license?"

"Not yet, but I'm starting to take the class next week, which will help me get my permit."

I rolled my eyes. "What are you, fifteen and six months?"

Ina chose to ignore me and proceeded to dump three packages of Splenda into her iced tea.

"So, how's Larry? Still married?" I asked.

"Yes," she replied, deciding to engross herself in the menu. "I don't expect you to understand, but we're doing really, really great. Larry's taking a job shooting a documentary in Baghdad. He's going to embed himself and follow around some of the troops."

I took all this in. "So, when is he heading off to war?"

"He's leaving in ten days. It's tough to get a flight out. There're only so many flights in and out of Riyadh a week." Ina was too bubbly; she was hoping her enthusiasm would win me over. "And he's thinking he can use some of the material they shoot to inspire his creativity."

I knew Larry was a camera operator, but I'd never thought of him as the creative type. I couldn't help but think that in the middle of his divorce (the divorce Ina was paying for) he'd decided to flee the country, leaving Los Angeles for Baghdad, of all places, where he could always blame being incommunicado on the circumstances in Iraq. It all seemed too convenient, bailing out right when the divorce was supposed to be winding up.

"So, what's happening at work?" Ina was too obviously changing the subject.

"It's great. I also just got some great news." I paused for a little bit of dramatic effect. "The show has been so successful that it looks like they'll rush a spin-off into pilot season next spring. They'd launch next fall, and they've been talking about making it my show. I'd run the writing staff and I'd also be one of the executive producers."

Ina banged both hands on the tabletop in delight. "I can't believe you didn't lead with this! This is truly great news!"

"I honestly wanted to hear what the latest was with you and Larry. And all this is just preliminary. A lot of things have to click into place for it to actually happen, and casting a show is so important, ya know? So I'm trying not to get too excited."

Ina's face lit up. "Stop, wait! I think we're going to have to organize a party or something, for your great news. Maybe we could throw one party for you and a going-away thing for Larry?"

I smiled politely. "I definitely want to celebrate Larry's departure. That is a reason to have a party, but let's wait until I have more news."

She leaned back in her chair, relenting for the moment. "Okay, okay, but we're definitely going to do something."

I knew she really wanted to celebrate. "Okay."

Ina's sister, Denise, picked her up. I waved good-bye to them both and was suddenly engulfed by a crowd of paparazzi in pursuit of someone famous. There was a break in the crush and I saw the orange glow of Paris Hilton. She was all orange knees and elbows, and she looked like a very tan pelican.

After seeing Ina, I knew what I needed: new shoes. In Beverly Hills, there was no better place to shop for shoes than Neiman Marcus on Wilshire. The best thing about going to NM was that they had a bar on the fourth floor. Each barstool was equipped with its own monitor, for watching endless repeats of *Sports Center* or whatever game was on. One of the bad things about going to the fourth floor for a drink, however, was that you had to travel all the way back to the first floor to stumble around the shoe department. Also, the men's department was on the fourth floor. So usually the bar chairs were filled with Beverly Hills men who had nothing better to do in the middle of the afternoon.

I hadn't had anything alcoholic to drink with Ina, so I nursed a glass of chardonnay and then another, and scribbled some show idea in my notebook. Over the past ten days I had been doing my usual trawling of the cable channels late at night, and I'd come across a great story. While visiting Korea, a young American exchange student had been brutally murdered after a night of partying with friends. The group had been staying overnight in a youth hostel, the kind that usually rented by the hour. It was St. Patrick's Day, so the

Westerners had gone out looking to party. They'd found green beer at a pseudo-English pub and danced until late. The place had also been full of American GIs. Most of the group had gone back to the hostel around 2 AM. Two girls, Gina and Nancy, stayed another hour, bumping and grinding to the music on the dance floor and flirting with some of the GIs. When they left, which Nancy said was around 3 AM, the girls had said good night to each other in the hall and gone to their separate rooms. In the morning, Gina was found stomped to death. Korean authorities and the US embassy jumped into action, tracking down the soldiers from the club and interviewing various witnesses who'd seen men loitering in the hostel hallway. The wife of the hostel owner said she saw a Westerner leave the hotel through the lobby around 4 AM.

To kill someone by stomping her to death was a very personal crime. Gina's face had been so bloodied when she was discovered that her friends weren't sure it was her. Her face had been covered with her own Windbreaker. Detectives theorized that one of the GIs had obviously followed her back to the hostel, come on strong, and Gina ended up dead. But thorough questioning of all witnesses led nowhere.

Finally out of options, the detectives floated a new theory. After going over all the statements, they'd noticed several discrepancies in Nancy's story. Nancy said that when she left Gina, Gina was still wearing her bra and panties. But police had found her jeans in a heap on the bathroom floor with her underwear inside them, indicating they'd been taken off together.

Nancy also changed her story several times about when they'd left the club. The police began to think Nancy was the killer. They thought Gina had made some sort of lesbian overture and Nancy had become so enraged that she slammed Gina's head against the tiles in the bathroom, and then dragged her into the main room to stomp her to death. As the investigation went on, they assembled facts to support their theory and Nancy confessed to the murder.

I knew the network brass would love this. A lesbian encounter? Lesbians always did big numbers; *The L Word* was doing great for Showtime. We could promote the show as a "snatched from today's headlines" event.

My thoughts of lesbians were interrupted by the bartender, a model-actor whatever—"Hey, are you writing a script?" he asked.

"Umm, no," I said. "I'm just making some notes."

"Oh, cool, okay. For a second I thought you were the woman of my dreams. Beautiful and a successful screenwriter."

I smiled tightly. "Sorry to disappoint you. I'll take the check."

After two glasses of afternoon chardonnay, I buzzed my way to the main event on the first floor. Neiman Marcus had the best shoe selection of any store in LA: Christian Louboutin, Prada, and a huge Manolos section. I worked my way from one end of the department to the other. After carefully picking up every shoe in the place, I settled on four different pairs to try: an impossibly high pair of pink Louboutins, two pairs of Prada pumps, and a crocodile sandal from YSL. The guy waiting on me couldn't have cared less about helping me. I saw his eyes graze my ringless left hand. Because I wore no makeup and had no ring, he probably thought I was a lesbian, maybe a stomping, murdering lesbian. He dumped the shoeboxes at my feet and split for greener pastures in the Manolos section. I wasn't going to dwell on the slight. I slipped each pair on and strutted around the department, pivoting and checking out the angles in the different mirrors.

The other women in the shoe department fit into two categories: the Ladies Who Lunch, with their important jewelry and salon blow outs, and the ProHos with their non-tourages—girlfriends and personal trainers.

I slid the pink Louboutin heels on for the second time. The ribbons crisscrossed my ankles and the three-inch wedge heels made my legs look impossibly long in my dark jeans. My eyes scanned the department from one end to the other. My salesperson was in a far-off corner, helping someone who wasn't me.

I leaned down and picked up my purse, turned on the three-inch Louboutin wedge heels, and walked out of the department toward my car parked curbside. I let the door close behind me and exhaled a sigh of relief. After all, Saks right next door was where that sticky-fingered Winona Ryder had gotten busted.

My Louboutin wedges pressed the gas pedal and I pulled out of the metered space. I wondered if my distracted salesman would even notice my three-year-old Charles David shoes in the Louboutin box.

Easing my car onto Wilshire, I started to head back to Hollywood for home. I calculated that I could make it in about twenty minutes. I prided myself on my inner navigation system that was better than any computerized system for figuring out traffic routes. My own little voice in my head. Braking, I decided to change my route. Instead of taking Wilshire all the way east, I was going to cut across traffic. I was going to take Doheny all the way.

Monday morning, I rushed in the door twenty minutes late. This was uncharacteristic of me, but I'd slept all the rest of the weekend and had slept through my alarm. I was speed-walking through the maze of cubicles toward my door on the far side of the office with my shades on and my head lowered. I was determined to get to my office and put my things down before someone saw me and realized that I was, for once, late.

I hadn't even made my way halfway through the cubicles before I heard Steve call my name sharply.

"Dani, in here, now!"

I had heard him use this tone before, just never in my direction. I detoured to his office and took a seat.

Steve looked pale. He usually spent his weekends surfing (a holdover from his jiggle-fest show), so something was definitely wrong.

"Shut the door."

I complied and gave him a questioning look. "Steve, are you okay? You look like shit."

He took a deep breath and raked his hands through his hair. "Chloe Johnson was found dead yesterday."

"What? Our Chloe Johnson?" I was shocked.

"Yes, our Chloe Johnson," he said through gritted teeth.

"Do you know what happened?" I asked. "You said she was found dead. Was she in some sort of an accident?"

"The police think it was a follow-home robbery of some sort. She had plans with friends for brunch but didn't show up on Saturday. They thought it wasn't a big deal. No one went over there until late yesterday afternoon. One of her girlfriends found her body."

"So she was killed during a robbery? Was there a lot of stuff taken?"

"The police are trying to figure that out now. She was a petite thing—she obviously wasn't a match for the guy who did this to her."

"I know you were excited about all the possible new stuff with Chloe. I'm sorry, Steve."

Steve looked terrible. I wondered what it could possibly feel like, to be dating someone who was murdered. I'd seen plenty of those shows on *Court TV* where the families talked about losing someone they loved, telling their story by rote for the camera in a southern-twanged monotone. They were usually southern-twanged because an incredibly high percentage of murders that ended up on those shows occurred in Texas and Florida. When I questioned my producer friend who worked on *Forensic Files* why so many of the show's murders seemed to happen in the south, she just shrugged and said, "Because crazy people live there."

I slightly enjoyed watching Steve as he fumbled with the production schedule for *Flesh and Bone*'s latest episode, his hands a little shaky from too much morning coffee and his bad news. I wondered when he'd heard. In spite of being late, I felt good, and I hoped I wasn't coming across as too perky.

Steve sensed my mood and I wondered if he was wondering if I knew about him and Chloe. I wondered if Chloe ever told him about Dave. Steve's eyes flashed up from his papers, and he held my gaze. I smiled warmly back. Was this our exchange? Our agreement to continue in silence? I noticed his hands still trembling as he tried to be nonchalant. He met my eyes and gave me a tight smile.

"You don't have to worry about being sorry with me," he said. "We're just fucked. We had two days' shooting left on this episode, and now we're going to have to recast and rush the re-shoots into production. This show is important."

His personal concern for Chloe had quickly been replaced with his on-with-the-show efforts. The cool, pragmatic producer was thinking how this would affect the bottom line. You gotta love Hollywood.

"This is going to cost us a lot of money. I've got to find out from the network if this is coming straight out of our budget or whether our insurance will cover us."

"Do you think she was into drugs?" I asked.

"I don't have any idea." He shrugged. "None of us here really knew her. It's possible, I guess. Why do you ask?"

I shrugged myself. "She was young, pretty, successful. You know the profiles—someone like her usually doesn't end up the victim of a crime like this." I sighed. "My bet is she was involved with some nefarious types and got caught up in something."

He just stared at me, taking a moment to compute this. "Are you trying to write this into some sort of story line in your head?"

"No!" Now I was indignant. "I'm just running the possibilities. This is what I do. I know this shit."

"Well, let it go. We've got to move forward. I'm going to call Deb Miller in casting and see who she can get in here to start work tomorrow or, better yet, today."

Steve picked up the phone and I took that as my cue to leave. This was definitely a first for him: an actress dead in the middle of shooting. It was going to be some week.

Closing the door to Steve's office behind me, I full on bumped into Evil Janet, who'd been lurking outside. "Hi, Janet," I offered.

"Hi, Dani, how are you?" She had no emotion in her voice.

I murmured "Fine, thanks," and moved to brush by her.

"I bet. I bet you're really, really good," she said to my back.

I stopped and turned around to hold her gaze. "I'm great. Thanks for asking." I decided to play it cool. "Hey, are you feeling better?" I asked.

"What do you mean?"

"I thought I'd heard you'd been sick or something. Haven't you had a cold?"

Squinting at me she smiled. "I've had a bit of a cold, but I'm better now, thanks."

"Well, I'm glad you're feeling better," I replied. I turned again and gave her my back, moving down the hall to my office. When I reached my doorway, I chanced a glance over my shoulder. Evil Janet remained outside Steve's office, still staring at me. I smiled again and closed my door.

Normally it was tough getting going Monday morning at work. I'd have to down two lattes to even function. But today was just one of those days where the words came easy. Punching up dialogue was a breeze! I loved my job! A couple of hours into it, sensing a presence in my office, I glanced up from my computer screen, annoyed.

"Hey, Dani." Rich stood in my doorway, all hulking Italian male.

"Hi, Rich, how are you?" My eyes strayed from him back to the flickering page, then lingered on Rich.

"I'm good, I'm good. I've been meaning to talk to you, but I just haven't been around when you've been around."

"Well, here we are!" I joked.

Seeing Rich here, in my office, had made my heart start thumping all over the place. He certainly wasn't acting like he had put the license-plate, Chloe-working-here, murder thing together. That was good. It was just a big coincidence anyway. Rich's manner did seem subdued, however, and that was saying a lot, because he was pretty low-key to begin with. My mind raced forward to play the scene that was about to unfold.

RICH
I think you know why I'm here.

ME
(Shaking my head and gesturing helplessly)
I have no idea.

RICH
They've got your DNA, Dani. You left some of your
hair on the floor when you and Chloe fought.
She pulled some of your hair out during the struggle.
You didn't think of everything when you were
covering your trail.

WHACKED

ME
I didn't do anything, I swear. I went home on Friday
night. I left the lot and went straight home.

RICH
How did you know her murder was Friday night? Her
body was found Sunday. We've only just ascertained
that she died late on Friday.

I'd hanged myself. I'd made one of the biggest mistakes a suspect
can make during interrogation. I'd run off at the mouth and my
words had convicted me. Already I was calculating my options.
Should I make a run for it, through the door? Or bust through the
window behind my desk? My eyes traveled back to Rich.

"Dani? Are you okay?"

"Uh, yeah."

"I'm here because I wanted to talk to you about what happened
to Chloe Johnson."

So I was right. I did have that intuition thing. He was here to
bust me.

"I just think you can never be too careful these days. I know you
live up in the hills, just a canyon over from Chloe's house. Something
like this could have happened to you."

I had no idea where he was going with this. I reminded myself that
he had a gun on his person.

"I need to ask you a personal question." He looked dead serious.
I waited, nervous.

"Do you own a handgun or any kind of firearm?"

"Are you kidding? No way!"

"Well then, I think you should give it some serious thought. A
woman who lives alone can never be too careful."

I exhaled. "Just so I'm being totally up front, I can't stand guns. I give money to Stop the NRA. Look at me . . ." I pointed to my pink Louboutins. "Would someone who wears these hot shoes own a gun?"

Rich took a quick but thorough look at my new heels. "Look, I'm serious. Just think how that could have been you. Some creepy guy could have followed you home from the lot that night, instead of Chloe."

"She was followed home from the lot?" I sounded strained.

"They think this could possibly be linked to the woman from Universal who was murdered a few months ago. I spoke to one of the detectives assigned to the case. Chloe had some important friends who are pressuring the department to solve this case."

"I wouldn't have any idea about where to buy a gun. Can't I just take a Tae Bo class instead?"

Rich's eyes softened. "Tell you what. Why don't you let me take you down to the shooting club? I'll show you."

"You'll show me how to handle a gun?" I couldn't suppress a smile.

"Yeah."

"It doesn't scare you, that I would know how to handle a firearm?"

Rich stared at me evenly. He was so serious all the time. "Dani, I'd never be afraid of you."

He wasn't scared of me. Knowing this gave me a shot of pure pleasure. "I'll think about the gun thing. Okay?"

"Okay." He was smiling just as big as I was. Then he slipped out the door and shut it firmly behind him.

Azita knocked once and then poked her head in. "Hey, there are a couple of police detectives here. They've been talking to everybody and they'd like to ask you some questions. Are you cool with that?"

"Sure," I said, a little caught in the headlights. "Let them come in."

I took a deep breath and clicked off my laptop. I centered myself, placing my hands on my desk. Then I crossed one over the other—more ladylike. I wanted to make a good impression with the cops.

I was surprised to see Rich enter first. He nodded toward me and moved to take the chair in the far corner. He was followed by a couple of guys who were definitely cops. It was like our casting office had chosen these two: early forties, salt-and-pepper hair, and bad polyblend blue blazers.

"Hello, Ms. Hale," said one of them as the two men sat down. "I'm Detective Max Robinov, and this is Detective Larry Steiger. Thank you for agreeing to talk to us. We know this is a difficult time for everyone here."

"Really?" I asked, surprised. "I didn't know it was such a big deal to everyone. I mean, Chloe had only been here a few days."

The detectives exchanged a look before Robinov continued. "Well, a woman is dead, Ms. Hale, and she deserves justice. We just want to arrest whoever did this."

"Of course, please, anything I can do to help, just let me know."

Rich hadn't said anything yet, and I wasn't sure why he was there. As if he'd read my mind, he spoke up. "Dani, these guys and I, we know each other from way back—we've worked a lot of cases together. And, since I work on the show now and know everyone, I thought it would be a good idea if I walked them through the place."

Detective Steiger leaned forward. "Ms. Hale, did you know Chloe Johnson before working with her here?"

"No, I didn't know her."

The detectives exchanged another look. "Apparently Ms. Johnson mentioned that she thought she may have met you before," Steiger said. "One of the costumers on the show recalls Chloe mentioning that."

I shifted in my chair. I thought they were playing it that Steiger was the bad cop and Robinov the good cop. I knew all about that. It was supposed to draw me to Robinov so that I'd feel he was a nice guy and that he was looking out for me, and all this would lead to a confession. I inhaled deeply.

"When you say 'know' her, I had met her once, but that was ages ago. I remember she worked on a show being directed by a guy I was dating."

I knew my tone sounded a tad defensive, but I was being interrogated and I knew how innocent people reacted. They dealt with their feelings up front. "You two are making me feel like I'm a suspect," I said. I paused, making eye contact with the two detectives, one after the other. Rich watched silently from the corner. "I thought someone said that her murder may have been drug-related?"

"Where did you hear that?"

"I don't know, the news?" I shrugged. "Or maybe the drug talk was around here—maybe someone mentioned she'd been into drugs and my crime-writer mind just assumed the rest."

"But you *did* know her?"

"You ever hear of six degrees of separation? This is LA, and we worked in the same business. Everybody's met everybody after a while. Sure, I may have been introduced to Chloe, but I didn't know her. I didn't pick her up at the airport or anything."

"Can we please have his name?"

"His name?" For a second I felt like running. I could say I was sick. I could say I wasn't feeling well and had to go home. I could say I was pregnant, and then they couldn't be mean to me. Men never wanted to go there if you were on your period or pregnant.

"Are you talking about Dave Gallagher?" the cop continued.

"Um, yes, so you know about Dave. If you know about him, why ask me?"

"And you dated for how long? We're just here because she said she knew you."

"As I said, I knew her mostly from the show." I sighed. "This whole thing is so unbelievable. I'm sure you're aware that the network was planning a big future for Chloe. They were thinking about developing a show around her that would be based on a character I created. And now, with her dead, the spin-off show is too, got it? It's all kaput."

"We're trying to get in touch with Mr. Gallagher. Apparently he's on a plane to New Zealand to begin directing a movie of the week for FX, so we haven't been able to speak with him. We've left word and are expecting a call back."

"Good, good," I said.

"Ms. Hale, when was the last time you spoke with Mr. Gallagher?"

I bit my lip, doing Chloe doing her Angelina. I thought about the answer carefully. "We spoke not that long ago. He called to tell me he was getting married."

Detective Steiger raised his eyebrows. "So you two had a good breakup?"

I shrugged. "What breakup is ever good?"

"May we ask, Ms. Hale, why the two of you broke up?"

I had to end this. "Detective Robinov, please, do we have to go there?" I let my voice tremble. I was thinking of a show I'd written last season called "Deadly Deception." Paula Magnus was a woman who seemed to have it all, but when her wealthy doctor husband was diagnosed with hepatitis B, he had to leave his job. After their money ran out, he contracted diabetes, and Paula found him one morning, dead. The autopsy showed he had a paralytic agent in his system, one used in surgery. This particular drug immobilizes the patient, making their breathing dependent on a respirator. Paula said her husband used it to commit suicide, but at her trial an expert testified that the police had found no needle near the body and that the husband wouldn't have been able to inject himself and then get rid of the needle, because he would have been paralyzed instantly. By the way, Paula was in line to inherit two million dollars in life insurance upon his death. When her guilty verdict was read, Paula sat stoically and a single tear slid down her cheek. She shook her head and whispered, "I loved my husband. I'm innocent."

Now, with these men in the room, I thought of Paula's one tear. My bottom lip began to tremble and I gripped my hands together tightly, trying to compose myself. I looked directly at Robinov and my single Paula tear slid down my cheek.

"With the shock of Chloe, and now your bringing up Dave Gallagher, this is just a little much for me to take in, okay, guys?"

My breathing was coming in short rasps and I fought for air a little. Rich intervened. "C'mon guys," he said, rising to his feet. "Don't you think this is a bit much? She's upset. Let's leave her alone." He put his hand on Detective Robinov's shoulder and gave him a squeeze to signal that this interview was over. I still wanted to get in the last word.

"I had virtually no contact with her. Last week was a crazy week and I was totally swamped—I barely left this desk. The only time I saw her was with Steve on set. They were getting lunch and invited me but, but I was too busy."

They absorbed this information and nodded, then both passed me their business cards with the LAPD logo emblazoned on them. "Well, if you think of anything more that would help, please call us, Ms. Hale," said Detective Steiger.

The three of them rose and made their exit.

I couldn't help myself. "You know that Chloe was dating Steve, right?"

This halted the three of them in their matching navy jackets. They turned in unison to face me. Robinov (the good cop) shared a look with Steiger. I was so cool that I sat and busied myself with straightening my desk for no reason.

"Chloe and Steve Jacobs were dating." Robinov's intonation wasn't exactly a question.

"Yeah, they were dating, for a while." I enjoyed their quiet turmoil. I loved being the keeper of the clues. Rich just watched me quietly, in his way. Troubled, the two cops nodded, then exited and closed the door.

I went over the entire exchange in my head, line by line, seeing if I had made any mistakes. I was fine. Even though I was in my office with the door closed, I realized I wasn't going to get much done, because I knew everyone was now buzzing about Chloe. I could actually hear people saying her name through the walls. I shrugged it all off. It was terrible what had happened to her, but she'd worked here for only five days.

Leaving the office early, I swung by the drive-through at In-N-Out Burger to get a Double Double. It sat in its perfectly folded white bag on the passenger seat for the entire ride home. In the back of the fridge, I had a bottle of what I called "fuck-me champagne" on ice, just in case. I opened it with a loud pop. I filled my glass and settled in front of the TV. From the second I'd come in the door, Lucy had been following me around. Whenever I was still, she head butted my legs for attention. Lucy was thrilled; she wasn't used to having me home this soon.

I flicked the TV on and surfed, killing time before Bill Curtis came on with a new episode of *Cold Case Files*. He should really think about suing that lame Jerry Bruckheimer show. They'd stolen his title under the guise of "fair use" and that chick on there sucked. Her hair was always disheveled, as if having messy hair made her more real. I was home in time for the news, and Paul Moyer's voice boomed out at me. "She was bright, beautiful, and had a promising career, and now she's dead. Our Beverly White is live from Hollywood with this breaking story of a rising actress murdered in her own home. Beverly?"

"Thanks, Paul," Beverly said. "I'm here in the exclusive Beachwood Canyon area of Los Angeles, home to many movie stars and recording artists. They move here for the privacy and the serenity of the canyon setting. But now they are questioning all that—with the news of this talented young actress's shocking murder."

"Oh, give me a break!" I complained to the TV.

The piece went on and on. The coverage of Chloe's death consumed a full four minutes at the top of the show. There was nothing like the news in LA. I couldn't believe people were getting killed in Iraq and this was the lead story. When Beverly started going into Chloe's credits and got to her work with Scorsese, I knew it was time to change the channel.

"Lucy, let's move into the bedroom." She was purring in stereo and knew exactly what I was talking about. As soon as I stood up and switched the TV off, she was racing down the hallway toward the bed. I lit the candles on my nightstand and the dresser. I used to buy them to light my liaisons, but when those never materialized, I lit them for Lucy and me.

Pouring my second glass of champagne, I flicked on the bedroom TV. Lucy jumped up onto the bed and settled in next to me. When Bill came onscreen to intro tonight's real cold case, I smiled. This was bliss.

As usual, I passed out during the show. The next morning I woke up with the sun streaming right onto my bed. I threw back the duvet and glanced at the clock. I couldn't believe that I'd been asleep for ten hours. I raced around the apartment, yanking on jeans and searching for a bra while brushing my teeth. This was going to be tight. I sped through all the yellow lights on Barham and raced into the office on time, but just barely.

I spied Azita walking into the copy room. When she saw me, she said, "Hey mama, there's someone in your office." My first thought was that the detectives were back, but when I pushed open my office door I was surprised to find Lauren waiting for me.

"Hey, this is a first," I said. "You never swing by and say hello. What brings you around? Are you shooting a story on the lot?"

Lauren's face was tight. "Yes, I'm shooting a story on the lot. I'm here shooting *the* story everyone's talking about."

I could tell Lauren was mad. With her big star-reporter hair and camera-ready face, she looked harder than "my Lauren," the girl with the wide smile and glass of wine in her hand.

"When you brush your teeth you call to give me the blow-by-blow," she started, advancing toward me. "And now you want me to believe that Chloe Johnson was here, working on your show, and you just forgot to mention it?"

I held my hands up to stop her. "Is that why you're so angry? Listen, it wasn't that big a deal that she was on the show."

"It wasn't a *big deal*?" she mimicked. "I want you to be straight with me for once, Dani. Chloe was murdered here on *your* show and I'm supposed to think that's just a coincidence?"

I couldn't believe she was putting all this on me. I was standing here fighting with one of my closest friends because of Chloe Johnson. The girl was fucking with me even when she was dead.

Lauren folded her arms across her chest. "The dead actress is just the beginning. While I was waiting for you, I thought I'd talk to Steve and see how everything's going. Since he's your boss, I figured you might not confide everything to him, but I know how close you are with Rachel, and, guess what? Steve tells me that no one named Rachel has ever worked here. So how do you explain that? So who's Rachel? Was she just someone you made up? Is she an imaginary friend?"

"It wasn't like that!" I said. "It's just that sometimes you guys give me such a tough time about going out. She was an excuse for me, someone I invented so that I wouldn't have to hurt your feelings every time I didn't go out with you guys."

Lauren shook her head. "What's wrong with you? Are you out of your mind? Dani, we call you because we want to see you. Because we have a good time when you come along. Maybe we call you because we think you *need* a call from someone. You're not doing us any favors when you finally give in and agree to go out with us."

"You are being way too sensitive about this, Lauren."

"I'm not the sensitive one—*you're* the sensitive one."

She turned, heading for the door. With her hand on the knob, she stopped. "Well, since you say you're not sensitive, I can finally be straight with you about something." Lauren paused for dramatic effect. "Dave hit on me when you were together. At the barbecue at Ina's, he followed me to the bathroom and made a move. And after you guys broke up, he kept calling me to go for coffee, but I told him to go fuck himself."

I was flabbergasted. "I can't believe Dave hit on you when we were together and you didn't tell me before this?" My eyes filled with tears—my own tears, not Paula Magnus's. "You're my best friend! You should have told me."

We stood there, staring each other down, before Lauren pulled open the door. "You know what? When you want to give me a straight answer, you know how to find me. Chloe Johnson is dead, Dani—call me when *you* want to come clean."

And then, with a nasty parting look, she was gone.

My head was throbbing. I sat down at my desk and tried to distract myself with work, but it didn't help. Hours later, I was relieved when, after a rap on the door, Rich poked his head in.

"Hi there."

"Hey," I replied, feeling listless.

"I know how you feel about the gun thing, and that going to the shooting range with me didn't really appeal to you, but I have a compromise. I was wondering if you'd let me come by your place and check it out. I just want to see how secure it is."

"Um, well, I guess that'd be okay," I said, pushing back from my desk. "But I've got to tell you though, my neighborhood is great. I'm not worried at all."

He smiled. "I'm sure it's very safe. I'd feel better swinging by and giving it a sweep myself."

"Sure, okay." I shrugged. "So when do you want to come by?"

"I can't do it during the week, but I could come over Saturday afternoon."

"I won't get back from my Barry's Boot Camp until five. Do you mind coming that late?"

"That's perfect. I'll see you at six."

He was headed toward the door before I could stop him.

"Hey, wait a minute, don't you need my address?"

He turned. "I'll just get it from the cast and crew list," Rich said. "You can find out where everyone lives off of that."

Rich held my gaze, as if watching closely for my reaction. I gave him a cool smile. "See you Saturday."

I ended up not going to Barry's Boot Camp that Saturday. The prospect of Rich coming over made my stomach jump. I wasn't sure if it was excitement or if it was nerves about his mention of the crew list. In the bathroom, I checked my teeth for the third time and put on another coat of lipgloss. I heard the bell. I wasn't exactly skipping, but I definitely had a quick shuffle in my step as I hurried to the door. The front door was open and the security gate was locked, as always. The fresh air blowing through the living room was great.

I could see Rich waiting just outside my door. I was used to seeing him standing in my doorway at the office; seeing him here at home was an anomaly. He was wearing a charcoal sweater with a few dark hairs visibly poking through the slight V-neck of the collar. I'd never seen him out of a suit jacket.

"Hey," I said a little too brightly.

"Hey," he answered through the metal screen door.

I let him in. I noticed his clean scent and hint of cologne as he moved closely by me to enter the living room. He took in my whole place at one glance. "You were right—this place is great. You lock that security door all the time?"

"Yes, this is LA. It's not like I'm going to leave my doors unlocked."

Lucy bounded in from the bedroom and ran right up to bump up against Rich's leg. She was such a little whore. He reached down and scratched her under the neck. She closed her eyes and started to drool. I was sure Rich had that effect on everyone.

"So you've been happy here?" he asked, breaking their moment.

"My landlord, who lives in the other half, is never there. He's gay and his partner helped him remodel before I moved in. They did a beautiful job. You know how good the gays are at making things pretty."

Rich took this in. "Have you been here long?"

I nodded. "A few years. It was a stretch at first. It was a big step up from my last place." I moved to the window and pointed to the house one down from mine. "I was a little nervous because there were six Middle Eastern guys living right next door. They would sit outside at night and grill meat for dinner and chain-smoke. I was convinced they were some sort of hijack squad in training. And then one day, they all left. For weeks after they disappeared, I'd rush to turn on *Good Morning America* when I woke up, expecting to hear that they'd blown up LAX or the White House. Fortunately there was nothing. The only sign they were there is the four-foot-tall black panther lawn ornament they left behind."

Rich just stared at me through this whole thing. I could tell he was thinking carefully about his next words. "Dani, have you ever thought that maybe you should be a bit more careful what you say out loud?"

"What are you talking about?" I asked. "What's wrong with what I'm saying?"

"Well, I've noticed you make a lot of borderline racial remarks."

"What? I'm not a racist! I have no idea what you're talking about."

"It's just, here you are talking about the guys next door, who you think are going to blow something up just because they're Middle Eastern. I've heard you say that when your friend Ina gets her license she'll be a typical terrible Asian driver, and you just said your apartment was beautifully renovated because your landlord was gay. All those statements could be interpreted as being ignorant, bigoted, or prejudiced."

"Oh, come on! After 9/11 we were all looking closer at people around us. Shit, the government asked us to! And wouldn't you think it was strange if a group of those guys lived next door to you and then one night they up and moved out . . . totally disappearing?" I heard my voice rising. "And the Asian-driver thing is a fact—everyone knows they can't drive worth shit. I have a lot of Asian friends and they all acknowledge this."

Rich was looking at me patiently. He knew he wouldn't be able to stop me.

"And what's so terrible about saying gays have a great sense of style?" I went on. "*Queer Eye for the Straight Guy* was a ratings bonanza!" I held his gaze, waiting for him to agree with me, but he didn't. I pressed on. "Gay men have a particularly keen eye for detail that naturally lends itself to home remodeling and decorating."

Rich just sighed.

"Wait, tell me," I said, "have you ever done a lookiloo at a home or an apartment, and when the Realtor told you a gay couple had lived there and done all the work—didn't it make you feel a little more secure?"

Rich regarded me inscrutably.

"It's a positive thing, what I'm saying. And it's only racist if it's not true, and all the stuff you're throwing in my face now *is* true."

Rich moved toward the door. "Dani, I'm here to check out where you live and make sure you're safe. We'll save the Anti-Defamation League conversation for another time, okay?"

I backed down. "Okay."

"Now, how about dinner?"

"Tonight? Are you kidding me? Don't you figure someone like me has plans on a Saturday night?"

He just kept looking at me. "Would you like to have dinner with me tonight?"

I smiled. "Let me grab my keys; I'm driving."

"Deal."

I double-locked the doors when we left, to prove how careful I was. We made our way up the hill to my car.

"I like to drive because I love my car so much," I told Rich. "Even though I've had it a while, it still has that new car smell."

I was leading the way on the narrow sidewalk when he said, "You drive a convertible cherry red Mercedes, right?"

I stopped in my tracks and turned around. Rich was looking at me with those detective eyes of his. "Oh, no . . ." he said, dramatically hitting his head. "Chloe Johnson drove that car."

I wasn't going to let him trick me. "Beemers are more my speed."

"Beemers?" he echoed. "*That* makes sense."

"Are you implying that I don't make sense?"

Rich's face spread into a smile. "Oh, you make sense. You're just totally whacked."

"Whacked?"

"Totally."

EPILOGUE

The Next Day

I was working on revising the Assistant Number Two Doheny show when my business manager, Alec, phoned me.

"Hey, Dani, I've got some interesting news."

"Interesting good, or interesting bad?" I asked, more cautious than usual.

"Oh, no, it's good, it's good," he assured me. "I don't know if you've had time to check your portfolio recently. I know from watching the news that there's been a lot going on at work for you."

"Yeah, yeah, you're right, things have been a little crazy here, but we're dealing with it. The answer to your question is yes, I mean, no. I haven't been able to go online and follow my stocks and investment accounts."

"Well, that Anagen ended up being a big winner. You were right on that one. It's split again. I think you're going to clear almost two hundred thousand when we cash out."

"What?" I couldn't believe this. Me, worth two hundred thousand dollars? All from reading Grant's e-mail?

Late that afternoon, Steve called me into his office and told me they were giving me a bump in pay and making me supervising producer of the show. So I had job security for the first time. Not bad for thirty-four, I thought to myself. This was the best week ever.

One Month Later

"Hey, Dani, how are you?" asked a familiar voice over the phone.

I sat up straighter. Catching myself, I softened my posture and took a deep breath. "I'm good, Dave . . . how are you?"

"I'm okay. I just got back from New Zealand, shooting this TV movie thing."

"Still getting married?" I asked.

"Oh, yeah . . . Valentine's Day."

"Wow," was all I could think to say. This call wasn't a complete surprise. I knew he was going to phone me at some point.

"So I was calling you to see if you had time soon to get together and talk?"

"Why?" I scowled into the phone.

"Well, I mean, c'mon . . . Chloe? That shit was fucked up."

Leaning back in my chair, I stared at an empty spot on my bookshelf that used to showcase my favorite picture of us.

"Yeah, I guess it was messed up."

"Weird coincidence," he added.

"Totally weird," I agreed.

Shrugging to myself, I knew I could totally handle seeing Dave, and if I got a free lunch out of it, even better.

"Okay, fine. You want to try and grab lunch at Le Petit Greek on Larchmont?"

"Uhhh . . ." he stammered.

"Is that not a cool place?"

"Well, it's just that a good friend of Madison's works there, and it kind of wouldn't be appropriate."

"If it's cool for us to 'talk,' as you put it, I was just figuring that your wife-to-be must feel it's okay."

Silence.

"So Madison doesn't know you're calling me?"

"Not exactly," he answered. "It's not like she would care or anything. I just don't think it would be appropriate for us to go to that restaurant."

It dawned on me where he was going with this. "So you're wanting to get together, but we have to do it in hiding?"

"I just think it would be better if I came by your place," he said smoothly. "Maybe some night this week."

This was too funny. "Dave, are you thinking that you're going to come to my house and get some sort of comfort from me about this whole thing?"

"Dani, hearing that Chloe was murdered was devastating. I mean, the police *interrogated* me for almost an hour. Interpol in New Zealand acted like I was doing some kind of O.J. run-for-the-border thing." Dave was using his silky voice, his "you're my baby and I need you" voice that always made me melt. For months after we'd broken up I'd prayed for this call, hoping he'd say he missed and needed me. Now he was asking me to console him about Chloe. "I could really use your friendship now."

What a loser.

"I'm not interested."

"Dani, I need you right now."

"If you call me about this again, I'm going to call Madison's dad and tell him that you're trying to get a sympathy lay from your ex-girlfriend, about your dead ex-girlfriend. How do you think he'd feel about your marrying his daughter then?"

And with that, I hung up.

I shook my head. The future Mrs. Dave Gallagher was going to have *a lot* of fun with him.

Still smiling, I turned back to my computer.

Six Months Later

"I'll take it."

I'd waited a long time to say those words, and they were just as satisfying as I'd always hoped. I was standing on the balcony of the empty Spanish villa I'd just put a bid on. Of all the houses I'd look-ilooed over the years, this one was really perfect: a 1930s classic, behind a gate, with all the bathrooms and the kitchen remodeled. The living room had wide-plank hardwood floors in a dark cherry. The ceilings in the living room and bedroom soared over twenty feet high, with wooden beams. The Realtor had given me a tour that ended up on the large balcony of the living room. "That's what they call a million-dollar view," he whispered in my ear.

We were high above Los Feliz and I could see all the way from the ocean in Santa Monica to the tall buildings downtown. I'd once told someone that I wanted a house in the hills that people would get lost coming to. This was that house. I worried about the Domino's pizza guy finding his way, but I'd deal with that when I was in.

The Realtor had continued with the hard sales pitch, even though he had me at the view. Looking east toward where he was pointing, I could just make out the lights of Dodger Stadium above Echo Park.

"Do you like baseball? You're so close to the stadium that you could be in your seat in about ten minutes from here."

"I love baseball," I answered. "I've been dying to go to a Dodger game."

I shifted my gaze a few inches to the right and I could make out the crest in the hills that marked Beachwood Canyon. Dave's little log cabin was still there, as was Chloe's place, but I never drove up Beachwood anymore. Chloe's old house had been put on the market a few months ago, and the Realtor had wanted me to do a walk-through there, but I'd shot that idea down. Chloe didn't have a view.

I'd heard from someone recently that a Dumpster was parked in front of her old place, indicating that at least one buyer hadn't been turned off by the idea of a murder having occurred there. The new owners were expanding the place upward and out.

"Will you be living here with a special someone? Are you both going to be qualifying for the loan?" the Realtor pressed.

I continued to take in the gorgeous views. "No, I'm going to be living here alone. Well, I'll be living with my cat, Lucy."

A panicked look flashed across the Realtor's face. I was sure he was wondering how a woman on her own could afford a place like this.

"I can make a large cash deposit," I assured him, turning to face him. "So I'm sure getting the loan will be no problem."

I held the Realtor's gaze, daring him to comment about the cat or the big down payment. He kept his mouth shut. My eyes were drawn back to the view.

"This place is perfect."

Ten Months Later

All the press coverage from Chloe's murder brought attention to *Flesh and Bone*, and starting with the huge audience for the recast Assistant Number Two Doheny show, we had our largest viewership ever. I felt great and was treated like a superstar around the office.

The detectives still came by the office every few weeks with more questions. They spent most of their time in Steve's office.

That fall, I took my first real vacation in years, splurging on an Ocean Villa at the Palmilla in Cabo. I was sitting by the pool when I read in the LA *Times* the big news about the arrest of Chloe's murderer. It seemed Evil Janet left some sort of DNA evidence at the scene. The police had finally concluded Evil Janet had been in love with Steve Jacobs, obsessively stalking him for months. Chloe's coming to work on the show had pushed her over the edge.

Case closed.

WHACKED

Twelve Months Later

Interior. Day. A fire crackles in the hearth of a cozy living room. Overstuffed couches, slipcovered chairs, and pillows are scattered everywhere. It is a warm and inviting living room, a place where you'd love to sink into a sofa, put your feet up, and read a great book. An open bottle of wine sits on the coffee table, with two wineglasses nearby.

A camera pulls across the room and we hear a male voice yell, "Action!"

On cue, two women struggle into the living room. Their arms are entangled and they're swiping at each other, struggling to stay upright. The brunette is beginning to get the upper hand, pushing the redhead back two feet, but then the redhead gets a burst of energy and swings the brunette around, overturning a side table. The brunette backs the redhead up against the wall. The brunette grabs the redhead's shoulders and starts banging her against the wall.

Up until this moment we haven't been able to get a good look at the brunette, but, with a quick camera move, we reveal Jennifer Love Hewitt.

LOVE
Shut up, I want you to shut up.

LOVE continues to bang the redhead against the wall. REDHEAD is flopping back and forth now. With each bang she dramatically arches her back against the wall, bracing for the next assault.

LOVE
You don't know me? You don't remember?

LOVE is so close to the redhead that their noses almost touch.

REDHEAD
He pursued me. He was never in love with you.

LOVE
Shut up, just shut up.

LOVE gives the redhead one more shove against the wall. The REDHEAD slams against the wall one last time, her arms above her head, and she drifts down the wall and folds into child's pose on the floor.

LOVE
I bet you remember me now.

LOVE freezes, but stays intense.

"And cut!" we hear from stage left.

There's a small round of applause, as various crew members step into the living room and start moving furniture. Our director, Mick, gives me a look letting me know that it was all money and we got this scene on the first take.

I see Rich, casually leaning against the stage wall, taking everything in. He is always watching. He feels my eyes on him and meets my gaze. My smile gets bigger as I think about the two of us last night.

Makeup artists, hair people, and assistants flood the set, pulling up the redhead and fussing over Love. I lose sight of Rich, and feel my heart hammer out of control. It's great that he still has this effect on me. Taking a deep breath, I remind myself that I have nothing to worry about. Even if I can't see him, he is with me anyway.

Standing behind the monitors, I take it all in, enjoying the fact that the scene played so well and everyone on set really responded to it. We've been working for a long time to get to this day.

"Dani, do you have a moment?"

Steve's voice makes me turn around. He's standing with someone I recognize, and the two of them are trailed by half a dozen people in suits. The man steps toward me.

"Dani, it's so great to finally meet you," he says. "I just wanted to let you know how pleased we are."

He holds his hand out, and I smile. "Thanks, Les, that means a lot coming from you. I'm glad the network is happy."

He looks pretty much the same, a little thicker and grayer than I remember from my Christmas card days at Lorimar, but he definitely has the air of someone in charge.

"I know it was a big jump for you to leave *Flesh and Bone* and work on this pilot. We are all very excited about the show. It has 'hit' written all over it."

I say something humble back to him. Les mentions putting a lunch on our calendars, so we can discuss other show ideas I might have. Les says the "voice" in my writing really resonates with viewers. Again, I am humble.

Les tilts his head and squints at me, thinking. "Have we met before? Before you were writing here?"

"No, we haven't met," I reply quickly. But then I add, "I think I would remember meeting you, Les."

His minions laugh heartily at that one. Can you imagine someone not remembering Les Moonves? The group starts to make rumblings about leaving; they are obviously making the rounds of the stages.

"Okay then, take care, Dani, and I look forward to that lunch." He turns, and they move as one to follow the boss.

Les Moonves wants to have lunch with me; he wants to discuss my future with the network. Steve Jacobs, visiting the set to give me moral support as we finish shooting, gives my shoulder a squeeze, and leans in to whisper in my ear. "Very big, that was very big, Dani! Enjoy all this—you deserve it."

"Thanks, Steve, thank you so much for everything. It's a lot to take in, but I'm trying to stay as present as possible."

Jennifer Love Hewitt spies Steve and me behind the monitors and starts waving.

"Dani!" she gushes, rushing toward me. "Was I okay? Do we need to do it again? I think I can give her one last body slam, if it's not right."

I quiet her with my hands on her shoulders. "Love, you were fantastic, brilliant. I couldn't have done it better myself."

Steve gives me a funny smile and leaves.

"You sure?" Love asks. Her brown eyes are looking up at me, seeking affirmation. I nod.

"This is going to be so great!" Love wraps her arms around me, in the sincerest form of an actress bear hug. I reciprocate by wrapping my arms around her too, quickly changing the position of my hands behind her neck. I am still getting used to Rich's ring.

It is pretty big and I can feel it digging into my right hand. I close my eyes and whisper in her ear, "You were perfect."

FADE OUT